SHIP SHOW

REASSEMBLY BOOK 3

C.P. JAMES

SHIP SHOW: REASSEMBLY BOOK 3

REASSEMBLY RECAP

Knowing it may have been a while since you had Geddy Starheart in your lap, let's get you caught up.

Following a long stretch as henchman to one of the galaxy's most infamous figures, Tretiak Bouche a.k.a. the Auctioneer, Geddy had enough. He took off with Tretiak's ship and returned to his home planet, Earth 2, wanting only to put in his time as an anonymous grunt in the geothermal plant and coast into a comfortable retirement.

But, after inhaling an ancient alien spore named Eli, his plans changed. Eli wanted to return to his home world, and Geddy wanted Eli out of his head. Together, they built a ship capable of making the long journey. What made it special was a metal from deep within the planet. Eli called it shinium, and only it could pass through the barrier protecting Eli's home.

Unfortunately, digging into Earth 2 caused an industrial accident that flooded the atmosphere with methane, earning it the nickname, The Deuce. Missing and presumed dead, Geddy watched the entire planet evacuate to Earth 3.

That should've been the end of the story, but the morning of their maiden voyage, Geddy's ship was stolen.

He escaped off-world and wound up aboard a down-on-its-luck salvage trawler called *For Sale Make Offer,* or the *Fizmo* for short. Geddy's mission soon became that of his new crew mates, and they embarked on a grand adventure with Osmiya "Oz" Nargonis, a sexy and smart Temerurian first officer, Durandian pilot Denk Junt, and a remarkable synthetic organism named Morpho.

While Geddy languished on The Deuce, a mysterious group known as the Zelnads vastly increased their numbers and had become seen by many as a threat. Eli revealed that he and the Zelnads are from the same old-as-time world, Sagacea. Their mission has always been to seed the galaxy with the insight and knowledge required for civilization to form. The Zelnads were convinced that civilization must end, and are taking people over in order to advance their plans.

The crew's effort to salvage a derelict Zelnad vessel led to an encounter with their rival, a Kailorian captain named Beebit Tompanov, and his trawler, *The Red Raven.* The result of that encounter was an unplanned atmospheric entry on Kigantu, home to Geddy's old boss and the Double A auction.

On Kigantu, Geddy met Voprot, a rarely seen Kigantean native with limited vocabulary, and Dr. Tardigan, an Ornean exile with what can only be described as a shame fetish. Tardigan, a.k.a. Doc, offered to join the crew and help them deceive Voprot in order to get him off-planet and Geddy his ship back.

Geddy hoped to fetch a high price for his Zelnad vessel,

buy back his stolen ship, and repay his debts before taking Eli home. Instead, Tretiak locked him up and hinted he might know what really happened to Geddy's parents, whose ship crashed during an unsanctioned trip to the Ice Castles on Earth 2 when he was twelve. Before he could learn more, the crew showed up and rescued him, then helped him get reclaim his ship.

As they escaped, Tretiak's mercenaries went after the mostly defenseless *Fizmo*, and Geddy couldn't just leave them to their fate. In desperation, he bailed out into space, letting Morpho form a bubble around him while his ship became a missile that saved the *Fiz* from certain doom.

After reuniting with his crew and leading a harrowing escape from Tretiak's hired guns, the crew formally made Geddy their captain. His first act was to make them some money the "easy" way, by winning a dangerous race called Ponley Point on the planet Thegus.

Geddy won the race and got the *Fiz* some much-needed gear, but a mysterious figure named Zereth-Tinn later extorted the rest of their winnings by dangling a very tempting offer — to reveal the location of his missing ship. He took the deal but had a crazy idea where to get some top-shelf salvage and refill the ship's coffers.

Old Earth.

Following a dangerous series of jumps into the unknown, Geddy and the crew made it to humanity's original home in the Milky Way and plundered the cloud of expensive space junk in orbit around it. But under the pretense of nostalgia, Geddy led Oz down to the ruined surface to retrieve data from *Project Rearview*, the mission that brought humans to a new galaxy.

He reasoned he couldn't bargain for his ship empty-handed, but he remembered his old friend, Zirhof of Zorr, theorizing that only some unknown technology could have vaulted humanity into their galaxy. Armed with that knowledge, Geddy travels to Aku to find his missing ship and finally get Eli home.

On meeting some actual Zelnads, however, Geddy learned to his horror that the shinium he lovingly scraped from the bowels of Earth 2 was exactly what the they need to make a weapon that will destroy Sagacea and finally end the cycle of civilization. Geddy gets his ship back, but without its shinium armor.

When last we saw Geddy, he and the crew had gone to Zorr to give Zirhof the quantum cubes from the *Rearview* vault on Old Earth.

Now that you remember what the hell was happening, sit back and enjoy the *Ship Show*.

For Amy.

*Sometimes, you just need to turn
the page and see what happens.*

CHAPTER ONE

LIZARD LESSONS

I￼F THIS WHOLE saving-the-universe thing didn't work out and the Zelnads ended civilization, at least Geddy and Dr. Tardigan would never again have to teach a giant lizard how to use articles of speech.

"Vop– er, *I* see you across room?" asked Voprot hopefully.

They hadn't even introduced "the" into the mix. Too soon. Though, he did say *I* on occasion. It wasn't that he didn't grasp the concept. He just didn't like doing it.

"It's a classic for a reason." Geddy gave a shuddering yawn and leaned back in the stool behind the rarely used workbench. "And hey, if she's your age, she might not have heard that one before." Taking Doc aside, he whispered. "This still feels weird. Isn't he like twelve in Kigantean years?"

The lessons were his idea, but Doc was concerned about Voprot's social acclimation. In this scenario, he was supposed to talk to a female at a party. A ludicrous premise on multiple levels, but Geddy didn't have a better one.

"He is an adolescent. Using his language skills in social situations is essentially ... what is your human expression?"

"A Sisyphean ordeal?"

"No, I believe it is, 'Killing two birds with one stone.'"

"If you say so."

Voprot pretty much always sat on the floor of the *For Sale Make Offer's* capacious cargo hold during a crew meeting or the language lessons. His gigantic, swishy lizard tail limited him in many respects on the ship, which was made for short, snail-like Ghruk. But even on his haunches, his eyes came level with Geddy's and Doc's, which made it hard to think of him as the adolescent he technically was.

The hold felt depressingly empty. Empty crates were stacked to the ceiling along the starboard side. Sturdy shelves ran down the port wall and formed the back of the raised breakdown area called the deck. All empty, all spotless.

Their long and dicey trip to Old Earth had paid off. His old friend, Balzac, took all the metal from their scrapped satellites, which bought them a ton of needed repairs and upgrades to the *Fiz*. It still resembled an abandoned warehouse welded to the back of a service vehicle, but it was nicer on the inside now. The water ran clear-ish, he didn't have to crouch to shower anymore, and the slapdash hull repair they got as a parting gift from Prince Bransel, Oz's father back on Temeruria, had been reinforced. Morpho even got most of the items on his wish list.

It was only mid-afternoon, but Geddy could've racked out at any time. The fatigue that had kept him feeling run down and groggy for days had only deepened. It didn't make sense. Once again, he'd slept through the night only to wake up in a complete fog that never quite lifted. At least they were stocked up on coffee now. Hard to believe that counted as a win these days.

Bored with the monotony of Voprot's language lesson, Geddy's eyes drifted over to the *Penetrator*, his ship he stole back from the Zelnads. Without its shinium skin, it couldn't cross the barrier surrounding Sagacea, and he couldn't get Eli home. It was parked tight with a bunch of other junk, naked, useless, and sadly unfinished. Not unlike his reflection.

Thanks to Balzac, though, the *Fizmo's* engines' familiar low-frequency hum was even and strong. He'd gotten so accustomed to its cyclic vibration under his feet that its absence still made it seem like they weren't running at a full burn toward Gundrun.

As nice as it was to get on the ground and kick back on Zorr, it lost its charm after a couple of days. The *Fiz* was their only real home.

"Voprot have question." His giant reptilian head often tilted to the side, making him seem perpetually curious, and the shape of his mouth suggested a permanent grin. Happy, affable, curious people got under his craw after a while.

Geddy's open palm arced into his forehead. The slap echoed through the empty hold. "*I! I* have question! Actually, you have *a* question, but we only cover that in the advanced class."

Doc's burnt-orange, oblong face pinched in concern. "Are you okay, Captain?"

Dr. Tardigan brought a lot to the table. A flawless memory. Broad academic knowledge, including medicine. And, most vitally, infinite patience. Geddy hadn't told him about the fatigue yet, but apparently, it showed.

His instinct was to say yes. But he wasn't okay at all.

Worrisome thoughts pummeled his brain like a meteor shower. Maybe that's why he was so tired. Engaging with the world was a recipe for anxiety even in the best of circumstances. He scratched at his right ear.

"Just tired and crabby. My ear itches."

Squinting, Doc leaned in to get a closer look. The ridges across his forehead pinched into sergeant's stripes. "You have a rash."

"I do?" he reflexively brought his fingers back up and gave it another quick scratch. "Bad?"

He shook his head. "Just some contact dermatitis. I'd like to keep an eye on it, though."

Great. On top of everything else, he was allergic to something on the ship. Probably Voprot.

"Yeah, okay."

"I am more concerned about your mood. You've been more surly than usual, and that is saying something."

"I'm fine. Let's just finish up here."

Doc returned his attention to Voprot. "Let's try it in conversation. Imagine you were attracted to a female. What might you say to her?"

"Voprot lick you," he said without hesitations, unironically cleaning one eyeball, then the other with his prodigious forked tongue.

"*Like*," corrected Doc through gritted teeth. "*I ... like* you."

He grinned. "Voprot like you, too."

Geddy closed his eyes and let out a long, cleansing sigh before he hopped off the stool and strode away, fistfuls of hair bunched in his fingers.

— *I'm worried about you.*

Eli, his microscopic, freeloading spore friend, had been silent for hours.

— Oh, now you chime in.

— *You do not have the patience for teaching.*

— This isn't teaching, it's punishment. On second thought, maybe it *is* teaching.

"Take ten?" Doc said to Voprot.

"Okay. Voprot butt numb."

Had Geddy been alone, he might've cried.

— Shouldn't I be *rewarded* for heroically saving him?

— *Sav–*

— If you say saving him was its own reward, I'll sneeze you back into space.

— *But–*

— I'm not kidding.

Doc put a comforting hand on his shoulder. "He's trying."

Geddy turned to him. Voprot had gotten up and was stretching each leg out to the side like he was peeing on a shrub. "Is he, though?"

They'd only left Zorr three weeks ago. Usually, time had no meaning out here, but it felt like months had passed. After finding three quantum cubes in a vault at NASA's Jet Propulsion Lab, he brought them to his rich old friend Zirhof for analysis.

It seemed they were some sort of doomsday storage media, where a good chunk of the world's accumulated data was stored. Almost an entire cube was dedicated to porn, which had never been done better or to the same degree in this galaxy. That technically made it one of humanity's most enduring contributions to all civilization in the universe.

The other, Zirhof believed, was a jump technology so advanced that it could only have been conceived by an ancient Sagacean, beings created during the birth of the universe. Beings like Eli, who was so much a part of him now that they no longer seemed like separate entities.

It would take Zirhof a long time to pore through everything on the quantum cubes. Even then, there was no guarantee he'd find anything concrete about the mythical jump tech humans almost certainly used to reach their galaxy. The tech that could only have been conceived by a very clever Sagacean.

The sale of their scrap and the old Virgin Galactic space plane had their finances in fine order for once, and the novasphere hopper was full, but their sense of urgency was lacking because they needed a break. They'd only been a working crew for about three months, during which they'd hardly had a moment's rest. With the Zelnads out there threatening all civilization, taking time to relax felt indulgent. But everyone, especially Doc, said it was crucial that they rejuvenate. And so they'd enjoyed Sumbakh while on Zorr, which made them realize they still needed to live a life worth fighting for. That meant slowing down occasionally.

"You haven't been wearing the device I gave you, have you?" It wasn't a question so much as an accusation. "If you don't want to get to the bottom of this, then I won't waste my time trying to diagnose it."

The fingernail-sized disc stuck to his forehead while he slept. It was unobtrusive enough, but the whole idea of it made him uncomfortable. He couldn't even stand jewelry.

Or maybe he didn't want to know if something really was wrong with him.

"I'll wear it again tonight."

Doc still looked doubtful, and rightly so, but his reproachful expression softened. This fatigue issue flummoxed him. "The sooner I can get diagnostics, the sooner you can get some real rest."

The device recorded brain wave patterns, vitals, and everything about his blood chemistry as he slept. "At this point, I'd eat a pan of snapping assholes to wake up rested."

Tardigan cocked his head like a perplexed dog. "How would that ever be a condition of your treatment?"

Human idioms always got him in trouble. "Never mind."

He glanced over at Voprot, who had shifted to stretching his hamstrings with his hands pressed to the hull like a hurdler. Then he arched back so far that he met their eyes upside down, then licked them again. So gross. Contorted like that, he looked possessed. You had to hand it to the big Kigantean. He never missed an opportunity to be himself.

Geddy gave a grim shake of his head and muttered, "This was an absurd idea. Why would you let me try this?"

Doc's eyes roamed over Voprot with clinical fascination. "Because beneath that simple exterior is a shockingly sensitive and thoughtful being. And what he craves more than anything, besides globzoiks, is the approval of his captain."

— *That's what I told you yesterday.*

— Hmm? I wasn't listening.

— *I am literally in your head. You can't not listen.*

They were right, of course. Voprot was pure of heart and incapable of lying. Who else could he say that about? Geddy had neither been patient nor empathetic enough with him since they met, and he didn't know why. Maybe it was because casual jokes at Voprot's expense just sailed right over him like lob shots. It was fun to swing at someone when you knew they'd duck every punch.

The airlock door slid open and Oz, his Temerurian First Officer, strode through with the look of a disapproving mother. "You're still at it? Why don't you get some rest?"

Her limited rotation of outfits typically combined sturdy, lace-up boots with dark tights and a fitted vest. It suited her very well, and nothing she wore ever looked dirty or used.

Doc checked his watch and gasped. "My goodness, have we really been at it for three hours?"

"Are you trying to say it's our bedtime?" Geddy winked at the lithe redhead.

"I'm saying we might have a long day tomorrow."

He stifled another yawn. "Why?"

"There's still a lot of chatter on the salvage bands. Whatever's going down on Gundrun sounds big."

Oz liked to peruse the net or read while monitoring the old radio frequencies used by salvage vessels. Sometimes, she said, high-paying gigs were discussed, and you could get an inside track. One such conversation hinted at a lucrative commercial opportunity on Gundrun, and for want of any better ideas, they were en route to a clear vector there.

After nearly running out of novaspheres on the way to Old Earth on his account, she certainly deserved the benefit of the doubt now. But considering how far it was to reach their vector, the information didn't feel too solid.

"I've got a feeling about this one."

Burning an increasingly expensive novasphere on Oz's hunch wasn't the issue. It was whether they should still be going after salvage work when the world might be ending. But they couldn't fight the Nads if they couldn't find them.

Until then, there wasn't much else to do but try and make more money.

Geddy gave her shoulder a pat as he passed. "Then we'd better check it out. Voprot, we're done for today."

He righted himself and shrugged. "Okay." The giant lizard loped over to his sleeping area in the corner and disappeared behind the privacy walls Balzac's people installed.

"I'll see you in the morning," Geddy said.

"Eli, make sure he sleeps," Oz called after him.

— *Tell her I will do my best.*

"He says you aren't the boss of us."

CHAPTER TWO

YOU'RE MY SATELLITE

"Hey, Cap?" came Denk's voice over the tinny intercom. "Sorry to wake you, but you're gonna want to come to the bridge."

There was no urgency in his tone, but the words still dragged Geddy out of a deep state. Not sleep, exactly. Whatever it was, it could hold him in its spell all night without the courtesy of rest.

Bleary-eyed, he got dressed and looked in the mirror, canting his head far enough to see the rash by his right ear. If anything, it had freshened.

Since getting the upgrades on Aku, splashing water on his face felt and looked less like a golden shower, and for that he was grateful. He brought a couple dripping handfuls up with a slap, and a bit of the fog lifted.

The captain's quarters were slightly larger than the others but otherwise identical, with a bed in the corner and a screen on the wall beside the small closet. The side with the mirror also had a sink and a small desk he almost never used. It shared a wall with both the galley and the bridge.

After one more quick look, he exited and found his entire crew waiting in the bridge, the looks on their faces more hopeful and alert than usual.

"Are we there yet?" Geddy asked.

Denk Junt spun around in the pilot's seat, his rodent-like features pinched tightly together. His prominent incisors hung just over his bottom lip like he'd just poked his head up from a rabbit hole.

"No, we're still en route to our vector," he said. "But we ran across this."

Doc and the others fixed their gazes on the front screen. A couple hundred meters ahead was an enormous — and very old — satellite, motionless and stark under the *Fiz's* lights as Denk made a slow circle around it. The only markings were a six-character code stenciled on the side. It wouldn't have looked out of place over Old Earth, where they'd claimed dozens of similar satellites weeks earlier.

Geddy set his hands on his hips. "Talk about your antiques. What am I looking at?"

"It appears to be disabled," Doc said. "Its transponder is not active, and its power supply is largely depleted."

"Who does it belong to?"

"Without a transponder, we cannot know for certain. I ran the registry number through IRSV and it did not match any records, however, it may predate the database."

"How old's the database?"

"Approximately one hundred eighteen years."

Deep-space salvage had both rules and an ethos regarding claims. The only truly safe claim was a craft that was clearly disabled or damaged beyond repair. However, anything not in the Intergalactic Registry of Spacefaring

Vehicles was generally considered fair game. Every captain had their own policy.

Geddy's only policy was to keep his ship and his crew in business long enough to stop the Zelnads. Their financial situation was much improved, but that could change quickly.

"It still has some power, though?" Geddy asked.

"Yes. Either it is not functional or it only cycles on periodically. Deep-space satellites often do."

"Composition?"

"Primarily aluminum, though its armor appears to be high-carbon steel indicative of–"

"Gundrun," Geddy finished.

"Yes. However, Gundrun steel armor is present in virtually all spacecraft originating from this sector. It could easily be from Zihnia or Afolos, as well."

"How far are we from the nearest civilized world?"

Denk replied, "Just under half a parsec to Zihnia, then point eight more to Gundrun."

The satellite wasn't any big windfall. Depending on the components and the market, they might get a couple hundred grand or so. They were flush with novaspheres, but the repairs on Aku hadn't included any armaments. After their encounter with the pirates over Temeruria, that made him very nervous. But replacing the non-functional disruptor bank alone would easily run a million. They needed torpedoes and missiles, too, and countermeasures.

The risk was low, and they weren't close to anything. Running across dilapidated hardware didn't happen every day. Besides, once Voprot blasted it to pieces and they sorted the parts into bins, there wasn't much anyone could do.

— What do you think?

— *Legally, it seems like viable salvage. Ethically, it is a toss-up.*

"Do we know what *kind* of satellite it is?" Geddy asked Doc.

"Its design does not betray its function, Captain."

The looks on everyone's faces suggested a vote would be split. As Oz often had to remind him, it was his job to lead and theirs to follow. This was a golden opportunity to be decisive. And if the trip to Gundrun turned out to be a waste of time, at least they didn't walk away empty-handed.

"Let's bring it in."

SALVAGING the old satellite gave the crew a needed injection of purpose. It took no time at all to get back into the rhythm of work, from hauling the scrap bins out from under the shelves, to prepping the suits, to running the tractor beam.

The feeling of teamwork helped clear away some of Geddy's mental fog, and he felt sharper than he had in days.

Oz used the tractor beam to keep the satellite immobilized above the floor of the hold while Geddy clomped around it, partly to assess its condition and partly to convince himself he was making the right call.

Retrieving it couldn't have been easier. It was about fifteen meters long and three wide and was caked with a heavy layer of reddish-brown dust. Micrometeor impacts from more than a century in space had deeply pitted its armor, but almost entirely on one side, where it was especially thick.

Gundrun was the largest habitable planet in the galaxy,

three times the size of Kigantu. Its gravity routinely tugged asteroids in, hence its planetary shield, the khetaka. They said nothing bigger than a basketball ever reached the surface.

"The old girl's taken a pounding." Geddy glanced at Oz, who didn't even give him the satisfaction of a chuckle.

On the other side of the airlock window, Voprot's lizard lips curled into a grin, and he licked his eyeball, which meant he was happy. Or sad. Or had a dirty eyeball. Possibly all three. He was anxious to use the plasma cannon once again — their secret to quickly turning a big salvage into little pieces.

"Any chance at all this belongs to Gundrun? I'd like to stay on their good side," Geddy said.

Gundrun had the most powerful army in the galaxy and was instrumental in ending the Ring War, albeit at great cost. Whatever stand they eventually took against the Zelnads, Gundrun had to be on the front lines.

After a long pause, Doc said, "It is possible. However, I now believe it is more likely that the satellite was part of an old communications network that once connected Zihnia to Zorr."

The reference turned on a light for Geddy. "I remember learning about that. Because in the days before narrow beam, they had to bypass the Karrea Ion Storm."

"You know your history, Captain."

"I wouldn't go that far. How confident are you that it's not in use?"

"I cannot know its origin or purpose. Thus, I cannot be confident at all."

He rolled his eyes. "What do I pay you for?"

"You do not pay me at all, Captain."

"I'll take it up with payroll."

— Great. What the hell am I supposed to do?

— *Satellites are placed and aligned very precisely. In moving it, you have already decided.*

— Well, shit.

He let out a long exhale. "All right, guess this one's a keeper."

CHAPTER THREE

MAHA'KUT

GEDDY WOKE from a long and lucid dream that vanished the moment he opened his eyes. Right away, he could tell he slept because he felt good and alert. It was five ten a.m., much earlier than his preferred six thirty, but he'd also turned in early, around eight. The diagnostic disc was still attached to his forehead, so Doc should have some solid data to look at.

He swung his feet out and planted them on the cold metal floor, then flicked on the light to check his rash. It was still there but looked much better than it had two weeks earlier when they hauled in the satellite.

— *You seem renewed.*

"Thanks for noticing."

Had they been on-world, he would've taken a long walk or even a jog. How many years had passed since he felt so energetic first thing in the morning?

Turning away from the mirror, Geddy threw his right leg atop the bed and leaned forward in a half-assed attempt to stretch his unyielding hamstrings.

— *What are you doing?*

"Making a BLT on sourdough. What's it look like?"

— You do not stretch.

True enough, but he felt like moving. Eli's confusion was almost palpable. This did not compute.

After throwing on his most comfortable outfit — his comfiest fatigues and a threadbare NASA T-shirt he refused to throw out — he stepped into the darkened passage, eager to tell Doc how refreshed he felt.

But then he had an even better idea. On his way toward the bridge, he knocked on Oz's door.

"Crew meeting in the hold," he announced. "Ten minutes."

"Huh?" came Oz's muffled voice.

He moved down to Denk's room and gave the door two firm raps. "Crew meeting in the hold in ten."

Denk's nasally voice groaned. Geddy bopped down the hall and turned right. The airlock doors slid aside and he entered the dimly lit hold. The bins of sellable scrap metal from the satellite were secured neatly under the shelves, making it feel less empty and useless. He'd equivocated at the time, but the whole op went perfectly, and he was glad they hauled it in.

As expected, Doc was deep into his morning seseluh practice. The ancient Ornean martial art had been the subject of many jokes at his expense, but the *Fiz* didn't exactly have exercise facilities, and Doc was probably the fittest and most even-tempered among them. There had to be something to it.

A single light in the ceiling always remained on so Doc could practice without bothering Voprot. Not that his silent morning exertions could possibly wake the hard-sleeping lizard.

Tardigan was so focused, he didn't notice Geddy enter and pad across the hold to peek into Voprot's sleeping pit. The big, doofy Kigantean slept exclusively on his back with his arms and legs curled up like a dead fly, his head lolled to the side and his long, forked tongue dangling like an old man's nut sack. He could easily be taken for dead.

Geddy hesitated before waking him. Voprot might be daft and generally embarrassing, but Doc was right — he'd saved Geddy's bacon more than once. Like it or not, he was part of the crew, and they were going to start the day right.

He stomped on the metal grating beside Voprot's pit. "Voprot, wake up!"

Doc whirled in his direction, his face shiny with sweat. "Captain, you startled me ... what are you doing here?"

"Rousing the lizard, so to speak." He stomped again. "Yo! Big guy! Let's turn that cold blood warm."

Voprot's outer eyelid cracked open, registering the same abject confusion as he'd heard in Oz's and Denk's voices.

"What is happening?" he croaked.

"Crew calisthenics. Ha! I just came up with that. Ooh, or maybe *Fiz* fitness. Fizness? Whatever. We're doing this."

Oz and Denk emerged through the airlock door looking equally bewildered. Voprot rolled over and yawned himself awake while Geddy, Denk, and Oz converged on Doc.

When Voprot approached, Geddy clapped his hands together. "Okay! I'm sure you're all wondering what we're doing here at oh five thirty."

"Never occurred to me," Oz said drolly, her red locks a bit duller than usual. The fleshy tendrils that looked like dreadlocks had their own blood supply and subtly changed color to reflect her mood.

"I woke up feeling very rested, thanks for asking, and I thought we might join our science officer in his seseluh practice."

"Cap, are you feeling okay?" asked Denk, still bleary-eyed.

"I'm great. Look, I know we've all been a little on edge lately, and I think some exercise might help. Supposedly, sesehlu bridges the spiritual and the physical, right, Doc?"

Emotion seeped into his eyes. "Oh, yes. In fact, experienced practitioners have been known to–"

"Exactly." Geddy cut him off, knowing that if he didn't, Doc would spend the next thirty minutes walking them through the entire history of sesehlu. "Anyway, I think what we need is a mental reset, and learning sesehlu struck me as a good way to do it."

"At five-thirty in the morning?" Oz wrinkled her nose and turned to Doc. "This has to be a symptom of something."

"A symptom of a new attitude!" Geddy pointed and gave a wink. "Just keep an open mind. Doc, we're putty in your hands."

Tardigan put his palms together as though in prayer and gave a little bow. "It will be my pleasure to introduce you to the sacred practice." He closed his eyes, took a cleansing inhale, and bowed. "Everyone spread out. Give yourselves plenty of room."

Oz gave Geddy one more look, a chance to reveal that this was some kind of prank. Instead, he posted up directly in front of Doc and mirrored his bow. Reluctantly, she joined Denk behind him with Voprot off to the side.

"Excellent," Doc said, clearly pleased to be teaching them something.

"Wait," Geddy said, searching around him and on the ceiling. "Where's Morph?"

He hadn't been around much lately. Back before the repairs on Aku, Morpho was always flitting about the ship, tightening bolts or repairing frayed wires. Now, Geddy sometimes went a whole day without seeing him once.

"I don't think he'd get much out of this, Cap," Denk said, endearingly missing the point.

Being captain was about understanding what his crew needed from him and making sure they got it. Voprot needed his approval. Denk, his faith and confidence. And Oz? Oz needed unvarnished honesty, even if it made him an asshole. He'd learned that the hard way.

"Central to the practice of sesehlu is *maha'kut*, or psychic breathing," continued Doc. "The idea is to actively *inhale* negative energy with humility and acceptance. When you exhale, you release the positive so that it may one day be returned to you."

Geddy glanced over his shoulder at Denk and Voprot. Denk was already lost, and Voprot was either a sesehlu savant or could sleep standing up. Oz gave him a sidelong glance that said how much she would've preferred a warm bed to this.

"Close your eyes," said Doc. "Draw in the negative energy around you like a vacuum. Welcome it into your body and mind as you breathe in … maaaahhhhaaaa …"

Geddy didn't have to close his eyes to feel that. He inhaled deeply, the smell of cold metal and machinery filling his nostrils.

"... and out. Kuuuuut ..."

"Plenty of negative energy to go around this morning, eh, Doc?" Geddy asked rhetorically, glancing at Oz.

Doc made them repeat the psychic breathing word. After a few minutes, Geddy felt physically better. Was this crap really working?

"Lovely. Now we'll combine this with the first basic form, called *ovikha-nar*. With your feet shoulder-width apart, reach as far behind you as possible, then arch your back and open your heart to the sky. Mind your balance."

Geddy's back only allowed him to open his heart about halfway to the ceiling. He glanced to his left to find Oz with her arms nearly crossed behind her, her head well behind her slender hips as her blood-red tendrils hung nearly to the floor.

— *She is very flexible.*

— So I've noticed.

Voprot was bent so far back he could've licked the floor. Meanwhile, Denk's doughy midsection stuck out like a squat pregnant woman, his stubby arms barely behind his midline as he trembled with effort.

"Each practice begins and ends this way. Ancient scrolls even suggest that–"

Doc's erudition was cut short by an alarm Geddy had never heard before, a polite, but insistent *beeeee-oop* that fell in tone. It yanked him from his reverie, and an orange light he'd never seen pulsed over the airlock door.

"What the hell's that?" Geddy's eyes darted between Denk and Oz.

The two of them exchanged an incredulous look that gave way to broad grins.

"It's a package!" Denk's stubby legs motored toward the bridge like a cartoon mouse.

Geddy looked to Oz for further explanation. Her eyes sparkled with hope. "It's usually an invitation to bid on a commercial job."

"Gundrun?"

She shrugged and hurried after Denk. "We're about to find out."

CHAPTER FOUR

TOP GUNDRUN

The *Fizmo's* bridge was much smaller than it should've been for a trawler of its size, which was a function of the ship's piecemeal design. Everything in front of the inside airlock that separated the bridge from the hold was from a War-era Ghruk freighter. The Ghruk bore a resemblance to snails and were significantly shorter than everyone but Denk, so the ceiling was low. Geddy felt like it was always pressing in on him, so he rarely was in the captain's chair for more than an hour at a stretch.

The airlock itself, along with the hold, were of unknown origin — most likely custom fabricated for the ship's late Captain Bykite. No matter how many times Geddy went from the hold to the bridge, the mismatched proportions always felt a little jarring.

Denk leapt into the pilot's chair and turned off the alarm, then powered up the screen as the package was decrypted and extracted. Geddy sat on the edge, leaning anxiously forward with Oz and Doc on his left, and Voprot crouched on his right. Morpho was perched on his shoulder.

Had their energy cleansing already sent a message out to the universe? He was starting to believe it might.

The screen blinked to life and filled with the big, stern face of a Gundrun official. The men were giant, blue-gray caricatures of chiseled movie idols, with prominent cheekbones and keen, hawklike eyes that stared into your soul. Their wide, squared-off chins projected strength and fortitude. Thick, sinewy necks flared out into impossibly broad shoulders and brawny limbs. The women were slightly shorter and had moderately softer features, but they could hardly be distinguished from a distance.

Gundrun had the most badass, best-equipped army in the galaxy. Much like the Spartans of Old Earth legend, children were trained to fight from birth. Over millennia in high gravity, they'd evolved thick bones and powerful muscles that nearly gave them incredible strength on other planets, which meant no one ever messed with them.

It was only fitting that Geddy's childhood hero, Otaro Verveik, last supreme commander of the Alliance, was Gundrun. Since learning about him from his dad, Geddy tracked down every article and video he could find about the man and decided that's who he wanted to be like. Courageous but compassionate. Measured but decisive.

Geddy was none of these things, but he was always trying.

"My name is Commandant Arbizander of Khetaka Central Command. If you are in range of this message, Gundrun needs your help."

Concern darkened Oz's bright yellow eyes.

"As you know, the khetaka is our primary means of defense against asteroids."

Arbizander's face dissolved into an animation of Gundrun, which was fully three times the size of Kigantu. Its immense gravity attracted chunks of rock ranging in size from marbles to planetoids, all of which had only added to its mass over the eons. The khetaka was a vast network of powerful laser targeting satellites arranged around the planet in a gigantic outer sphere to protect it from impacts.

"We need to deploy four hundred new satellites here, to sector seven." A triangular slice of the sphere flashed red. "Ordinarily, we would not require outside assistance, however, our current circumstance requires it." The words stuck in his throat.

The camera zoomed way out to show Gundrun at the center and its relatively tiny moons circling it. A dotted line at the edge of the screen inched inward.

"This is XCR-190, a planetoid some eight hundred kilometers across that recently broke away from the Elenian Belt. Our models have it striking Valniuq, our largest moon, with a glancing blow, ejecting colossal amounts of debris into space. Most likely, it will overwhelm the khetaka and destroy all life on Gundrun. We're evacuating as many people as we can."

Geddy looked anxiously to Oz. Her big eyes were peeled wide, her fleshy hair a dull rust.

— *My god, Geddy. This is extinction-level.*

The screen dissolved to a 3D image of a slowly rotating ovoid satellite. "This is the new KT-200. Only four hundred have been made so far, but we're putting them into service immediately because it's our only hope." Shame and embarrassment colored his face. "The asteroid will strike Valniuq in six hours and eighteen minutes."

"Six hours?" Denk asked. "How does something that big sneak up on you?"

"You may be wondering how something so large could sneak up on us. It seems one of our deep-space early warning satellites monitoring the Elenian Belt malfunctioned, leaving us with a large blind spot. It didn't appear on our near-range scopes until a few hours ago."

Geddy's heart dropped into his shoes.

"We beseech any and all class two salvage vessels to help with the deployment. For each satellite you place, the government of Gundrun will pay five hundred thousand credits." Denk turned back to Geddy with his eyes wide and gave a low whistle.

"Wow, that sesehlu really works, huh, Cap?"

Judging from the looks on the crew's faces, only Denk had yet to realize that the early warning satellite in question was the one they'd blown to bits two weeks earlier. Apparently, it had been working after all.

"Captains who return signed contracts will be given further instructions. Remember, the more satellites we deploy, the better our chances of saving Gundrun. Good luck, and thank you."

A leaden silence descended over the bridge. Geddy, Oz, Doc, and Voprot stared at the screen. Denk, in front of them in the pilot's seat, swiveled back wearing a dumb grin.

"Well, gang, whaddya ..." On seeing their expressions, he trailed off and his grin flattened. "... say?"

— Give me the strength to do this tactfully.

— *You can do it. I think.*

He took a deep breath, then spoke in a calm, even tone

like a doctor telling someone they were going to die. "Denk, do you recall the satellite we hauled in a while back?"

"Sure. Why?"

"Because there is about a hundred percent chance it's the early warning satellite that supposedly malfunctioned."

Denk's eyebrows raised hopefully as though Geddy might reveal it was a joke, but quickly fell. "Oh, no."

Logic dictated he also check with Voprot for understanding. The big lizard's mouth hung slightly open, his forked tongue lolling a bit out the side. He understood well enough.

"Think we can put it back together?" asked Denk.

Geddy gritted his teeth, adding a firm rub of his temples through which hot blood angrily pulsed. His rash flared.

Oz came to the rescue. "No, Denk. We can't. And even if we could, it would be pointless now."

"Well, shoot." He threw up his hands. "I'm all out of ideas."

"Captain?" Geddy pivoted to Doc. "What are your orders?"

The asteroid was coming either way. Again, he couldn't imagine a scenario in which they defeated the Zelnads without the Gundrun army.

"How far to our jump vector, Mr. Junt?"

Denk spun back and checked the scopes. "Almost there. Forty minutes out."

"It's bad luck," Oz asserted. "We decided together."

"Bad luck that might destroy an entire planet. Mr. Junt, prepare to jump."

"Are you sure about this?" Oz leaned close to him. "We don't know anything about deploying satellites."

"We'll figure it out."

"But our shields …"

"It's fine. Doc, pull up the contract. I'll sign it on the other side. Oz, Voprot, let's make sure the hold is buttoned down."

Voprot took off immediately. Oz's gaze lingered on him a moment.

"What?" Geddy asked.

"If anything, they're downplaying this," she warned. "You heard the desperation in his voice."

"I agree, Captain," Doc said, joining them at the back of the bridge. "The khetaka is designed to repel isolated large objects or clusters of smaller ones. Not both. Their efforts are almost certain to fail."

"We lose Gundrun, we lose any chance of stopping the Nads," Geddy stated. "We have to do this."

"Aye aye, Captain," said Oz doubtfully. She turned on her heels and marched through the airlock.

"I'll secure the galley, Captain," said Doc, who followed her out the door.

— *Are you sure this is worth the risk?*

— No, but we have to try.

Geddy closed his eyes and whispered, "Maaahhaaa … kuuut."

CHAPTER FIVE

A BIG LOAD

THE *FIZMO* CAME out of its jump about a thousand kilometers from Gundrun, which was just inside the khetaka. Even at that distance, the planet could not be taken in at once.

"My god, it's massive," Oz said. Geddy had barely opened his mouth when she thrust her open palm into his face. "Don't."

He unclipped from the harness and rose, steadying himself against the chair back. Jumping was hard on the human body. Their trip to Old Earth proved he was only good for one, two at the most.

The crew gathered behind Denk and stared at Gundrun with their jaws slack. Geddy had run Gundrun armor and weapons many times but had never been to the planet itself. It was larger than even Kigantu, its iron-rich soil making it almost uniformly rust-colored. A single ocean connecting the poles split it in two. Virtually all the planet's cities were arranged around it, the rest apparently being too dry to support life.

"Geez. I knew it was big, but ..." Denk trailed off.

Meanwhile, outside the khetaka sphere, the lasers fired every ten or fifteen seconds, the asteroids they vaporized appearing as tiny flashes against the blackness. And they were only looking at a tiny sliver of it. They must take out thousands of rocks every day. Impressive tech for sure.

"Doc, is that contract ready to sign?" Geddy asked.

"Yes, Captain."

"Anything out of the ordinary?"

"The terms are quite straightforward. The satellites' transponders will be associated with our ship. Each one deployed to the khetaka is worth half a million."

"What if it doesn't work?"

"It does not say."

"Fine." He took a few shaky steps over to Doc's terminal and applied his digital signature. "Send it."

Doc sent it off. To their right, near the inside edge of the khetaka, a massive military cargo vessel sat stationary. A handful of trawlers and repair ships, Gundrun and otherwise, flowed in and out of the open hold. Denk angled toward it.

The light around the front screen flashed red to indicate a hail. Geddy glanced at the ID, expecting to see someone from Khetaka Central Command, but grimaced when he saw who it was instead.

Beebit fucking Tompanov, commander of the thieving *Red Raven*, which he'd last seen when it swallowed the *Penetrator* like a hot dog over Kigantu and brought it to the Nads. Bile flooded his gullet.

"I'll deny that sucker, Cap." Denk reached for the button.

"No. Put him through."

Tompanov's long, dumb Kailorian face appeared

onscreen. He'd grown a thick blue mustache. On seeing Geddy and the crew, his face brightened as though a pile of orphans had just gotten floated.

"Well, look who it is!" His voice dripped with sarcasm. "Geddy Starfart and the can't-do crew of the *Jizzmo*. Gundrun must be desperate indeed."

"No one takes a load as well as you, Tompanov."

As they drew near the Gundrun repair ship, the much larger *Raven* came into view just outside its cavernous entrance. It was nearly identical in color to the planet itself. Naturally, he'd gotten there first.

He gave an exaggerated sigh. "Regrettably, the *Raven's* hold is quite full at the moment, but we made enough room for four satellites so we can do our part for Gundrun."

Geddy turned to ask Doc how many they could handle. Anticipating the question, he was already holding up four fingers.

Something had to soften the broken glass churning in his guts, say nothing of Tompanov calling just to taunt him. He badly needed a win.

— I know what you're thinking, and it is not appropriate. You do not even know how to deploy a satellite.

"Tell you what, dipshit. How about a little wager?"

A mischievous grin decorated Tompanov's dark blue lips. "I'm listening."

"A hundred grand to whoever finishes first."

— Ugh. Why do I bother?

Tompanov considered this a moment, then nodded. "You're on, Starfart. I'll send you my deposit information."

The transmission blinked out. He could already feel Oz's eyes burning a hole through him.

"You are unbelievable."

———

THEY PASSED a Gundrun freighter on its way out of the repair vessel. Two stern Gundrun stared at the *Fiz*, haunted expressions on their faces as though they'd been at it for hours. Denk threw a wave that wasn't returned.

The steady *tink tink* of small rocks slipping through the khetaka continued against the unarmored parts of the Fiz, adding to the ominous nature of their task. It ceased as soon as they passed through the big ship's shields.

Yellow lights directed them where to go. A dockworker in a spacesuit and giant magnetic boots motioned them toward a loading dock along the starboard side where the enormous satellites were lined up for loading. The *Red Raven* was tethered next to them waiting for the last satellite to be loaded in.

As soon as it was in place, the *Raven's* door closed, and the tethers fell away. It joined the parade of other trawlers and maintenance ships headed back out to complete the job.

"Let's wish him good luck." Without any additional cues, the whole crew joined Geddy and gave him double-barrel middle fingers.

In response, Tompanov turned around, dropped his pants, and pressed his surprisingly sculpted blue buttocks to the window.

"He's in pretty good shape," Denk offered.

Geddy looked to Oz, but her eyes were averted. His bet with Tompanov had her seething, and rightly so, but maybe she'd feel differently when they won.

Denk swung the *Fiz* into position for loading and set her

down, activating the magnetic tethers. Like four charmed cobras, they rose from the floor and clamped onto the fuselage, then tightened down. He opened the hold, and the rush of escaping air met their ears.

Geddy headed back to the airlock to watch the loading procedure through the window. The others crowded around him.

Two workers walked the first weightless satellite into place, partially blocking their view. They gave a grim nod, their broad, angular faces lit from inside their helmets. Two more came in right behind with the second, which they placed in front of the window, leaving only the camera feed to watch.

"All right, Doc, talk us through this."

"Of course, Captain. According to the mission brief, the new satellites were designed to self-deploy. However, there was not time to complete their programming, which is why they must be placed manually. Fortunately, the placement does not have to be especially precise. Once it nears the neighboring units, it should activate and auto-orient."

"And we have coordinates for all of them?" asked Oz.

"Yes."

"What about the beam?" Geddy asked her. "Any concerns about deployment versus retrieval?"

"Mainly momentum." She still wouldn't look at him. "We can't rush it. If we push it out too fast, like, say, if we were trying to win some stupid macho bullshit race, the beam might not be able to stop it. It's not that strong."

Doc continued before their bickering began. "Oz is correct. The mission specs recommend only half a meter per second."

"That's slow. How long will it take us at that rate?"

"Approximately one hour per satellite."

He checked his watch. Five hours and fifty minutes before impact. Barring any complications, that gave them ample time to deploy the sats and get out of there.

"Anything else?"

"Once the asteroid strikes the moon, the debris coming through the khetaka will increase quickly. I recommend diverting full power to the rear shields once we're in position."

"Is this gonna work?" asked Denk.

That was a great question. They all turned to Doc, who shrugged. "I do not know."

"All right, *For Sale Make Offer*, you're locked and loaded."

Geddy said, "Roger that. You can count on us."

"Best of luck, Captain."

Once the dockworkers cleared the hold, Geddy closed the door and hightailed it back to the bridge. "Denk, let's catch up with the *Raven*."

"Way ahead of ya, Cap."

As they were pulling out, Voprot sheepishly approached. "Voprot regret blowing up satellite."

Geddy gave his scaly shoulder a reassuring pat. "Me, too, pal. Not your fault."

Voprot's scaly skin felt oddly rough. Geddy glanced at the giant lizard's shoulder to find a flaky white patch a couple centimeters wide.

"Hey, is this some kind of Kigantean eczema or did you fall asleep in the tanning bed?"

"Voprot molting soon."

— Does that mean what I think it means?

— *It seems Voprot's reptilian traits include sloughing off his outer layer of skin.*

— Why does he have to do that?

— *So he can continue to grow.*

— Ugh. Geddy regret asking.

CHAPTER SIX

THE TICKING KHETAKA

THE KHETAKA WAS ALREADY BEING PELTED with rocks. A single blast turned most to pebbles, although some needed two. But the sector had thousands of satellites, and they were deploying hundreds more. It was hard to imagine a rock large enough to need that kind of firepower.

The thought of seeing them firing in unison at a planet-killing asteroid got him a bit excited. How many lifetimes would you have to live to see something like that even once?

Full mission parameters had been delivered to each ship. The Fiz's assigned region was represented onscreen by a green hexagon.

"Five minutes out, Cap," said Denk. "We almost caught up to the Raven!"

"Nice work. I'm gonna suit up and help Oz. Doc, be ready to deliver the positioning data to our helmets."

"Already loaded in, Captain."

The four big lasers barely fit in the hold. He slipped between the two positioned nearest the airlock and crossed to where Oz was kneeling in front of the tractor beam controls.

She'd already removed the EVA suits from their closets and was topping off the reserve O2 tanks.

Things between them had been pretty good since Aku, but that all ended when he made the bet. He got it. Gundrun could be wiped off the map, and them along with it. But that weasel Tompanov made his blood boil and having some skin in the game gave him extra motivation.

She didn't look up as he approached.

"I'm almost done." Her tone was flat and cold.

"Hey, look, you were right back there. This isn't a game. In fact, the stakes may be even higher than you think."

She rose, wiping her hands on a rag, and squared up to him with an irritated look. "Yeah? How's that?"

"Because the only way we stop the Zelnads is by reforming the Alliance. That starts with Gundrun."

She blinked, shaking her head. "What?"

"Think about it. They have the best army in the galaxy. We come through now and we've got some real juice with them."

"I knew you had an ego, but wow." Oz barked a laugh. "You think a trawler captain's singlehandedly gonna convince Gundrun to rejoin the Alliance."

"Not singlehand–"

"One minute out, guys!" Denk's voice interrupted over the loudspeaker.

Oz left to step into her suit, signaling the end of the conversation. "Showtime."

Geddy turned to tell Voprot to clear out, but he was already safely behind the airlock.

They got in their suits, ensured good seals on their

helmets, and activated their magnetic boots. With a final glance his way, Oz let out a long exhale. "Ready?"

"Ready. Denk, we're opening the doors."

He hit the button and waited for the rush of air to blow past. Once it stabilized, he stepped up to the edge and got his first close-up view of the khetaka. Lasers as powerful as any battleship's fired with staggering rapidity, leaving clouds of rock to pass between. Small debris ricocheted off the shield, causing faint yellow ripples that overlapped like a handful of stones breaking the surface of an electric pond.

Oz's face pinched skeptically. "Gundrun may not be around long enough to help us."

"All the more reason to do this right. If we can take Tompanov's money in the process, all the better."

"If he welches on it," she allowed her lips to curl upward, "I get first shot at him."

Geddy winked. "I'd practically insist."

CHAPTER SEVEN

PLACEMENT RACE-MENT

"Captain, the *Raven's* first satellite just came out of the door," said Doc over the comm.

Oz had locked on to the first of their satellites and eased it toward the door. Moving heavy cargo around in zero G wasn't the kind of work you could rush, especially with so much at stake, but he wanted her to try.

Geddy opened his mouth to speak, but Oz stopped him short. "We're moving as fast as we safely can." She sighed. "But, assuming their recommended rate is conservative, I think we can push it a tad."

It was Oz's show now. But angry as she was, she didn't want to see Tompanov win. Whatever led to his falling out with Captain Bykite, her and Denk's old boss, the result was that Tompanov screwed the *Fiz* out of millions. Denk thought he just had a knack of being in the right place at the right time, but Oz figured he'd pimped himself to the Nads and was using their technology to get *all* the best stuff *all* the time. Geddy was inclined to agree with her.

"What was the velocity they recommended, again?"

asked Geddy, stepping back to ensure the satellite was aligned properly with the hold door. The pockmarked gray sphere of Valniuq, the doomed moon, hung innocuously in the background.

"Half a meter per second. I'm doing point six."

— *There's plenty of time to do it right.*

— Doesn't anybody want to put that jackwad in his place?

Once the satellite cleared the ship, Oz eased it toward its assigned place.

"*For Sale Make Offer*, watch your velocity," cautioned their liaison on the command ship, a lieutenant named Karraj.

"Respectfully, lieutenant, food moves through my intestines faster than your recommended rate." Geddy hated backseat drivers. "I mean, it's nutrimush and this is a satellite, but still. We know what we're doing."

But the lieutenant was right. The tractor beam was finicky on its best days. Anything too massive or fast-moving would slip from their grasp.

Nearly thirty interminable minutes later, the slowly tumbling satellite reached its spot in the matrix of lasers. Oz let go and reversed the beam. As soon as it was in place and auto-orient took over, a green ring around the exterior illuminated indicating it was active.

"Looks like you do. Nicely done." Karraj was just the latest to underestimate Osmiya Nargonis.

"One down, three to go." Geddy rubbed his gloved hands together.

"Captain, the *Red Raven*'s second satellite is on its way." Doc's updates were starting to get on his nerves.

"I only want to know when we catch 'em." Geddy released the metal strap holding the next satellite in place. Oz snagged it again with the beam and the entire process started over.

Again, Oz guided the satellite through the door, just a touch faster than the first. She was getting comfortable now.

"Looking good, Oz."

"Don't get excited. This is as fast as I'm gonna go."

Karraj's voice broke through on the master channel. "Two hours, twelve minutes to impact. Debris is already picking up. Watch your shields."

Indeed, debris had picked up since they began their deployment. Every few seconds, several lasers would blaze, followed shortly by a shower of shimmery green ripples against the shield.

"Shields nominal, Cap," came Doc's voice. "Eighty-four percent and holding solid."

Geddy positioned the next satellite for Oz, and she pushed it out as fast as she dared while Geddy watched from through the door. Glancing over his shoulder, Voprot grinned at him through the inner airlock window, giving a big thumbs-up that he reluctantly returned.

Each passing minute saw still more space rock turned to dust. It inspired confidence, but Geddy doubted it had ever been tested like it was about to. As soon as they were done, the needed to hightail it out of there or the same rocks that threatened Gundrun might take them out, too.

The moment Oz expertly guided their third satellite into place and it came online, Doc's voice came giddily over the comm. "We have placed our third satellite before the *Raven*."

Geddy met Oz's gaze from across the hold as he released

the latch on the last satellite. She seized it in the beam and began guiding it out.

— *When are you going tell her?*

— Tell her what?

— *That you're crazy about her.*

— What? No, no, I'm not–

— *Geddy ...*

— There's no time for that crap. Especially now.

— *Feelings are crap?*

— Now you're getting it.

"Oz, you're killing it."

"Interesting choice of words."

"Whup, hang on." Something on the beam's display distracted her. "There's a flashing red message here."

"What's it say?"

"How should I know? It's in Udsar."

He'd almost forgotten the device was Udsarian, which was partly why they needed Zereth-Tinn's help with the installation back on Thegus. But for that same reason, it couldn't connect to any of the ship's internal systems. Translating its baffling menu system had to be done the hard way, and Doc's Udsar was iffy at best.

"Doc, can you translate what she's seeing?"

"Okay, let's see ..." came Doc's voice. "I believe it reads, 'Dear Estimated Customer. Temporary make loss of velocity ... cleanliness error, please must renew reset procedure for make happy."

"Cleanliness error? How long does it take to reset?"

"It doesn't say."

How many times had they used the damn thing to haul in

junk over Old Earth? Worked without a hitch. Only now, with everything on the line, did it decide to crap out.

"Well, is there anything that says, 'reset?'"

With Doc's assistance, they navigated the menus to what he believed was the reset command. But it took forever to find, and their gains against Tompanov were erased.

"Oz, what are you seeing?" Geddy's foot tapped anxiously inside his magnetic boot.

"The screen's blank right ... Okay, here we go. Looks like a ... loading bar?"

"Loading bar? What's this thing run on? Windows 98?"

Geddy could take no more. Bets aside, Gundrun was the linchpin in the inevitable war with the Nads. They couldn't exactly bring their hulking bodies and badass weapons to the fight if their planet was dead. The *Fizmo* wouldn't be the one ship to fail them in their darkest hour. Especially not with a big paycheck on the line.

A terrible idea took hold. "Screw this. I'm doing it manually."

Oz looked, a scowl on her face. "Say what?"

"I'll take the EMU and push the satellite in front of me. It'll shield me from the debris."

— The what?

— The extravehicular mobility unit. It's like a backpack for moving around in space.

— But what about the–

Incredulity coated her voice. "What about the trip back, genius? We're in the middle of a damn meteor shower."

— Exactly.

He shrugged off the risk. "One puff of the jets and I'll be inside the shield again."

"There's no way you can be precise enough with the EMU." Concern took over. Maybe she did still care. "Look, let's just tell Gundrun what happened. They'll probably have us leave the last satellite for another ship."

"There's no time for that." Geddy clomped across the hold toward the cabinet that housed the two packs. "I signed a contract for four satellites, we're deploying four satellites."

He reached the short steps to the deck where Oz stood, but she blocked his way and crossed her arms defiantly. "I said no."

"Oz, come on. This isn't a big deal."

"We haven't run those in months. Years, maybe." She was right. Since Morpho could work outside the ship, they never had to put on the suits to make repairs. And he hadn't used one himself in at least a decade. It had to be like riding a bike though, didn't it?

"If a single part of you pokes out from behind the satellite and a rock blows through your suit, you're dead."

Oz wasn't going to move, and he couldn't yield. She didn't understand how important this moment was. They'd been losing ground against the Zelnads since the get-go, and their plans were accelerating. The only road to victory went through Gundrun.

Though he knew he'd regret it, Geddy shot out his hand and slapped the button on her belt that released Oz's magnetic boots, followed by a tiny push in the process. Her eyes shot open as she lifted free of the platform and drifted away at an angle toward the ceiling.

"Hey!!"

"I'm sorry." He continued to the where the EMU's waited without looking at her. "I have to do this."

She floated toward the far side of the hold, spewing invective into his ear. Geddy backed into one of the EMUs and buckled himself in, then gave the controls a brief test. They worked pretty much like an atmospheric aircraft — roll, pitch, yaw, up, down, fast, slow. He released his boots and gave himself a couple puffs toward the hovering satellite.

— *So much for sharing your feelings with her.*

— I wasn't gonna do that anyway.

"Eli, talk sense into him. Take him over if you have to!"

— Don't even think about it.

"Just trust me for once, would ya?"

He reached the satellite and backed off his speed. The controls were a lot more sensitive than he remembered, but it was all coming back. Besides, all he had to do was push the damn thing in a straight line.

Oz, who was nearly upside-down, reactivated her boots as she touched the shelves and started clomping her way back down to the floor.

"Starheart, I swear to the old gods ... you do *not* have to do this!"

Meanwhile, he put one hand on the back of the satellite and gave a little forward puff of the jets with the other.

"Denk, expand the rear shield buffer and match my velocity. If we do this right, I shouldn't have to go outside the shield."

"Are you sure, Cap?" Denk's voice shook. "Oz makes a pretty good–"

"That's an order, Mr. Junt."

Outside, the ripples on the shield had just gone from a sprinkle to a deluge. If this didn't work, it might be the last order he ever gave.

CHAPTER EIGHT

HEAVY OBJECT LESSON

As Geddy drifted past the threshold pushing twenty metric tons of satellite ahead of him, he got a good look at Oz's face. He'd expected anger but only read a gut-wrenching combo of disappointment and fear. No matter the outcome, he might not live this one down.

She thought it was just about the stupid bet with Tompanov and his ego, but it wasn't about that at all.

It was about Otaro Verveik, little Eddie Kepler's childhood hero. Eddie was now Geddy Starheart, but heroes were heroes.

Before the Ring War, Verveik's sure-handed leadership took the Alliance from an unremarkable trade agreement to what almost became a unified galactic government. He was as close to a universally respected figure as the galaxy had until the War forced an Alliance intervention. What began as a trade dispute between three planets escalated to a war that engulfed dozens of worlds. Verveik ended the bloodshed through military force, but many planets believed the conflict would have played itself out. Resentments old and new bubbled back up. The Alliance folded, and Verveik disappeared.

Some believed he returned to Gundrun in disgrace. Others said he went into exile. Geddy couldn't know for sure, but he clung to the belief that his hero was still alive somewhere. Gundrun men often lived to two hundred, so it was possible. And if Verveik was alive, he was their best hope.

Maybe it was naïve to think a new Alliance might succeed where the old one had failed, but for the first time, the galaxy had a common enemy. They just didn't know it yet. The war to come, terrible though it would be, would bring all worlds under the same banner.

Verveik would've defended Gundrun to the last breath. He'd have to respect anyone willing to do the same — even a lowly trawler captain. Wherever he was, Geddy needed an audience with him, and in that moment, this felt like the only way to earn it. Not any man could ask a man's man to man up.

The second the satellite pushed through the shield, Geddy could feel the vibrations of tiny stones hitting it. The only good handhold was a little maintenance panel at the back. When the time came, he'd have to grab it tightly and hit the brakes.

"Captain Starheart, what's going on up there?" Karraj's sharp voice filled his helmet. "We're getting a weird signature on our scans. Is something attached to the satellite?"

"Yeah, me. Our beam malfunctioned, so we're gonna do this the old-fashioned way."

"An EVA?!" the man was apoplectic. "Are you out of your mind?"

"No, just a man of my word. Am I not on the right course?"

He paused to check the scopes and took a deep breath. "No, you're on course. And Gundrun appreciates your dedication to the task, but as Commandant Arbizander made clear, it's unlikely to matter."

"I understand. How are we on time?"

"Impact is in forty-four minutes."

Geddy gulped. He didn't realize how much time had elapsed. "How long before the debris field reaches the khetaka?"

"Another fourteen or fifteen minutes, but that's an estimate."

"Hey Cap," Denk chimed in, his ordinarily upbeat tone wavering. "We need eight or ten minutes to reach minimum safe distance. Once that rock hits home, you'd better get back on board."

"Understood, Mr. Junt." He gave the stick a tiny tap and increased his velocity to 0.9 meters per second. Any more was too strong for the tractor beam, which meant if something went wrong and he couldn't slow down, Oz couldn't haul him in. That would not be cool.

He glanced over his shoulder to ensure the *Fiz* was following right behind. But in so doing, he moved his fingers just a tiny bit off-axis, and the satellite rolled into a lazy tumble.

"Oz, how's our beam?"

"Meter's half full," she said flatly. "The satellite's turning."

He winced, his throat suddenly dry. "I noticed that, thank you."

"And it is on course to hit one of the current satellites," added Doc.

Keeping the big machine on course took almost constant bumps on the EMU jets, which he'd only been able to control with one hand. Now it would overshoot the khetaka at best, and at worst it would take out one or more others in the process.

"Geddy, you swung and missed. Now get back inside the damn shield and let me take over," Oz admonished.

But he couldn't stop now. At this point, he had a front seat to the show. He reached for the handle on the panel.

— *You don't have enough mass!*

— All I need is an equal and opposite force, right?

— *Didn't you get a C in physics?*

— Yes, and that was hardly paying attention at all.

— *The only way this would work was if you and the handle–*

His fingers curled around the handle, and he tapped the stick up. The instant he did, he realized his error.

— *... were aligned precisely with the center of mass.*

The sudden change in direction mostly stopped the long-axis rotation but added a wobble. And he could already tell it was on another incorrect course. The khetaka was more empty space than satellites, so it would probably just drift right through, but still.

— *Oz told you this would happen.*

— She knows perfectly well I don't listen.

"Impact in four minutes. Captain Starheart, get out of there."

As much as he wanted to keep going after the satellite and right it, he was out of time. Geddy pulled back on the small stick and stopped, then swiveled his eyes over toward Valniuq. The asteroid called XCR-190 caught the light as it lazily turned over, a jagged, planet-killing space turd nearly as long as Valniuq was wide.

"Uh, Cap, you're still outside the shield."

"Roger ... that," Geddy said absently, transfixed by what was about to happen.

A ship appeared from the corner of his left eye and came to a stop several hundred meters away. The *Raven*. Predictably, Tompanov's voice was the next one he heard.

"I must admit, Starfart, I thought Arbizander was kidding when he told everyone what you were doing. Don't worry, though, we've got your back. Dave?"

A bright yellow beam shot from the gigantic trawler and seized the out-of-control satellite a moment before it sailed past the perimeter, but Geddy was too mesmerized to care.

"Impact in three ... two ... one."

The initial shockwave raced across the moon's surface as though it were liquid. For a moment, it seemed the asteroid had just embedded in the moon like the spaceship in *The Astronomer's Dream*. But then a spray of dirt and rock the size of Earth 2 exploded off the side, so much that it briefly obscured the asteroid itself.

Oz was screaming in his ear, but he didn't hear it. The futility of the whole operation crashed over him like a wave just as the first stray pebble glanced off his face shield with a faint *ting*. A crack appeared at the edge of his vision, jolting him from his celestial train-wreck trance.

A sting like a Kigantean wasp sent an electric jolt up his left arm. "Ah!"

His fingers, which were resting on the EMU controls,

reflexively stiffened, activating the jet that rotated him to the left. He began to spin, crystals of blood shooting out of the finger-sized hole where the rock had pierced his forearm. The suit immediately blew up like a balloon and started venting air through the puncture as the unforgiving cold clamped its fingers around his forearm.

A warming tingle hit him as he spun. Oz had him in the newly rebooted tractor beam. His vision alternated between the back of the *Fiz* and the dark shape of XCR-190 as it emerged from the cloud of dust like a vengeful space god. It was not one asteroid now, but two, and neither would veer wide enough to miss Gundrun. Not even close.

When Oz finally arrested his spin, the first thing his eyes settled on was Voprot, whose horrified expression from behind the airlock glass said it all. The hold door was already halfway shut when he passed through, and Oz lowered him to the floor a moment before they slammed home. She re-engaged artificial gravity and the pain from his arm surged anew.

"Denk, get us the hell out of here!" Oz yelled, and the sudden acceleration rolled Geddy nearly onto his stomach.

As air flooded the room, his ears filled with outside sounds. Through his cracked shield, he saw the light over the hold door turn green. He unlatched the collar of his helmet and yanked it off, taking a deep drink of glorious oxygen.

"Where are you hit??" Oz twisted her helmet free and cast it aside.

"Arm," Geddy managed.

She knelt and grimaced, then looked up at the airlock. "Voprot, get Doc!"

CHAPTER NINE

THE INTERVENTION

"THAT'S GOOD ENOUGH FOR NOW."

Doc finished squirting some kind of pink goo into the clean hole in Geddy's left forearm, which passed directly between his ulna and radius. There was blood, and plenty of it, but the rock ha missed anything major. Of more immediate concern was the skin around the wound, which had already turned a disconcerting shade of maroon.

He put two final wraps on the bandage and frowned. "There may be nerve damage."

"Meh. I only use that one when I need to change things up."

Doc placed his arm in a sling and adjusted it, then Geddy got up and left the tiny infirmary, hurrying away with Doc at his heels. He rounded the corner and strode onto the bridge. Denk and Oz were fixed on the screen, but both whirled toward the sound of him entering.

"You okay, Cap?" A hopeful look filled Denk's rodent face.

"Through and through," replied Geddy. He glanced over

at Oz, whose mouth formed a straight line. "What's our status? Are we clear?"

"Yeah, we're clear. Everyone got out."

Geddy's eyes drifted back to the screen. The salvage vessels that responded to the emergency call were arrayed over the planet along with the Gundrun repair ship. Well below them, the scopes tracked a final handful of transports still evacuating citizens from the surface.

— *How many do you think will be left behind?*

— Too many.

The chunks of moon that broke off Valniuq hurtled toward the khetaka. Mixed among them like ice cubes in a frothy gray drink were the two halves of XCR-190, so nearly on the same trajectory that they might as well have been one.

"I do not understand," whispered Doc, coming up beside Geddy. "How could they miss this?"

He'd asked himself that same question several times. Space rock got knocked out of belts and rings all the time. And when it did, it gravitated toward the most massive celestial body. The Elenian Belt was no more than a tenth of a parsec away, which was why they'd only had a few weeks to prepare.

It all made sense, and it could all be chalked up to bad luck. So why did it feel so improbable?

"We're not getting paid, are we?" asked Denk.

"Look." Doc pointed a shaking finger at the screen. "The debris cloud."

Lasers old and new began to light up, first a handful, then dozens. Within a few seconds, it seemed every targeting satellite in sector seven had gone hot, sizzling beams of white light bisecting the void and painting streaks on Geddy's retinas.

For a few awe-inspiring seconds, it seemed the khetaka might actually keep up. Nothing from the initial wave appeared to slip through. But then the bigger ones came in dense clusters. Chunks large enough to see with the naked eye sailed through the array unimpeded. The flashes of exploding asteroids were quickly replaced by the fiery destruction of overwhelmed satellites. Everything to come would be like water through a sieve.

Barely a minute into the barrage, and khetaka was already toast. At best, the whole operation forestalled the inevitable by a few measly seconds. In a way, it was comforting to know that neither the junked satellite nor his ill-advised spacewalk would matter.

The sheer, inexorable power of it stole Geddy's breath. Valniuq looked like a piece of fruit with a bite taken out. Now, all that material, and quite possibly the moon itself at some point, was all going to hit Gundrun followed closely by the two colossal pieces of asteroid.

What would become of Gundrun's military after this? Had they moved weapons and ships to Zihnia, too? Without them, how could they hope to stand against the Zelnads?

Every satellite in the sector fell before the onslaught.

"The khetaka has failed," Arbizander grimly reported from one of the transports, his voice trembling with emotion. He'd been broadcasting on an emergency channel since before the initial impact. "No more can be done."

— *You're really going to just watch the planet be destroyed?*

— What else can we do?

"Whoa, that's weird," said Denk, noting a small readout

on the control panel. "Big burst of gamma waves from in front of the debris cloud."

"Gamma waves? From wha ..." Oz trailed off, her jaw falling open.

Eight or ten colossal warships had appeared over Gundrun as though by magic. They were pyramid-shaped with a slightly concave side that only a few people had ever seen.

Zelnad destroyers. Geddy called them schnozzes.

Adrenaline flooded his body, and he drew in a sharp breath. "What in hell ...?"

"Cap, I've never seen readings like this from a jumpgate."

"That wasn't a jumpgate," Geddy muttered. "They just appeared."

The ships dwarfed all but the largest transports, including the Gundrun repair ship positioned nearby, and even some of the manmade moons like Pretensia. Assuming they were tukrium, it was more in one place than anyone had ever seen.

— What are they doing?

Eli didn't respond at first. That usually meant he was deep in thought, and Geddy had learned to wait.

— I think they are going to save Gundrun.

The debris cloud had closed half the distance between the khetaka and the surface. The schnozzes assembled near the edge of the planet's ionosphere, moving closer together with surprising speed.

"What the heck are they doin'?" asked Denk.

Geddy took a step closer to the screen, no longer noticing the pain radiating up his arm. The moment Eli said it, the whole ploy slammed home. The Nads would see Gundrun as the biggest potential threat to their plans. But why fight them when you could earn their loyalty? They must have nudged that damned rock out of the Elenian Belt themselves on a perfect vector toward Gundrun. Now, they'd look like heroes.

But even ten destroyers looked tiny against the cloud of material barreling toward the atmosphere. What were they planning to do?

The schnozzes arranged themselves along the long axis with the flat part facing in. By the time they stopped, they were almost touching. A barrel-like hole ran through the middle of a pointy pyramid, the apex aimed at the cloud.

"They're making a supership?" Geddy said, more to himself than anyone else. Then he looked helplessly to Oz. "They're making a goddamned supership."

A glistening, white-green ripple gathered in the base of the supership, then briefly flashed before unleashing a beam so dense with energy, it bored straight into the heart of the first chunk, and it shattered as from an inner cataclysm. He gasped.

Again, the beam gathered like a breath, then spat from the barrel of the Zelnad supership in a stream of fury beyond reckoning. And, again, the massive rock was turned into a million smaller ones.

"Captain ..." Doc muttered.

Now, the Zelnad formation unfolded like a night lily, the flat bellies of the schnozzes opening like petals. More energy collected, then released in a shockwave that consumed the advancing wall of rock. Two more bursts took care of the rest.

The remaining rocks became faint, impotent streaks in the upper atmosphere, leaving only the Nad destroyers, the gaping hole in the khetaka, and a nearby moon with one flat side.

"What just happened?" Oz looked at each of them in turn.

Geddy swallowed hard. "I think we already lost the war."

CHAPTER TEN

MAN IN THE MIRROR

KNOWING that the Zelnad scheme would've happened either way, and that his comedy of errors made no difference in the end, was of little consolation to Geddy. Back on The Deuce, there was no one to let down. No one to look at him as Oz had when he made the bet, or again when he drifted out the door pushing a satellite in front of him.

Now, however, there was plenty of time for self-recrimination. After the Zelnads seemingly materialized to save Gundrun from certain annihilation, he ordered Denk to get as far away as possible in any direction.

That Tompanov won the bet only added insult to his literal injury. Transferring the hundred thousand credits from his own account into that of his despised rival stung worse than the hole in his arm.

Whether Gundrun would still pay them for the three satellites they successfully deployed was an open question. If it happened, it wouldn't be for a while.

No one had talked much since leaving. They were

making a lazy figure eight where several trade routes intersected, roughly in the middle of a square formed by Knetos, Eyeria, Doxx-Mora, and Ornea. With a bit of luck, they'd talk one of the transports into ejecting their junk or learn about an upcoming terrestrial job. But the feeling of momentum and buoyant optimism that followed them to Gundrun had evaporated.

After Doc changed his dressing, Geddy lay in bed a long time. He'd hardly slept at all, and the rash around his ear had returned with a vengeance. The same bleary-eyed malaise that had plagued him in the days leading up to Arbizander's desperate plea had wrapped him up like a straitjacket and he occasionally felt like he couldn't breathe.

— *This, too, shall pass.*

— Ah, yes. The lament of the constipated.

— *You should talk to her.*

— Not now.

— *Especially now.*

— She hates me.

— *She needs you. That's why she's upset.*

If he was being honest with himself, Geddy hadn't felt needed by anyone until Eli went up his nose. Even then, it took Eli saying *we are bound together* for him to truly understand. That's how disconnected he was. The way he saw it, Oz didn't need anyone, either, but maybe that wasn't true. Maybe nothing he believed really was.

Getting up out of bed, he paused at the mirror. The pale, doughy reflection staring back at him grimaced and moved away. Walking the two doors down to Oz's quarters was one of the hardest things he'd ever done. The belt around his chest only tightened as he gave the door a gentle rap. Maybe she was sleeping.

"Come in."

He took a deep breath and opened the door. She was seated at her little desk in the corner, idly swiping past screens in the net. A large headline read, *ZELNADS SAVE GUNDRUN*.

"Is this a good time?" Part of him hoped it wasn't.

She turned off the holobar, then pivoted in her chair and stared at him with her arms crossed. "Just my daily dose of bad news. How's your arm?"

He sheepishly entered and sat on her neatly made bed, placing his good hand on his knee and feeling the full weight of her withering stare.

"It hurts."

"You got lucky." He gave a rueful chuckle and looked away. She leaned forward. "Aren't you gonna say you haven't gotten lucky in seven years?"

"Seven years, seven months, and twenty-two days. But who's counting?" When she didn't laugh, he nervously rubbed his knee. "Listen, I know I owe you and the crew an apology. Again. But I came because I wanted to answer your question."

"What question?"

"Why I did what I did."

She shrugged. "I know why you did it."

He gave his scruffy face a scratch. "I'm not sure you really do."

"Because you thought you could save the day."

Geddy had flights of fancy once in a while, and yes, he fantasized about being a big hero, but that's not what this was.

"I wish it was as simple as that."

Oz heaved a sigh and threw up her arms. "Then you're gonna have to help me out, Ged, because I still don't get it."

She didn't have the full context because there hadn't been time to explain.

"I'm not sure you understand what it will take to solve our Zelnad problem."

She slid back in her chair and regarded him with her head cocked. "You mean reforming the Alliance."

"Okay, maybe you do understand."

"And how does your little stunt help make that happen?"

"Without Gundrun, reforming the Alliance is pointless. If there was even a one in a million chance to save them, I had to take it. And then there's Verveik."

Oz frowned, confused. "Verveik? As in Otaro Verveik? He's been dead for decades."

"We don't know that. Nobody knows that. All I know is, we need him."

Understanding descended over her. "And you thought giving your all for his home world might help your cause."

"I'm torn, Oz. On one hand, we've got a commercial operation to run, but on the other ..."

"... we need to build a coalition against the Nads."

Now they both sank back, Oz in her chair and Geddy against the wall with his legs hanging off the bed. The needs of the *Fizmo* didn't jive with what they knew about the Zelnads' plans. They were like the peasant who spotted the advancing army but couldn't get an audience with the king in time to warn him. Only there was no king, and no kingdom —

only loose or long-dead associations and a powerless salvage trawler.

"The real problem," Geddy began, "is that we don't know where they are. We need concrete proof of what they're doing."

"How can we find them?" asked Oz.

"By scanning deep space for large amounts of tukrium."

"Is there a way to do that?"

"Not that I know of." Oz scratched her chin thoughtfully. "Why? What are you thinking?"

"IASS."

The Intergalactic Association of Spacecraft Suppliers was the largest trade association in the galaxy. Their annual expo on Xellara attracted tens of thousands of visitors ranging from major shipbuilders to distributors and startups. Other attendees included a full roster of the rich and famous, some who came to check out the latest tech and others who only wanted to see and be seen.

Geddy tried to recall what time of year it was, which, once you were at space long enough, was sometimes a struggle. The first day of the show always fell on the Xellaran spring solstice, which had to be coming up soon.

Tretiak, his old boss, went regularly to rub elbows with collectors and brokers, but Geddy never had a good reason to go.

"That's not a bad idea."

She smiled appreciatively. "That's why I said it."

"Isn't going back to Xellara a problem for you?"

Oz had run away from her overbearing parents on Temeruria at a young age and joined the Xellaran resistance. The planet's working class had long been embroiled in a long civil war against the oppressive government, which they ultimately lost. She'd never talked about it, so he figured it was off-limits.

She shifted in her seat and gave a weak smile. "I'm a big girl. Besides, it's our best chance of finding what we need."

"All right, then." Geddy rose, and Oz joined him. "Let's call a huddle."

CHAPTER ELEVEN

TOTALLY JELLIN'

"THERE IS NO SUCH TECHNOLOGY," asserted Doc, dabbing away the sweat on his prominent forehead.

Geddy and Oz exchanged a quizzical look. Tardigan was smart, but he'd been exiled from Ornea, captured — sort of — by Voprot, and been with them ever since. It seemed unlikely he had his fingers on the pulse of new ship tech.

They'd just finished their morning sesehlu practice, which had further eased the tension between the crew. After explaining to Oz why he risked death to place the satellite, Geddy pulled everyone together and outlined the situation. But he decided to wait until after sesehlu to tell them about Xellara.

"You seem very sure." His arm still throbbed, but the practice had flooded him with endorphins. Not as well as Kailorian gin, but arguably healthier.

"That is because my brother's been working on it for nearly twenty years without success."

Geddy blinked in confusion. He really needed to get to know his crew better. "Your brother?"

"Parmhar, yes. His research is focused on deep-space scanning technology. Currently, we can only make educated guesses at the precise composition of distant bodies, be they planets or ships. Knowing their specific composition would have massive commercial and scientific potential."

"But he no do it?" asked Voprot, his forked tongue lolling grotesquely from his mouth.

"Parmhar has a brilliant mind, but his obsession has alienated him from family and colleagues alike. The last I heard, his funding had nearly run out and he was denied tenure."

"Is that bad?" Denk's eyes darted between them.

Tardigan regarded him almost pityingly. "Oh, Denk. What a gift to understand so little."

Denk smiled appreciatively. "Mom said it was my superpower."

"Where's Parmhar now?" Oz asked.

"Still working at the University of Tathe, at least he was." When Geddy and Oz only stared at him, his face slackened. "You can't possibly be thinking of going to Ornea."

"It can't be more than a few days from here." Denk gave a nod, confirming Geddy's guess.

Doc bristled at the notion and unconsciously balled his sweat towel in his fist. "Begging your pardon Captain, but that is not an option. Visitors to Ornea are carefully vetted. Considering your past, it is unlikely you would be granted the proper visa. And you would certainly need a guide. However, as a condition of my exile, I cannot even enter the atmosphere. There is facial recognition ... and paperwork! My god, you can't imagine the bureaucracy."

Geddy scratched his chin. He desperately needed a

shave. "Faces and paperwork, eh?" A sly grin came to his lips. "That might not be as big a problem as you think."

———————

THE LAST SNIP of beard hair tumbled into the sink, and Geddy regarded himself in the mirror. Clippers would've been the way to go, but he still hadn't thought to buy any, so scissors it was. But he'd taken his time and it looked pretty good.

— *I'd nearly forgotten your face.*

"I don't look half bad. Have I lost weight?"

— *I can only speak for your head, but there is more room than usual in here.*

"Very funny."

An unexpected smile formed as fond memories played across his mind. He gave a long, hard yawn, sleep deprivation having carved dark crescents under his eyes.

Jeledine Berwynd. How long had it been? Thirteen years?

Once, Jel would've followed him anywhere. But there was no place for a girl like that in his world. With her talents, she would've wound up working for Tretiak herself, or at least someone similarly connected to criminal enterprise. Better to break her heart than let that happen, though it broke his to let her go.

Jel liked to refer to herself as, "the best in-and-out girl this side of Stemir," which spoke to their shared comedic sensibility while also having the virtue of being true. If you needed to get in somewhere and back out safely, she was your gal. From disguises to drop-offs, credentials, and clean getaways, Jel got it done and demanded top dollar for her service.

Aside from being capable and daring, she was also born and raised on Stemir, which produced the most desirable women in the entire universe.

Geddy splashed water on his face then ran wet fingers through his hair. It wasn't quite long enough to gather into a ponytail, though he wondered how it would look. He was probably too old to pull off a man-bun.

— *This is just means to an end, right?*

"Totally."

After sesehlu, he pulled up the subspace frequency sometimes called the "band of thieves." He used it often working for Tretiak and was relieved to find his old passkey still decrypted the stream. He hailed Jeledine, and she came onscreen almost immediately, feet up and fingers laced behind her head. Her pure white hair tumbled over her smooth, olive-hued shoulders in perfect curls, her signature goggles perched just so atop her head.

"How in hell are you still alive?" she asked.

"I guess I've always wanted to see what happens next. How are you? Busy with the ol' in and out?"

"As always."

It wasn't a good idea to hang out on the subfrequency for too long, encrypted or not. He cut straight to the chase.

"Listen, Jel ... I need into Ornea."

"Ornea? That's a new one. Just you?"

"I'll have a plus one. He's Ornean, but he's been exiled. Suffice it to say, they take that pretty seriously."

She barked a laugh. "Exiled? What'd he do — cheat on a math test?"

"You are shockingly close. So, can you do it?"

"You, I could do." Her seductive smile seemed to come right out of the screen.

Geddy gulped, wishing he had a glass of water. "What about the Ornean?"

She hemmed and hawed before answering. "I can make him look Soturian and probably get him in, but their algorithm checks visas recursively against a randomly generated string. You'll have two hours, maybe less."

Not exactly the response he was hoping for.

"We can work with that. Can we meet?"

She'd delivered rendezvous coordinates and signed off. As soon as he disconnected, he sent them to Denk with little explanation before attempting to take a nap. He woke an hour later to a tap on his door.

Oz's voice followed without waiting for him to respond. "We're almost there."

Geddy scrambled to the door, catching Oz before she could walk away. She turned to face him.

"You shaved."

Instinctively Geddy ran a hand over his short stubble.

"I've been meaning to since we left Zorr."

That was more or less true, but guilt set in as she eyed the fresh shirt he was wearing. Whatever they had was still developing, but he and Jel had actual history, which he couldn't quite ignore.

"Why do I get the impression this girl's more than just an old acquaintance?"

"She was more … but that was a long time ago. Right now, we need her help." He yawned again and rubbed his eyes.

"Still not sleeping?"

"Apparently not."

"Cap, I've got a transponder match to your friend's ship. Two minutes out." Normally Denk's voice over the comm came at the worst times, but today his timing was perfect.

Most ships would've had to soft dock on the *Fiz's* roof and come in through the old escape pod hatches since the original airlock had been walled off. Fortunately, Jel's ship was small enough to fit in the empty hold.

"Great." Geddy brushed past Oz on his way to the airlock. "Let's unroll the welcome mat."

A few minutes later, he stood with the entire crew pressed against the airlock windows, including Morpho. Denk popped the hold door and the alarms sounded. Before they had even opened fully, Jel swooped in and nosed her ship inside. The *Bogart* was a custom racing ship that Jel took in payment for a job. He'd always been a little jealous of it.

The big doors slowly closed behind her as the skids settled onto the floor. Geddy re-engaged the gravity and was the first through the airlock door. The *Bogart's* ramp lowered as he approached. Standing tall, he unconsciously smoothed his signature Apollo Program jacket. Denk and the rest of the crew joined him, standing shoulder to shoulder waiting to greet their guest.

Jel came down the ramp at a crouch to keep her head from hitting the fuselage then rose as she fluffed out her perfect silvery hair. As usual, she was outfitted in tight, ratty leather that seemed like it came preinstalled on her lithe body.

"Geddy Starheart," she said, beaming.

"Jeledine Berwynd."

They embraced, and it felt so good, he nearly forgot to let go.

CHAPTER TWELVE

A FEW STIFF ONES

As with most Stemirian women, Jeledine hadn't aged a day since Geddy last saw her. Her impossibly smooth skin still had its luster, and her strappy leather getup still wrapped just so around her modest curves. The bright, ice-blue eyes that always twinkled with mischief were clear as ever.

And yet, a certain darkness had attached itself to her, not unlike looking through a tinted window. Shit happened, and it seemed shit had happened to her. Geddy wasn't sure how much he wanted to know.

After introducing her to Oz and the rest of the crew, a peculiar sound came from Jel's ship, like ball bearings stirred in a pot. They turned toward it, and a shapeshifting cluster of magnetic bots climbed down the ramp like a slinky.

"Hughey?" Geddy asked.

Hughey was Jel's shapeshifting synthetic companion. She'd taken him as payment for a job before she and Geddy ever met, and he'd rarely seen her without him.

"Actually, Hughey Twoey. Hughey One sacrificed himself to save me from pirates."

The bots were metal slivers roughly the size and shape of snake scales that could mold themselves into shapes, roll like a ball, or even fly like tiny helicopters. Each provided a share of the hive-like AI, which was programmed for companionship and protection. Sometimes it took the shape of a dog, sometimes a bird or exotic creature. It all depended on Jel's mood.

Morpho, who was perched on Denk's shoulder, hopped off and landed on the metal grating with a splat as Hughey Twoey rolled toward them, like jangling chainmail. It stopped a few centimeters from Morpho, mimicking his blobby shape. They made a slow circle, mirroring each other's movements as they checked each other out.

— *They seem to like each other.*

— I can't decide if that's good or bad.

Jel leaned close to Geddy. "What is Morpho, exactly?"

"Synthetic organism. Beyond that, we're not too sure."

Jel squatted beside the two synthetics. She reached out and poked Morpho, who briefly curled around her finger before returning his attentions to Hughey. A crooked smile decorated her face as she rose.

"Fascinating. Basoan? Nichuan?"

"Zelnad," Oz answered.

Jel's smile vanished, her gaze narrowing accusingly at Geddy, demanding explanation. Clearly, the Nads had something to do with the cloud that had attached to her.

"Relax, he's cool. He's saved all our lives multiple times."

She took another good look at Morpho. "Is it an AI?"

"That's a discussion best had over a stiff drink. Whaddya say?"

Her expression brightened. "I'd take a stiff anything right

now. How about you show me around, then I'll get started scanning Dr. Tardigan's face while we catch up."

— *A stiff anything?*

— It's just her way.

— *It is also your way. Perhaps you rubbed off on her.*

— Oh, I definitely have.

Denk turned on his heels and marched toward the airlock with a sweeping gesture of his stubby arm. "C'mon, Jeledine, lemme show you around my ship."

Jel kept up with Doc and Voprot right behind. Neither Oz nor Geddy moved.

"'A stiff anything?'" Oz asked drolly. "Sounds like a graduate of Geddy Starheart's Comedy Camp."

There was nothing between them anymore, but his standing with Oz had taken a hit and had yet to swing back. Geddy knew these two women well enough to believe they would get along, but it never would've occurred to him Oz might be jealous. He wasn't sure if he should use it or ignore it. Either way, the next few hours could get very interesting.

———

AFTER DENK SHOWED Jel around the ship, they circled back to haul some of her gear out of the *Bogart*. Doc sat patiently, if nervously, as a portable scanner made a detailed map of his face. All the major races were pre-programmed into her printer, which would need a few hours to make the prosthetics. She let it run while they convened in the galley for drinks.

Jel had initially taken one of the seats around the table

but quickly got back up. "Sorry, I've been sitting for days. You guys don't mind if I stretch a bit, do you?"

"That seems reasonable," Doc nodded at Geddy and Denk.

Standing, she spread her legs and folded her arms back behind her, twisting and leaning side to side as she spoke, casually baring her flawless midriff with each move.

"So, what were you doing when I called?" Geddy swirled the gin around in his glass.

"Not much. I'd just tied off on a job on Myadan." replied Jel. "My god, that feels good."

"Myadan?" Oz asked. "What kind of job?"

"The kind I'm paid well not to talk about."

Myadan was the destination of the derelict biotransport ship they'd encountered a few months earlier. Other than the ranse that turned Captain Bykite into a canoe, they didn't know what else it carried or why it was headed to that planet.

Oz flared her eyebrows and looked away as she took a drink. Operators like Jel were never too forthcoming about their work. Then again, what criminals were transparent about their activities?

Jel extended one sleek leg up on the edge of the counter and touched her chin to her knee. Denk, who presumably had never seen a Stemiran girl in the wild, couldn't take his eyes off her. She had that effect.

"Anyway, it's weird right now. Nobody knows who to trust, y'know? Did you hear what happened over Gundrun?"

The crew exchanged an uncomfortable look and shifted in their seats. Geddy cleared his throat. "We were kinda there."

Her eyes peeled wide. "You were? Ohmygod, tell me everything."

Geddy took another drink of his gin, then hesitantly recounted the events leading up to the Nads' perfectly timed arrival, omitting the part where he could've died. Thankfully, Oz chose not to fill in the blanks.

"The Gundrun aren't stupid," asserted Jel, her face pinching into a determined pucker. "I don't know what the Zelnads are up to, but clearly, they're up to *something*. I mean, swooping in to save the planet from a collision they somehow didn't see coming? It stinks to high heaven if you ask me."

She had that right. The Gundrun weren't stupid. But even if they smelled a rat, they'd just seen a Zelnad supership turn a planet-killing rock into sand. If there came a time when they had to pick sides, their choice would be clear.

Oz sat up and leaned toward Jel. "You believe the Zelnads are evil?"

"Ha!" Jel threw her head back. "They're crooked as a Basoan's dick. I saw it firsthand." She downed half her gin in one gulp and wiped her mouth on her sleeve, then switched legs.

— *She is a free spirit.*

— I could tell you stories.

— *You have. I feel like I know her.*

"Geddy!" Oz slapped his shoulder, jolting him back to reality. He'd zoned out there for several seconds. "Did you hear what she said?"

— Um, help?

—*Jeledine's youngest sister disappeared. She thinks she joined the Zelnads.*

"Of course, I did. I'm just glad to know you don't trust them either. Most people think they're a cult."

Jel considered this, then shrugged. "I don't know they're *not* a cult. Hell, I don't know if they're shapeshifters from the eighth dimension. But I don't have to know *what* they are to know they're up to no good. And if there's as many of 'em as I think, that's a real problem for me."

Geddy and Oz shared a look. At this point, the only reason not to share the truth about the Nads was if you thought you were talking to one, and even then, it probably wouldn't have mattered.

Oz refilled Geddy's glass. He took a long pull, then told Jel everything. That there were timeless beings called Sagaceans who planted the seeds of intelligent life as part of a grand experiment. That the Zelnads were a rebel faction of Sagaceans who decided it was time to call the experiment a failure.

Jel downed two glasses while Geddy talked. She could've put any of them under the table.

When he finished, she stared at him through narrow slits. "How could you possibly know all this?"

"Because one of the good Sagaceans is in my head as we speak. His name is Eli, and he wants everyone to live."

Jeledine's slow, serious nod faded to a smile, then cut to a fit of full-throated laughter. She slapped the table. "Oh my god, G-Star is in a relationship he can't escape! That's a friggin' riot!"

For the first time since Jel arrived, Oz's hardened expression softened, and she laughed, too.

— *G-star?*

— It's a dumb pet name ... Although, it works on a few different levels.

Before long, everyone joined the chorus of laughter at his expense. Finally, Jel settled down and tipped her glass toward him.

"Well, Eli better not change his mind about the experiment just because he wound up in your dumb head." She cupped her hands and yelled, "He doesn't represent the best of us!"

— *Oooh, I like her.*

Oz cackled, clapping, and Denk was doubled over. Even Doc allowed a wide grin, which looked as foreign on his pasty face as a kabuki mask.

— *Wow, they must've really needed to laugh at me.*

— *Or maybe what everyone needs in this moment is for you to laugh at yourself.*

Eli's point hit home immediately. Early on, it was much easier to see the humor of their situation. At a certain point, it stopped being funny. But the world might end at any moment now, and the time in which to laugh might be short.

He cracked a smile that became a chuckle, and that chuckle morphed into a full-bore belly laugh that coaxed tears from his eyes. God, he needed it. For a few precious moments, it seemed like everything might be okay.

— *Music to my ears.*

CHAPTER THIRTEEN

EAVESDROPPING

WHAT GEDDY EXPECTED to be an hour or two of catching up turned into a marathon session fueled by two whole bottles of Kailorian gin. Once Oz finally warmed to Jeledine, which everyone eventually did, it was off to the races. Doc turned in first, soon followed by Denk and Voprot, leaving him and the ladies to keep each other in stitches until the small hours.

When they finally decided to call it a night, Geddy realized Jel didn't have anywhere to sleep. She planned to just crash on the *Bogart*, but after a long turn in space and in light of her help, he offered to swap rooms for the night.

The *Bogart* smelled a bit like Jeledine's ever-present mint gum, as did the cramped quarters behind the cabin, which was just big enough for a single fold-up bunk and a shower that had to be small even for petite Jel. A few trinkets, mostly bracelets and necklaces, hung from little hooks on the wall to either side of the cubbies where she kept her clothes. Otherwise, it was basically empty, the bulk of her equipment and food stored elsewhere.

She was a no-frills kind of girl, and this was a no-frills setup.

The gin made it easy to fall asleep, but when he'd been drinking, Geddy often woke up after a few hours later as though his brain was trying to sweat it off. This time, however, he woke to a conversation taking place in his head. At first, he dismissed it as a dream.

— **Are we in agreement, then?**

— *Yes.*

The rash on his ear, which had nearly healed, flared hot. When he reached his hand up to scratch it, his fingernails touched something muscled and faintly sticky, like a dry-aged steak.

— **What was that?**

— *What was what?*

— **He just scratched me. Is he …?**

— Awake?

The other voice in his head was Morpho. The first time he spoke to Geddy was over Kigantu when he plugged into his brain and had a conversation with him and Eli. That was weird enough, but then, on Aku, when Eli briefly took Geddy over, Morpho intervened and revealed himself as a fellow Sagacean. Had he not done so, Geddy might be a Zelnad himself.

Since then, however, Morpho had made himself scarce and Geddy hadn't communed with him again. But now, it appeared Morpho and Eli had been using his brain as a boardroom, and he was mildly allergic to whatever Morpho was made of.

— **How much did you hear?**

— That you agreed on something.

— *Geddy, I am sorry. This is the only way Morpho and I can talk. I fear it has affected your sleep patterns.*

— **I am sorry, too. I will disconnect from you immediately.**

— Hold up a sec. How long have you been talking?

— *Most nights since leaving Zorr.*

His strangely persistent fatigue was starting to make a lot more sense. Some part of his subconscious had been awake for these conversations and rarely got to rest.

— About what?

— **The plan.**

— Don't you think I should know the plan?

— *We have only just settled on it.*

— And?

— **We do not believe the Zelnads want a war. It is too inefficient.**

To that point, Geddy envisioned a vast Zelnad armada sweeping through the galaxy, leaving a trail of destruction in their wake. But theirs was just one galaxy of thousands, maybe millions, and going about it that way would take a long time. Considering what happened over Gundrun, it seemed they were being more strategic.

— You think they just want to destroy Sagacea?

— *Destroying Sagacea only prevents the rise of future civilizations. There are many to erase.*

— But you heard the Metallurgist back on Aku. They already have all the shinium they need to build their weapon.

— **The Metallurgist wanted you to believe all was lost.**

Geddy's heart leapt. The hopelessness he'd felt about their chances against the Nads opened just a crack.

— So, they don't have all they need?

— *We have calculated that a weapon capable of destroying Sagacea would require a great deal more shinium.*

— **We believe they are so focused on tukrium because trace amounts of shinium may be mixed in.**

The Metallurgist said tukrium, the galaxy's most valuable metal, was formed by forces present during the birth of the universe. In rare cases, Sagacean spores landed in molten tukrium and became trapped inside like insects in amber. Their spirits in the metal would, in theory, allow it to pass through the barrier protecting Sagacea.

If Morpho and Eli were right, then the Zelnads' obsession with tukrium wasn't about building an army so much as finding enough shinium for their Sagacea-killing weapon. The good news was, he hadn't just handed them what they needed. However, he'd revealed where he acquired it.

The Deuce.

— Oh, no. They're going to plunder Earth 2!

— *Yes. Chances are, they have already begun.*

— So how do we stop them? What's the plan? At this point, a match might take care of The Deuce.

— **We must rebuild the Alliance before the Zelnads consolidate their power.**

Was it possible that the part of his brain that couldn't sleep through Eli and Morpho's nightly powwows had absorbed this? Was that why he felt the same way, or did they all arrive at the same conclusion?

—That's what I've been saying!

— **But there is a problem.**

— *What happened to Jeledine's sister has happened across the universe. Fathers, mothers, and siblings have been taken over. To harm the Zelnads is to harm their hosts, who are innocent.*

— So, what do we fight back with? Name-calling?

— **We need concrete evidence to galvanize support for a new Alliance.**

— *Morpho is right. We must prove the threat.*

— That's exactly why we're talking to Doc's brother. Tukrium is the key to everything, and we need to find out where it's all going.

— **What about Earth 2?**

— I might have an idea about that, but let's worry about one thing at a time.

— *Geddy, I am sorry we have been meeting in your head. Your brain is the perfect medium, and besides, it is largely uncluttered.*

— Well, look at you with the zingers.

— *I am here every Thursday. Try the veal.*

Geddy couldn't help but laugh. He'd created a monster.

— **For the time being, we no longer require your head. I will disconnect now.**

— Hold your horses there, Cowboy. Where do you go all day?

— **What do you mean?**

— Back when you guys first picked me up as space junk, I figured you were always working on the ship. But the ship's in decent shape, yet I see way less of you. Why is that?

— **She is a demanding mistress.**

— That's an interesting way to put it, given that you crawl around her guts.

— **I perform my role without rest, without question, and, frankly, without direction. I am the only reason this ship is in one piece. Are you really questioning how I spend my time?**

— *Morpho!*

— **I apologize, Captain. Sometimes my emotions get the better of me.**

Neither Eli nor Morph were much for emotions, which made Morpho's defensiveness even more notable.

— No worries. Carry on.

A sticky, slurpy sound filled Geddy's left ear as Morpho withdrew, creating a brief vacuum that broke with a pop. "Ow!"

Morpho slithered off the bed and out the open door into the cabin.

Geddy scratched at the rash Morpho just freshened and lay there in the dark contemplating how deeply weird his life had become. Two microscopic aliens had been holding court in his head. His ex was sleeping in his bed, alone, and she might be BFFs now with the girl he was currently in love with.

"You there?"

— *Always.*

"I like that."

— *Do we need to talk?*

"How much do you know about Morpho?"

— *That he is a Sagacean, and that he opposes the Zelnads.*

"Yeah, but besides that. Like how he came to be a Zelnad tarball in the first place."

— We have never spoken of the past. Present and future are our sole focus. Why are you asking?

"I know where everyone on this crew is from and how they got here. Everyone but Morph."

— You still do not trust him?

"I trust him with my life. But he's being cagey, and I feel like I should know why."

— Morpho takes his duty very seriously. His intentions are pure.

"Then we have nothing to worry about."

— I hope you sleep soundly, Geddy.

"Me, too."

CHAPTER FOURTEEN

TARDIGAN THE SOTURIAN

GEDDY AWOKE to the sound of Jeledine's laugh echoing through the hold like a bell. He'd expected the wall to be much further away when his eyes opened, so his brain took a while to register that he was still in Jel's bunk in the *Bogart*.

"You can't be serious. All thirteen appendices used the wrong citation format?" she asked.

"As well as the footnotes!" came Tardigan's surprisingly jocular voice. "His children were taken from him!"

Again, Jel laughed. "Man, Doc, you have got some doozies. You should write a book."

"I have written eleven books. Reading them is a high crime!"

Jel howled again as though this was actually funny. She had no way of knowing they were actual terms of his exile.

Regardless, she had a way of making everyone feel good, or interesting, or funny — even when they weren't. Especially when they weren't. As much as he loved her for that, it always made him wonder if she was on the level. Such was the curse of cynicism.

Geddy pulled on his clothes and halfheartedly made the covers, then folded up the bunk and peered out through the front shield. Doc sat in one of the stools beside the workbench with his back to the shelves. Jel flitted around him, dabbing at his face and smoothing the areas where his real skin met the edges of the prosthetics.

He ducked his head and took the ramp down into the hold.

Jel glanced over and smiled. "Morning, Sunshine. You're just in time for the big reveal." She glanced back at Doc. "You ready, Professor?"

Bleary-eyed, Geddy padded over to the workbench. Jel spun Doc's chair around, a brilliant smile illuminating her pretty face.

The quality of her work stopped Geddy in his tracks. It might as well have been Zereth-Tinn or Sammo Yann seated on the stool. Soturians shared Orneans' ridged brows, and nearly the same skin tone, but the similarities largely ended there. Doc's eyes had gone from light brown to ice blue and even appeared larger. His teeth were pointy, his hair tightly packed and graying. Even his shoulders were more squared-off to help sell it. He was on the tall side for a Soturian, but not enough to raise many eyebrows.

No wonder it took half the night. She must've printed off ten different pieces, maybe more, including contacts and a dental appliance.

Geddy whistled in amazement as he circled Doc, who was truly unrecognizable. "Damn, girl. You've done this before."

"I've come a long way since you knew me. But I'm not gonna lie, Ornea's a tall order. Especially in his case."

Geddy leaned his good elbow against the workbench. "You've got credentials for both of us, right?"

"Yeah, but like I said, their system re-authenticates visas every half hour or so. I could only manage four challenge codes, so you've got two hours at the outside."

Geddy nodded. "What's my cover?"

"You're a government bureaucrat in charge of the Bubbles on Earth 3, which have had some major leaks. Doc here's an engineer sent by the Soturian company that makes the pressure couplings. You want his brother to review the new designs before you place a big order."

— *Bureaucrat? You could maybe pull off liquor distributor.*

— Give me a little credit. I'm not as dumb as I look.

— *Dumber?*

"You got clothes to give us?"

"Of course," Jel said, a playful note in her voice, "but as you know, I'm better at taking them away."

Geddy gulped. "Doc, why don't you grab Oz and prepare the *Dom* for the drop."

"But my disguise ..." he protested.

"Consider it a test run. See if she knows it's you."

Tardigan stiffly rose and rolled his eyes, then took off toward the airlock. Voprot snored quietly in his corner.

Geddy turned to face Jel. It was the first time they'd been alone since she arrived.

She took Doc's seat and put her feet up on the workbench, rubbing her temples. "I haven't worked that hard in a while. It's almost like the bad old days with you."

Geddy came around behind her and took the other stool like he and Oz did sometimes. It almost felt like cheating.

He laced his fingers behind his head and yawned again. "Were they, though? I seem to remember us having some pretty good times."

Jel gave a rueful chuckle. "That sounds about right."

"What?"

"That you'd remember it that way."

Geddy had let plenty of people down and burned his share of bridges back then, but not Jel. He always thought he'd done right by her, more or less.

He frowned. "How do you remember it?"

"That you only came around when it was convenient. We'd ... dock somewhere in the ass end of space, have a few laughs, and go on our merry way. You probably thought it was a perfect relationship."

True, it was the very definition of friends with benefits. If pressed, he would've said he loved Jel, but he could see that wasn't true. Maybe she knew it never would be, even back then. Women had a way of knowing stuff.

"You wanted more."

She shrugged, smiling, like the thought of it could trouble her no longer. "We never would've wanted the same things. You'd already come to terms with that. It took me longer is all." Jel held up her slender hands. "But hey, in the end, all that matters is—"

"Today and tomorrow," he finished. She used to say it all the time. For a guy who spent a lot of time ruminating, it struck him as a damned good philosophy.

Her smile faded, and her face turned deadly serious. "'Course, from what you say, tomorrow's not a guarantee anymore."

Geddy gave his head a slow shake. "That's for sure."

"This thing with the Zelnads ... we don't have much time, do we?"

"It doesn't feel like it."

Her eyes drifted downward to where her hands were sandwiched between her legs. "What can we do? What can anyone do?"

He hesitated before answering. Not because he didn't trust her, but because after hearing what Morpho said, it no longer sounded so plausible. "We're going to rebuild the Alliance."

Jel squinted as though she hadn't heard him correctly. "The Alliance. As in, the long-dead intergalactic organization?"

"Everything old is new again."

"What's Ornea got to do with it?"

"The less you know, the better."

Jel nodded, running her lower teeth along her upper lip like she always did when something bothered her. "Level with me, Ged. From one operator to another — can we really beat these guys, or should I gather me rosebuds?"

"I have to believe we can."

"And this ... little voice in your head. What does he say?"

"He tells me to drink less and never hurry a shit. But he also believes we can stop them."

Jeledine slid off her stool and planted a tender kiss on his forehead. "In that case, I wish you both luck. Him, especially."

— *Tell her that was very thoughtful.*

— You tell her.

Oz strolled through the airlock door thumbing over her

shoulder. "We just passed Ornea's outer marker ..." She stopped short. "Did I interrupt something?"

"No," Jel said, strolling casually her way. "In fact, *Captain* Starheart was just telling me more about the op. I assume you saw your Soturian stowaway."

Oz laughed and fist-bumped her, shaking her head in disbelief. "I wouldn't have recognized him. Well done."

"Thanks." Jel's eyes darted between Geddy and Oz. "I'm gonna hit the shower. Anyone care to join me?"

The awkward silence was immediately filled by Jeledine's bemused cackle, which followed her out the door.

CHAPTER FIFTEEN

ME SO ORNEA

The Dominic plunged toward the capital city of Tathe, shuddering as it entered the atmosphere and descended through puffy white clouds. Ornea was an Earth-like planet with long days and short nights, warmed by a relatively small, young sun. Two small moons orbited the planet at vastly different distances, though neither was visible during their approach.

Ordinarily, Doc would've been walking Geddy through its entire timeline dating back to early geological history, but he hadn't uttered a word since dropping out of the *Fiz's* belly. The faraway look in his eyes confirmed his trepidation about it. He had barely veered off the path of academic integrity and was pilloried for it. More accurately, he had been loaded into a rocket and shot off to Kigantu never to return.

Talk about the door hitting you in the ass on your way out.

— *Get him talking. It calms him.*

— It doesn't calm the listener.

— *Even so.*

Their approach vector was rendered onscreen as a long, nearly straight tunnel. Usually, he preferred to do things manually, but this time, he set the autopilot and swiveled toward Doc.

"You doing all right, Doc? I know we sort of railroaded you into this."

"I'm here of my own accord, Captain. And I am fine."

"If you say so. Tell me more about your brother."

Even from beneath the prosthetic, his face seemed to relax. "Parmhar is three years my senior. My father always favored him despite his interest in applied sciences, which he calls for-profit science. I might have done the same were it not for my desire to please my father. That's why I chose the humanities."

Great — another overbearing parent. Better than having no parents at all. "Are you and Parmhar close?"

A faint smile crossed his face. "We were. But we haven't spoken since ..."

He didn't need to finish. It had been about three months since Doc became Voprot's prisoner, a situation he'd been strangely comfortable with. Probably because Voprot kept him alive, and in the Kigantean desert, that was the best you could hope for.

"If nothing else, he'll be glad to know you're alive, right?"

"Yes. The same could not be said about my father."

The *Dom* eased into the troposphere, and the fuselage began to shake. Doc's fingers dug into the armrests, his lips pinched tight, and his eyes closed. When they emerged through a final cloud, the shaking stopped, and the carefully planned sprawl of Tathe City opened below.

Geddy's work for the Double A never took him to Ornea.

Thieves and super-rich collectors didn't exactly hang out there. From what he understood, everything Orneans did was supported by facts and logic. The value of a thing was measured not in money, but by how it benefited society. In that regard, they were like human-sized Sagaceans. If Doc could've crawled into Geddy's ear and had long conversations with Eli, he would've in a heartbeat. And then he'd never sleep again.

The city was arranged in neat geometric shapes that fit together like an elegant puzzle with just enough variety to interest the eye. The spaceport doubled as a transportation hub for the entire city, which relied on a combination of mass transit and low-impact personal transportation like bicycles.

Doc explained that any large endeavor was the product of engineers, city planners, estheticians, arborists, and countless other experts who sought sensible compromises. It begged the question of how anything got done.

"There are stories of committee meetings lasting for weeks," he raved. "Can you imagine how electric that would be? A diverse collection of peers engaged in a free and open exchange of ideas leading to a mutually agreeable solution? I get chills just thinking about it."

Geddy flared his eyebrows. "Like running a high fever."

The *Dom* swung low over an elongated park near the spaceport and slowed nearly to a hover. Geddy unbuckled as the automated ground-based traffic control took over. There weren't that many ships coming and going, which made it seem unnecessary, but when in Ornea …

The system even extended the skids and set them down gently on pad 2A, a stone's throw from the gate labeled Visa

Control. Doc's ice-blue contacts stared straight ahead, his breathing shallow and rapid.

"You gonna be okay?" Geddy asked.

"Just a ... routine panic attack."

Geddy placed a calming hand on his shoulder. "You've got this, Doc. Remember, you're not you. You're Polvo Grenn, my Soturian engineer. I'm Jevar Sodenvoch from Earth 3, and we're here for a little consult. That's it."

Doc closed his eyes again and took a couple long, deep breaths. "You're right. We're just playing parts."

He actually hadn't given it that much thought until then. Structural engineer was a stretch, but he could fake it. As long as no one asked him pointed questions about math or physics, he'd be golden.

"Game time," Geddy said. "Remember, our clock starts the moment they scan our visas. We need to be in the air in two hours or less. Getting caught is no bueno."

Tardigan squared his jaw. "I'm ready."

THE THREE LINES into Visa Control merged into one with an arm scanner flanked by two guards. They fell in line behind two gangly and clearly annoyed Dudirans, their four arms folded defiantly.

"Twice a week we have to do this," complained one. "I've got two words for you — trusted traveler."

"I know. Like anyone in their right mind would sneak into Ornea."

Doc looked pleadingly back at Geddy, but he took that as a good sign.

— If I need to say something smart ...

— *I'm ready, don't worry.*

"Hey, do I know you?" asked a cheery voice behind them.

They whirled. Another Soturian, substantially shorter than Doc, had joined the line behind them. His eyes narrowed at Doc, ignoring Geddy utterly.

"Did you go to the University of New Kitama?"

"Me?" Doc was so startled that he almost spat out the Soturian denture he had in. He covered his mouth and mumbled, "No, sorry. I'm a Cayapolis man through and through."

"Cayapolis?" He frowned. "I thought that was a women's college."

"Yes, of course," Doc stammered. "But they're test marketing it to men."

"Interesting."

The line steadily advanced. Only three people remained in front of them.

The guy kept touching Doc's arm in a decidedly unsubtle way. "I love your coloration. So vivid. Are you from Overogdan?"

"My family is."

— *Wait ... is he ...?*

— Hitting on Tardigan? I think so.

"Ha! I knew it. What brings you to Ornea?" asked the flirty Soturian.

Maybe this was a good thing. A test of Doc's nerves before the important part.

"Er, my colleague and I are having some challenges with a pressure coupling. We're here for a design review."

Again, the man touched Doc, this time a playful slap on

the shoulder. "Ha — I'm in the exact same business. What are the chances?"

"Astronomical," Tardigan said, anxious for them to be motioned up.

"What kind of challenges? Maybe I can help." He raised his eyebrows hopefully.

"Slow leak." Geddy herded Doc away from Sir Talksalot. "Whup, looks like we're next. Have a good one."

"Next!" The immigration officer's nasally voice bounced off the walls.

Doc grabbed Geddy's hand and pulled him ahead. "Sorry, we're traveling together."

— *I believe Dr. Tardigan is pretending you are a couple.*

— Yeah, I picked up on that, E.

The officer nodded at the scanner. Moment of truth. Doc set down his wrist and the scanner read his fake credentials. A photo of him in disguise appeared on the officer's holo-screen, whose eyes moved back and forth between the screen and Tardigan a couple extra times.

"Destination?"

"The University," replied Doc.

"On what business?"

"A design consult."

Seemingly satisfied, the officer glanced up at Geddy and had him do the same. The scanner read the chip embedded in his forearm and also brought up his phony credentials.

"Earth 3, eh? How's the mogorodon situation?"

"Sticky," Geddy quipped. "It's mating season."

Tardigan coughed again. The Ornean officer allowed the faintest of smiles to alight on his face, then it vanished as quickly. "Thank you. I needed a laugh."

— That was a laugh?

—Maybe there's an open-mic night around here. I'd have 'em smirking in the aisles.

The officer gave them one final look up and down, then digitally approved their entry. "Welcome to Ornea."

They nodded politely then scurried through the gates into the attached ground transit hub. Geddy noted the time. 11:17 a.m.

Most places like this were chaotic and loud, with un-chipped aliens trying and failing to communicate with other travelers about which shuttle or train to take. Not here. Clear and concise signs and wayfinding kiosks abounded, and there weren't many people around.

Tardigan, of course, didn't need any signs. He pointed to a row of sliding doors near the end of the terminal and looked anxiously over his shoulder to ensure the Soturian hadn't followed them. "This way."

They proceeded through the doors and stepped onto the platform where the train awaited. They got on, and the doors closed just as the Soturian came running up. He stared long-ingly after Doc and raised his hand in farewell.

Doc leaned back and heaved a sigh, the back of his head hitting the glass with a little thud.

Geddy patted him on the leg. "You did great."

"Did you start the timer?"

"Yeah. We should be on the *Dom* by one."

Doc exhaled heavily. "That doesn't leave us much time."

The train pulled out of the station, accelerating to an impressive speed with no discernible vibration. They shot through a tunnel of overhanging trees and emerged into a bright, sunny Ornean day.

It was exactly how Geddy imagined the good parts of ancient Rome or Athens used to be. Nearly every building was a high-rise separated from other skyscrapers by lush, neatly pruned green spaces. Small groups of people were arrayed on short mounds, seated and listening attentively to others teaching. And they weren't even to the university yet!

Doc spotted him looking and leaned over. "They're mostly employees of downtown companies. They're only allowed four hours each workday for D and D, if you can imagine."

"D and D?"

"Debate and defense. How are you supposed to develop your mind with just four hours of vigorous discussion per day?"

"It's criminal." Geddy said what Tardigan needed to hear.

The train continued around the downtown loop, turned right, and glided through an unpretentious residential area before it emerged into a sprawling urban campus. Doc leaned excitedly forward in his seat.

"The University of Tathe," he said reverently. "Flagship of the Tathe university system. Of the thirty-four campuses in the city, this is the largest."

Tathe wasn't all that big. A million people, give or take. How many institutions of higher learning did they really need?

— *I think I would like it here.*

— You're welcome to stay.

They came to a gentle stop at University Station. Geddy and Doc got out descended wide stairs onto a quadrangle webbed with sidewalks. Again, Tardigan knew exactly where they were headed and took off across it. Flowering trees, alive with bees, lined their path.

Students and professors strolled along, rarely alone and always engaged in conversation.

"... I have run the assay three times but still can't account for the delta in the samples."

" ... but did Ehrmograth ever adequately undergird his defense of the Mingarten theorem? After reading all eighty-four of his collected works, I am unsatisfied."

"There!" Doc pointed across the quad. "That's Parmhar's building."

He took off at a clip, leaving Geddy to jog after him. As they neared the building, they passed a long, ornately carved wall lined with reliefs of faces and carvings of their many accomplishments. Tardigan breezed past it without so much as a glance.

"Hey, what is this?" Geddy took a couple steps toward the wall.

"The University of Tathe wall of fame." Doc thumbed down the path. "We ought to keep moving."

Geddy was about to follow when a familiar name appeared.

TARDIGAN.

"Whoa, hold up. Is this your family?"

Reliefs of two men and a woman were under the family name.

Doc gave a long sigh and pointed at them in turn. "That's Sabin, my uncle, Reni, my mother ... and Pyrus, my father. Can we go now?"

From the other side of the wall came a thin, wet *splat*, and bits of orange goop landed on Geddy's forehead.

"What the hell?"

He touched it and gave it a sniff. Some kind of vegetable, maybe a tomato or its Ornean equivalent. He frowned at Doc. Another splat came, this time clearly from the other side of the wall, and more spray.

"What's going on?"

Doc chased at his heels as he rounded the end of the wall and found two students, a man and a woman, pelting a parallel monument with rotten vegetables.

Geddy marched angrily up to them. "Hey, what gives?"

Noting the look on his face and the flecks of tomato, or whatever, on his borrowed clothes, the color drained from their faces. "Oh, goodness." said the young woman. "Sir, we are so, so sorry."

The other monument, separated from the wall of fame by a decorative shrubbery, was much smaller. It, too, featured reliefs, but they were exaggerated like caricatures. And one of them, caked with both paint and vegetable matter, seemed awfully familiar. The name beneath was KRONS TARDIGAN.

— *Oh, no.*

"What is this thing?" Geddy demanded.

"The Academic Exiles display," answered the very contrite male student. "We call it the Wall of Shame."

"We're encouraged to deface it," the woman explained. "Like a rage room."

Tardigan gritted his teeth. "Yes, and they face off-campus to signify that they turned their backs on academic integrity. Now, can we *please* go."

Doc grabbed Geddy's arm and practically dragged him to the sidewalk on the other side. As they receded, one of the students remarked, "How could a Soturian know that? I didn't even know that."

"Now hold up, Doc. Is that really how they did you?"

Academics never made much sense to Geddy. What kind of psychopath dedicates their life to the study of one super specific thing? But apart from that, Ornea's commitment to shame and dishonor was starting to rub him wrong.

"People like me must serve as a warning to others. It's no more than I deserve."

Geddy stopped in his tracks. Doc kept going for a few steps, then turned on his heels.

"Don't start that shit again," Geddy said.

Doc was taken aback. "I'm sorry?"

Geddy closed the distance between them in two quick steps, pointing at the Wall of Shame. "That is not you." He gave Tardigan a sharp poke in the center of his chest. "*This* is you. Right here, right now. Fuck these people for shaming you. Do you regret what you did?"

"Every second of every day."

"And given the opportunity, would you make the same choice?"

He gasped. "Good heavens, no!"

"Then that's all there is to it. Now look, it's the fourth quarter and we're behind. I want to put you in, but I need your A-game. Not this woe-is-me crap. You feel me?"

"Yes," he stammered, trying his level best not to smile. "Yes, I do."

"Good. Now let's find your brother."

— *You handled that well.*

— This place is ridiculous. If I was from here, they'd paint my face on toilet bowls.

CHAPTER SIXTEEN

PARMHAR

The College of Applied Science was a small, boxy building tucked in the corner of campus, about as far from the hallowed halls of law, medicine, and philosophy as it was possible to get. Geddy and Doc entered through a central lobby and took the stairs up to the faculty offices on the second floor.

Tardigan marched confidently down the hall, stuck his head into an office, and immediately pulled back, his eyes wide with shock. "Oh. Uh ... I'm sorry. Wrong office."

Geddy caught up and found the spacious office occupied by a woman who almost certainly was not Doc's older brother. She wore the same sort of robes they'd observed throughout campus.

"Do I know you?" she asked. Doc took a step back.

A brief flash of panic crossed his face, but he righted the ship quickly. "No, no. I was expecting someone else."

"Who are you looking for?"

"Dr. Tardigan."

A knowing look softened her expression. "Ah. This *used* to be his office. He's at the end of the hall now."

"I see. Thank you."

Doc turned to leave, but she stopped him. "You're sure we don't know each other?"

"It's my first time to Ornea," he said. "Good day."

He hurried down the hall, taking a deep breath and letting it spill from his lungs.

"Good save," Geddy said.

Doc shook his head. "This is not good. The last office is normally for grad students, maybe post-docs. Not professors."

"So what?" Merely having the last in a long row of identical offices didn't strike Geddy as meaningful.

Tardigan regarded him like an idiot. "It means he's already got one foot out the door. I'll bet he's even been relegated to teaching underclassmen. Underclassmen!"

"That's bad?"

He heaved a sigh. "It is the death rattle of any academic career."

Luckily, the last door in the hall was open a crack. Doc leaned in and gave the door a soft rap as he pushed it open. "Dr. ... Tardigan?"

"Office hours are Tuesdays from two to five," came a sullen voice from the other side.

"I'm not a student. My colleague and I are here for an engineering consult," he announced loudly.

The door still hadn't opened fully. A rustling sound indicated things were being moved out of the way. Doc glanced back at Geddy, his face knotted in concern. After a few more seconds, the door opened, and Parmhar stood up to his knees in papers and journals. Not a square centimeter of horizontal surface remained.

"Sorry about that. Just doing some ... rearranging." He gave a pile of boxes a halfhearted kick, then pretended they didn't tumble right back down. "How can I help you?"

Tardigan's brother looked like he had more than three years on him. His cheeks were hollow, his eyes gaunt, the way people look after a million all-nighters. A scruffy beard was in desperate need of trimming, all the more noticeable by virtue of a hairless, deeply ridged scalp that reminded Geddy of an old-timey washboard.

Doc hesitated, himself taken aback by his brother's haggard appearance. No doubt, the last few months had been hard on him. He didn't recognize Doc at all, which was quite the credit to Jeledine's skill.

"Parmhar, my god, you look awful."

Parmhar's eyes narrowed, and he cocked his head. At the sound of Doc's voice, the recognition was instant. He gasped. "Krons?" Doc nodded, and Parmhar wrapped him in a tight hug. "Oh, my dear, dear, brother! You look ridiculous. What are you–"

"Shhh!" Doc cautioned, looking anxiously back down the hall. The female professor's head leaned curiously out from her office. "We need a word in private."

"Of course. Let's go to the garden. Who's your friend?"

"How rude of me. This is Captain Geddy Starheart."

"Captain? Of what?" Parmhar asked.

"Of my soul," Geddy joked.

"From the human poem, 'Invictus,'" Parmhar said, seemingly impressed. "You must be a man of letters."

Doc launched into another coughing fit. Geddy had no

idea the phrase had significance. He'd probably seen it in an ad for a male-enhancement drug. "No, but I do know most of the English ones."

"Follow me." Parmhar hurriedly locked his door and led them down a stairwell directly across the hall.

Geddy checked his watch. It was noon on the dot. They skirted the edge of campus until they reached an arched, vine-choked trellis that marked the entrance to a stunning ornamental garden. Flowers and ferns, exploding with color, formed winding paths through the fragrant space. They continued until they reached a small aluminum table and chairs. Overhead, chirping birds fluttered from limb to limb among the tangle of trees, nattering loudly.

Parmhar settled into his chair and leaned forward. "How are you? Your disguise is exceptional."

"Ah, yes." Doc unconsciously touched his face. "I'm afraid we don't have a lot of time."

Doc quickly caught Parmhar up on the tumultuous few months that had followed his exile. Geddy couldn't tell from his expression whether he was fascinated, horrified, or simply upset.

"Why didn't you reach out as soon as you could? I took you for dead."

Doc's eyes drifted down to the table. "I was merely honoring the terms of my exile."

Parmhar's expression went slack, and he played with the cuff of his robe. "I certainly cannot judge you from the end office."

"I am so sorry, brother," Doc replied gravely. "At least I do not have to imagine your shame."

"Ugh, enough!" Geddy said, annoyed. "Tell us about your research."

Parmhar raised his eyebrows hopefully, eyes darting back and forth between Doc and Geddy. "My ... research?"

It was Geddy's turn to explain about the Zelnad plot. "We need to find them and get evidence. Until we do, no one's gonna believe us. Your research could change everything."

His hopeful look fell once again. "I would dearly love to help. Unfortunately, my funding has run dry. I cannot get more without a working prototype ..."

"... and you cannot make a working prototype without more funding," Doc finished.

Parmhar nodded sadly. "I am headed to the IASS show in a couple weeks. If I cannot secure new funding, my research will come to a screeching halt. At best, I will be demoted to associate professor."

Now it was Doc's turn to gasp. Tears welled in his eyes. "Oh, Parmhar, no."

— I have no idea what's happening.

— *For academics, reputation is the only currency that matters.*

— That's why I could never be one.

— *Yes.* That's *why.*

"It gets worse," Parmhar lamented. "I am supposed to teach a section of freshman calculus next term."

Doc sucked air through his teeth like he'd just been cut. He reached across the table and took Parmhar's hand. "My god, their cruelty knows no bounds."

They shared a moment of fraught silence.

"Anyway ..." Geddy said, still trying to drive a wedge into

this weird situation. "The IASS show's exactly what we came to discuss. What's your plan?"

Parmhar wiped away a tear with his robe and sat back up. "No plan, really. I reserved a small booth in the corner with my own money and whittled my presentation down to one hundred seventy-eight slides. With luck, the right investor will happen along."

Geddy wrinkled his nose and shared a doubtful look with Doc. "Right ... What kind of money are you going for?"

"Seventy million."

His eyes just about popped out of his head. True, he didn't know much about this stuff, but that seemed pretty steep. "Yowza!"

"Is that not feasible?"

Geddy shrugged. "I dunno. Something tells me anyone with that kind of scratch won't just be wandering around the show floor. You've got to find out where the movers and shakers go."

Parmhar was crestfallen. Maybe if he was more business-savvy, he wouldn't be in this situation. "Then I am as bereft as Ortessia's widower in *The Many Unhelpful Ruminations of Melpf Lowderthistle*."

"Parmhar has a penchant for Ornean literature from the middle baroque period," Doc explained. "The tale he references chronicles the struggles of a–"

"How solid is your tech?" Geddy asked impatiently, cutting Doc off.

"Very solid ... on paper."

"Good, because we need that prototype yesterday."

Parmhar's hope rose again. "You can fund me?"

Geddy barked a laugh. "No, but I know my way around

the upper echelon. I can pitch it for you."

Parmhar appeared skeptical. "Forgive me, but how does a trawler captain know people with that kind of money?"

"That's a story for another time. What we need to do now is ..." Geddy trailed off, noticing that a dozen or so older students had begun filing into the garden.

Parmhar and Doc both seemed to know what was going on. "A garden lecture," Parmhar explained. "What day is it, again?"

Geddy rose and checked his watch again. It was 12:34 — nearly time to get back to the train. "We should be going. Let's plan to rendezvous on Xellara."

Parmhar nodded excitedly. "I'm staying at the Excelsior. Find me there."

Tardigan again wrapped his brother up in a hug. "It is good to see you."

"You as well, brother," Parmhar said. "See you on Xellara."

Doc turned to leave, and the moment he did, he ran squarely into a man in cream-colored robes trimmed in gold. In contrast with Parmhar, his beard was crisp and pure white. His whole person radiated importance. Images of Aristotle and Cicero flashed through Geddy's mind.

"Careful there." He regarded Doc with thinly veiled disdain. "I'd think a Soturian would have better spatial awareness."

"Father," Parmhar stammered. "I didn't know you had a garden lecture today."

"Of course, I do. It's the second Tuesday of the month." His eyes still hadn't left Doc, who had frozen like a statue. "Aren't you going to introduce me to your friends?"

CHAPTER SEVENTEEN

PAP PYRUS

Now it was Parmhar's turn to be dumbstruck. Pyrus peered down over his angular nose, waiting silently for the answer. Tardigan continued to stare back.

— *Do something!*

"Hello, sir." Geddy took a step forward with his hand outstretched. "Jevar Sodenvoch, Earth 3. My colleague here is Polvo Grenn. We're consulting with Dr. Tardigan on an engineering project."

Pyrus ignored Geddy's hand. "Engineering? I doubt he will be able to help you. He is rather busy clinging to relevance in for-profit science." Parmhar's already ruddy complexion flared red, but he said nothing. Pyrus turned to his class and cleared his throat. "Class, we are in the presence of engineers. Look upon them and tremble."

The class chuckled appreciatively, and Geddy wondered if they hadn't done Doc a favor by shooting him randomly into space. Pyrus turned back with a self-satisfied grin.

"I'm curious what project is so vexing as to require the

great *Dr.* Parmhar Tardigan?" His lips curled mockingly around "doctor" like he'd discovered a hair in his soup.

"The Bubbles on Earth 3 are leaking," Geddy said. "A particular pressure coupling design keeps failing and we're not sure why."

Pyrus guffawed. "Humans are well-versed in repeated failure."

A dour-faced young man behind him nodded and said, "Humankind is central to our studies about futility."

Geddy's building ire bloomed hot in his cheeks. He felt the sudden urge to defend engineers and rip on philosophers, although he knew precious little about either.

— I'm not sure I have the brain power to dance with this cat.

—*I am certain you do not.*

"You want to talk futility?" Geddy nodded at the gaggle of smug students. "How about philosophy students finding a job?"

The students gasped. Pyrus pursed his lips and looked him up and down. "Birds and rodents perform feats of engineering by instinct. Higher thought is what sets intelligent life apart. And my students will have no trouble contributing to the intellectual wealth of Ornea."

"Come, Jevar. The rarefied air here is getting to me." Doc brushed past his father.

"Not so fast, Soturian." His voice had a commanding edge. Doc stopped but didn't turn back. Pyrus approached and studied him closely. "Have we met?"

Doc locked him in a spiteful glare. "Certainly, I would recall having met the great Pyrus Tardigan. Or, perhaps I did, and you left no impression either way."

One of the female students stifled a snigger, which Pyrus further silenced with a single flick of his bushy gray eyebrow. "Get out of my classroom, the both of you."

Doc ignored him and extended his hand toward his brother. "Thank you for your advice, Parmhar. We will see you on Xellara." Parmhar gave a pained smile and shook Doc's hand.

They pushed past the bemused students and wound back through the paths until they reached the garden entrance. Doc was hoofing it so fast, Geddy had a hard time keeping up.

"Don't take this the wrong way, but your old man's a dick."

"It is a wonder Ornea's crust can bear the weight of his ego."

Once they were well clear of the garden, Tardigan slowed his pace and swiveled his head back and forth, taking in the majesty of the campus' stately buildings, fountains, and towering trees.

"I grew up wanting to be surrounded by this," Doc mused. "Now, I see it for what it is — a pretentious exercise in self-aggrandizement."

— *That means creating the appearance of superiority.*

— I knew what he meant. Basically.

"Would you still think that if you hadn't been exiled?" Geddy asked.

"It is hard to say. But working alongside you and the crew has taught me that knowledge is not the only virtue."

"Um, thanks?"

They boarded the train at 12:55 — later than ideal, but

hopefully under the wire. The business in the garden took longer than it seemed.

Doc plunked down on one of the ergonomic bench seats and held his head in his hands. "I am sorry you had to see that. I did not expect to see my father."

"Hey, we did what we came here to do, right?" Geddy sat next to him. "With a little luck, we'll put some air under your brother's research and restore a bit of his reputation."

Tardigan looked away, turning it over in his prominent noggin. "I had not thought of it that way. Too bad my own reputation cannot similarly be restored."

— Ugh, more of this self-pity crap. I can't take it.

— *It comes from an inner pain. He has lost the respect of his peers.*

— Obviously.

— *Including you.*

— What's that supposed to mean?

— *You cut him off earlier when he was talking about the book.*

It took a few seconds to remember what Eli was even talking about. Parmhar mentioned some book, Doc started going on about it, and then ...

Eli was right. He always cut Doc off when he was about to give one of his mini-lectures. How was he supposed to regain some respect when his own captain didn't show him enough of it? Geddy didn't judge Doc in the slightest, yet he rarely let the man do what he did best — teach them stuff.

"Hey, listen, I didn't mean to cut you off back there when you were talking about that book."

His face lit up. "*The Many Unhelpful Ruminations of Melpf Lowderthistle?*"

"If you say so. Anyway, I meant no disrespect."

"I understand, Captain. I know I can be long-winded and … dare I say … dry in my delivery."

"That's no excuse. I owe you an apology. Now tell me about this book Parmhar likes so much. Please. I'm ready to listen."

Doc glanced up at their progress on the floating display over the door, then continued. "I suppose you could call it a fable. It takes place in a society that reforms criminals by making them relive their worst choices through technology. It's called Rumination. They believe it cements the wrongdoer's perception of consequences. The character Parmhar referenced has very little to do with the plot. You might call it a 'deep cut'." He unnecessarily supplied the air quotes.

"Then who is this …?" He fished for the weird name.

"Melpf Lowderthistle? He begins as a man with everything in life. A man of respect and honor. But he is convicted of a crime he didn't commit and sentenced to Rumination. Compared to most people, his mistakes are minuscule, but over the years, they take on colossal proportions. By the time he is exonerated, he is so broken that he becomes the criminal he never was. It's about our relationship with the past."

— That sounds … not horrible.

— *And you occasionally surprise me in a not-horrible way.*

Geddy arched his eyebrows. "Maybe we should read it together."

Tardigan's slips upturned. "Perhaps we should, Captain. You're right. I've had enough of regret."

"I've said those exact words over an empty cake pan," Geddy gave a wink, eliciting an even broader grin from Doc.

"Next stop, Tathe spaceport," said a digital voice. It was 1:13 p.m.

Geddy and Doc rose and waited in front of the doors. The moment they opened, a retinue of Ornean guards pushed through and made a beeline for the two of them. Apparently, the jig was up.

"Jevar Sodenvoch and Polvo Grenn," said the one in front. "Please come with us." The other three guards formed a wall around them.

"Did we do something wrong?" asked Geddy.

"There are irregularities with your credentials. Please." He gestured toward the open doors.

Doc shrugged helplessly at Geddy, but there wasn't much to be done. They'd pushed their luck a bit too far, and now they were going to the long-division mines or wherever Orneans sent lawbreakers.

— *What will you do?*

— Wait for you to think of something.

"WHAT THE HELL is taking so long?" asked Geddy through gritted teeth.

They'd been sitting in an unused office for the better part of an hour, during which no one had come in to explain why they were being detained or even ask them a question. Doc browsed the net while Geddy paced anxiously back and forth. It was time to get back to the *Fiz* and make plans for Xellara.

"Either they are making us sweat, or they know the truth, " Doc replied.

The door slid open, and the guard who had taken them from the train entered.

"The truth about what? Your faked identity? Your violation of an exile order? Or maybe all of the above?"

Geddy squared up to him. "Look, this was all my idea. There are nefarious forces at work here, and–"

The guard flashed a patronizing grin. "Forces, you say. Oh, there are forces at work here, gentlemen, but in this case, they are working in your favor."

Doc's face twisted in confusion. "What do you mean?"

"I mean you are free to go under the condition you never return." His eyes never left Doc. "I am talking to you, Krons Tardigan. Not even the births and deaths of a million suns could bleach away your stain."

— What is with these people?

— *It seems they are not big on second chances.*

For a brief moment, it seemed Doc might crumble and cop to being the worst Ornean who ever lived. Instead, he squared his jaw and rose. "The only shame I carry is that which I am willing to bear. And I will bear it no more."

"Hmph." The guard narrowed his eyes at Doc, then about-faced and left in a huff. A moment later, Pyrus Tardigan entered, his robes fanning out behind him like a cape.

His eyes first met Geddy's. "Mr. ... Sodenvoch. Or is it Starheart? I would like a word in private with my son."

Doc didn't hesitate. "Whatever you want to say to me, you can say in the presence of my captain."

Pyrus gave an empty shrug like it didn't matter in the slightest. "Suit yourself, Krons. I came to say that this is not a reconciliation. In fact, when the authorities contacted me, my inclination was to let you face justice." He raised a knowing finger. "But then I thought to myself, 'My son is many things. A cheat. A liar. An affront to academic integrity. But he is not foolish.'"

Geddy and Doc exchanged the same befuddled look.

"I do not understand," said Doc.

"Why, Krons? Why risk such dire consequences and engage in such a ... grotesque charade?" He regarded Doc's prosthetic and apparel with sickly disdain. "Why would you subject us all to your presence when it is so deeply unwelcome?"

The conflict over what to say and how much played across Tardigan's face. "We believe Parmhar's research can help save the universe."

Pyrus searched Doc's Soturian face for a sign of insincerity. He'd spoken the gospel truth, but it wasn't going to matter. "Then perhaps you *are* a fool. Be that as it may, you are free to go. But do not return."

"Come, Captain. My father's benevolence is finite." Doc stopped beside his father and looked warmly up at him, placing a hand gently on his robed shoulder. "I leave my shame here with you, father. I know it will be well cared for."

Feeling quite proud, Geddy patted Pyrus on the shoulder, and gave him a phony grin. "Good luck with your philosophy."

He followed Doc out the door.

CHAPTER EIGHTEEN

XELLARA

GEDDY and the crew parked in geosynchronous orbit over Donglan, Xellara's largest city and home of the IASS, for three hours before they were cleared to land. He'd intended to take the *Fiz* down, but only Joanie-class ships or smaller were allowed to land. Since most ships that small weren't designed for sleeping, Geddy figured it was a ploy to sell more overpriced hotel rooms.

For them, it created a problem because the *Dom* wasn't roomy enough for everyone, especially with Voprot in the mix. But the big lizard hadn't left the *Fiz* since Thegus several weeks ago, he was starting to molt, and for everyone's sake, he needed a cleaning. Denk wasn't about to be denied the opportunity to see hundreds of cool ships and gear in one place, and Oz was the only one who knew her way around, so as usual, it fell to Morpho to hold down the fort.

The *Dom* handled like shit with the five of them packed into the small cabin, and Geddy could barely keep it in the approach tunnel. Voprot's eye-watering BO was inescapable, so when they had to hover over Donglan for an hour and a half waiting for final clearance, it was all he could do not to crack the windows. Finally, they got their landing pad assignment and his whole body relaxed.

Xellara had accumulated a tragic history, of which Geddy only knew the broad strokes. It began as an agricultural society but now manufactured unglamorous ship parts by the millions. Rivets. Conduit. Positronic cabling. Shipbuilding planets like Kailoria, Ghruk, and even Gundrun came to Xellara with specifications and quantities, and the Xellarans delivered — on time, every time.

But in order to hit those deadlines, Xellara was constantly expanding its production capacity. At a certain point, the government began offering workers tempting bonuses for taking cybernetic mods that made them more productive at their jobs. Most did, and the mods kept coming until some workers were barely flesh-and-blood Xellarans anymore. Now, only the ruling class was still organic, and the workers basically androids.

The infrastructure that rose around this lucrative industry laid the groundwork for what would become the IASS show, and now it was too big to be held anywhere else.

The same leaders and celebrities who decried Xellara's appalling labor practices were all too happy to get dolled up and party there during the show. That, unfortunately, was the crowd they'd have to rub elbows with in order to get Parmhar his funding and them a prototype of his long-range scanner.

The automated landing system took them in a wide loop over the convention center and the battlement of towering hotels around it. The scale and engineering prowess defied description. The area called to mind a terraced hillside, with organic-looking curves cut from each of its seven levels with a glassy dome at the top. In front, a massive lagoon dotted with skinny palm trees sent lazy waves rippling across its surface like a placid ocean while an endless stream of attendees curled around it en route to the cavernous entrance and the glittering sign that read *Welcome to IASS 2427*.

"Holy hell," Geddy muttered.

"Wait 'til you see it at night," Oz said.

"I was talking about Voprot's ... musk, but this is cool, too."

"Voprot smell self now. Not good." The lizard was pressed against the back wall wrinkling his nose.

The distracting architecture and glitz of the convention area drew the eye away from the depressing sprawl just beyond. Rectangular factories with shiny metal roofs extended nearly to the horizon in all directions, each encircled by tenements where the workers lived. Rail lines outside each all fed toward Donglan's other commercial spaceport in the distance, used exclusively for shipping.

Geddy turned to Oz with his eyebrows raised. "Looks a little different outside the conference zone."

She gave her head a rueful shake. "You don't know the half of it."

The main convention spaceport was several times larger than even the oversized one on Thegus, with similar architectural touches as the convention center itself. Long rows of uncovered landing pads radiated from the central building, giving it the resemblance of an asterisk. The system guided the *Dom* down one of the rays to the very end, then eased them onto pad 78R, which had to be two kilometers away.

Geddy immediately opened the hatch and climbed down

the ladder, taking in lungfuls of fresh air. Though it carried the faint scent of industry, it was like jasmine compared to Voprot's funk. They were so far from the main spaceport building, say nothing of the convention zone, that he wondered if they'd make it by dark. It was blisteringly hot, too.

Before they'd even buttoned up the *Dom*, an empty, driverless shuttle came gliding up beside the pad.

"Welcome to Xellara," cooed a female AI. "Would you like a ride to the convention zone?"

"How much?" Oz asked.

"Fifty credits per passenger."

She flared her eyebrows and looked to Geddy. Considering what their rooms would likely cost, if they could even get rooms, it seemed frivolous. Plus, he was ready to get some blood moving.

"How much for a Kigantean?" he asked. It couldn't hurt.

"Cleaning protocol required. Seventy-five credits."

"Cleaning protocol for him or the shuttle?"

"Geddy!" Oz admonished.

It was almost worth it. Almost. "Nah, we're good. What direction is the wind from today?"

"The wind is out of the southwest at four kilometers per hour. Have a nice day."

The shuttle continued down the line of cheap landing pads and quickly filled with passengers.

"Voprot, feel free to hang back. I want to find lunch, not ..."

Voprot's giant mouth already hung open, but now two basketball-sized sacs had inflated from vertical slits on the sides of his neck. The skin was so thin that sunlight shone through, highlighting veins and capillaries.

"What the what?!" Geddy asked no one in particular. "Did he always have those?"

"Make Voprot cool," he explained.

"You're already cool in my book, V," said Denk.

Geddy could only shrug as they began down the marked walkway ahead, shimmering heat radiating off the concrete.

He peeled off his jacket immediately and looped it through the shoulder strap of his duffel, then unzipped his coveralls to his doughy midsection. When he left The Deuce, he was as ripped as he'd ever been. Since then, high-calorie nutrimush and Kailorian gin had taken a predictable toll.

Oz undid her vest a bit, revealing the top of her ample cleavage. The view was decidedly more appealing.

The longer they walked, the more crowded the path became until they were shoulder to shoulder with the throngs of conference attendees scrambling for food and lodging after a long turn in space. They curled around the base of the spaceport itself and angled off toward the convention zone.

When they reached the edge of the lagoon, they sat on the retaining wall and enjoyed cool mist from the dancing fountains. Voprot fell to his knees and stuck his entire head in the water, taking big gulps before coming up dripping and deflating his neck sacs. Onlookers, as they so often did when he was around, recoiled at the sight but couldn't turn away.

"Really?" Geddy asked, sweat dripping from his forehead. "How is this too hot for a Kigantean?"

"Kigantu a dry heat."

"We could just have him wash up right here," offered Denk.

Geddy pictured Voprot covered in suds with a contented look on his face, eyes closed while the three of them ran stiff-bristled brushes over his scaly skin and peeled it off him in wet sheets.

"At least then we'd know what rock-bottom looked like."

Oz threw her head back and laughed, which was the best sound in the world. He'd rarely heard it lately, but it quickly brightened his day. All he wanted was a tepid shower, a change of clothes, and some decent food. Considering the volume of people milling around, one or more of those might not be possible.

None of them had ever seen anything quite like this, not even on Caloth. There had to be ten thousand people just around the lagoon, say nothing of those who had already filed inside or had yet to arrive. Technically, the show didn't even start until the next morning.

He was about to ask Oz where the cheap hotels were when a familiar voice cut through the thrum of the crowd.

"Well, if it isn't the crew of the galaxy's hardest-trying ship!"

Zereth-Tinn came strolling through the gaggle wearing baggy shorts and a threadbare T-shirt with a fading illustration of Ponley Point. Thegus felt like a million years ago, though it had barely been two months. Seeing him dressed so casually took Geddy aback.

The man's loyalties were still unclear. He seemed to know more about the Nads than pretty much anyone and had even been approached to put a long-range tracking device on the *Fiz*. However, he hadn't done it. Instead, he'd helped install the tractor beam *and* confirmed that the *Penetrator* was on Aku. All Geddy knew for sure about him was that he was an outstanding pilot and decent lounge singer with enough pull to lock down the Thegus spaceport on a whim.

They rose to greet him, and Geddy shook his hand. "Zereth-Tinn. Are you an attendee or the entertainment?"

He gave an aw-shucks grin and winked at Oz. "Oh, you know ... a little business, a little pleasure." She rolled her eyes.

He greeted the rest of the crew, pausing at Voprot, who was still slaking his thirst in the lagoon. As usual, a buffer had been opened up between them and passers-by. Parting a crowd was arguably Voprot's superpower.

"Friend of yours?" asked Zereth-Tinn, wrinkling his nose at either the sight or the smell. Likely both.

It dawned on Geddy they hadn't met back on Thegus. "More of a mascot."

Oz gave his shoulder a playful smack. "Yes, he's my friend." The words felt strange in his mouth. "And a part of the crew, I'm told."

"Friends are hard to come by these days. It's hard to know who to trust."

If he recognized the irony in that statement, he didn't let on.

"Ain't that the truth."

"So, what brings you here? Did your ... ship come in, as they say?"

Geddy gave a halfhearted chuckle as he calculated how much to share. "Trying to find investors for a friend's startup."

He nodded, his mouth downturned, as though the premise was flawed. "Interesting. And how do you intend to do that?"

That was a good question. He figured he'd run into a few

people he knew from his Double A days, buy them a drink, and make a pitch. Beyond that, he really didn't know.

"I suppose we'll play it by ear."

Zereth-Tinn laughed, probably not so much at his phrasing as the looseness of their sales strategy. "Well, Starheart, having been to about ten of these over the years, I can assure you that's not how business gets done at IASS. If you really want to drum up some funding, you need tickets to the gala."

"Gala?" Oz tried not to seem *too* interested.

"The opening gala tomorrow night in the Echodrome," he pointed to the smooth, glassy apex of the convention center. "Exclusive guest list. Every deep-pocketed player at the show will be there."

Geddy's eyes swiveled to Oz. Visions of her in clingy formalwear passed through his brain, followed closely by visions of a rapidly emptying bank account.

"Sounds expensive."

He smirked. "Oh, it is. A hundred twenty grand per ticket. However ..." He reached into his pocket and withdrew something, then took a step closer to Geddy to be less conspicuous. He opened his palm to reveal two shiny silver coins with the IASS logo stamped on them. "My VIP package included two passes that I regrettably can't use."

Geddy had held many valuable items in his life, but at that moment, they all paled next to these coins. They might prove pivotal in stopping the Zelnads, which made them priceless.

Everyone had their heads on a swivel to ensure no one tried to swipe them, but the buffer around Voprot still held, and he was drawing everyone's attention.

Geddy tucked the coins in his pocket and locked eyes with Zereth-Tinn, searching them for his true intentions. Was he their guardian angel or was he playing them like a piano? His icy Soturian eyes betrayed nothing.

"Why are you helping us?" Geddy asked.

In lieu of a reply, Zereth-Tinn broke his gaze and looked them up and down, distaste contorting his smooth features.

"You're gonna need better clothes." He nodded toward a row of fancy-looking shops on the other side of the lagoon. "Across the way is a clothier called Taverna. Tell her I sent you and she'll make you look good. You can even put it on my tab."

"Thank you," Oz said, clearly wowed by the offer. "We owe you big-time."

"Yes, you do," he said with a disarming smile, then slipped on a pair of designer sunglasses. "Anyway, have fun at the gala. Maybe I'll see you around." He melted into the crowd like a ghost.

CHAPTER NINETEEN

SHIP SHOW

AFTER FINDING the least-overpriced hotel rooms and lunch
they could, Geddy charged Denk with the unenviable task of
getting Voprot cleaned up. He accepted the chore with
customary enthusiasm.

"There must be an alley and a hose around here somewhere," Geddy offered, giving his shoulder a firm squeeze.
"We're talking industrial detergents. It should burn a little."

Doc had just contacted Parmhar at his hotel, so he went
off to meet him for dinner. Meanwhile, Geddy and Oz
headed over to Taverna for some fancy duds. The owner
turned out to be the rarest of Xellarans — flesh-and-blood
middle class. She grimaced at their poor appearance, but the
mention of Zereth-Tinn's name changed the equation
entirely. Before long, tiny, floating bots were making laser
maps of their entire bodies while Taverna examined their
skin with something like a loupe to determine the precise
shade of fabric that would suit them.

Upon their return to the hotel, Denk explained that he

and Voprot had to go back to the main spaceport and pay to use the self-serve ship-wash bay, but the job was done, and Voprot's eye-watering reptilian musk was erased. However, his normally shiny dark-green skin had turned cloudy, and more raised bits of dead skin had appeared.

"Voprot in molt," he'd said, a bit too excitedly. "Water make faster."

The thought of Voprot sloughing off welcome mat-sized sheets of skin was unsettling enough, but the timing made it that much worse. Geddy spoke a wish to the universe that the process hold off for just a few more days. Once he was back in the *Fiz's* hold, he could do all the gross lizard stuff he needed.

Following a meager dinner in the hotel lobby, they all fell into bed, exhausted by the events of the past several days and the crush of humanity on Xellara.

The following morning, they waited in line for almost two hours to purchase the cheapest general admission tickets they could get. Geddy abhorred lines and grew so irritated by the time they reached the window that he wondered if it was worth it. All that changed when they finally set foot inside.

He'd been in some colossal buildings before. Giant spaceports like Caloth and Thegus, yes, but also the Promenade on Pretensia or the Myadan zoo. But any one of them could have fit easily inside the Donglan Convention Center.

From the outside, the terraces suggested individual floors, but they were only a design feature. The interior formed an oblong dome so large that small ships were being test-flown overhead. The floor was so dense with booths and ostentatious displays that you could hardly even judge the distance across, but it had to be pushing at least a thousand meters, maybe more.

"Voprot feel so small," He absently scratched at a loose piece of skin that came off in his claws.

"You're gonna deal with that in private, right?" Geddy asked hopefully.

His face turned serious as he dropped a piece of skin the size of a dinner plate into a trash bin. "Voprot never, ever embarrass friends."

— Voprot never see irony of that statement, either.

— *Nor you, space-walker.*

— Okay, that's fair.

The floor was separated into sections identified by slowly rotating holograms overhead. Power Systems. Weapons. Crew Life. Scanning. Food Court. And something labeled Ship Showcase.

"Let's see if we can find Doc and Parmhar." Geddy started down a wide aisle in the direction of Scanning. Parmhar was assigned to booth 6673.

Power Systems took front and center. Animations of new quasion drives boasted 63% greater efficiency and 140% less vibration. A Degarret 19F engine had been vivisected to show atmospheric dust buildup, while right beside it was a smaller, completely clean Hovensby with supposedly the same number of operating hours.

Denk stopped to gawk. "Whoa, baby! We should get some of these for the *Fiz*!"

"Better save up." Geddy nodded at the small, almost hidden price tag below, which said the engines started at two million credits.

"Yikes. Maybe they have some used ones."

"I kinda doubt it, pal. You know much about Hovensby?" Denk shook his head. "Super high-end, super innovative, and super expensive. Remember that sweet-ass ship of Prince Bransel's?"

Back on Temeruria, Oz's father's ship had left quite the impression. The fit, finish, and motion correction were state-of-the-art.

Denk's eyes widened. "That was a Hovensby?"

Geddy nodded. "Pretty sure. You know what the engines cost ... imagine a whole ship." Denk gave his head an incredulous shake.

They continued toward Parmhar's booth. The crush of attendees made for a slow shuffle across the exhibit floor, which was as diverse a crowd as he'd ever seen. Geddy thought he knew all the spacefaring races, but there were aliens in attendance he'd never seen in his life. Spiny ones that resembled giant crabs. Translucent blobs with pulsating organs inside their gelatinous bodies. In some cases, it was hard not to stare.

"It's a big galaxy, isn't it?" noted Oz.

"Getting bigger all the time," replied Geddy with a wink. Doc would've liked that joke.

Fortunately, the floor was well-signed. The further they got from the center, the smaller the exhibits became until they reached Parmhar's cringeworthy space. Like his office, it, too, was at the end of the row.

He and Doc sat behind a sad little table with a small sign taped to the front that said:

PT Deepscan
Prove Your Metal

A SMALL BOWL of untouched candy sat beside a fan of brochures. A holo-display behind them played through his 178 slides, the text far too small and dense to read at a distance.

This was going to be harder than Geddy thought.

Doc's face lit up when he saw them. He and Parmhar rose, and introductions were made. Parmhar was polite to Oz and Denk but found Voprot fascinating.

"My stars, Krons. I must admit, I thought you were pulling my leg." He made a slow circle around Voprot, who seemed to relish the attention. "I never thought I'd see a flesh-and-blood Kigantean."

"Voprot always visible."

Parmhar hooted at that. "Ha! You are a delight."

"Yeah, he's a real gas." Geddy smacked his hands. "Anyone come along with your seventy million yet?"

"Someone picked up one of the candies," Doc offered, "but he brought it back. Said we probably needed it more. What about you? Everything set for the gala?"

"Oz and I are picking up our duds this afternoon. I figured Parmhar had better give us his elevator pitch now."

"Elevator pitch?" Parmhar asked, confused.

"Sorry, human expression. It's like what you'd say about your business if you only had like ten seconds to say it. Go."

Parmhar's face went pale, his fingers tugging absently as his collar. "Ten seconds. Goodness, that's ... uh ..."

Geddy figured he might need a prompt. "PT Deepscan is ..." He made a rolling motion with his hands.

Parmhar's panic deepened further as he stammered, "Right. Okay. Well, PT Deepscan is based on proprietary ... well, you see, the myriad limitations of common spectrographic scanning technologies are limited by the Aneshpidad paradox, which–"

"Errrrk." Geddy cut him off with a buzzer sound. "Time's up, and I still don't know what the fuck it is. Look, I've been around rich people most of my life. They care about the broad strokes. Market potential. Now, who's gonna buy it?"

"Mining companies, mostly. Salvage operations."

"All right, so it's deep-space scanning tech that can identify metal composition from up to ... how far away?"

"A hundred parsecs," Parmhar said proudly. "Theoretically."

"And current tech only reaches what? One parsec at the outside?"

Parmhar nodded.

"Okay, so your tech makes it easier to find and identify valuable materials like tukrium, preventing overmining in the known galaxy while potentially lowering prices."

Parmhar smiled appreciatively. "I guess so. I've focused on the technology so long, I suppose I'd lost sight of the applications."

Geddy nodded and turned to Oz. "You got enough?"

She nodded and gave a shrug like it was obvious. "I think so. More distance, more accuracy. Mining and salvage applications. Ground-floor opportunity. Fifteen mil gets you what? Twenty percent or so?"

"Something like that," agreed Geddy. "Forty for a controlling interest or seventy for the lot."

Parmhar's expression turned incredulous. "But that's too reductive. What about the math?"

"Nobody needs math," Geddy asserted. "We'll find your angel investors or Oz'll die trying."

CHAPTER TWENTY

THE GALA

GEDDY WAS INDULGING in a cocktail in the lobby of their cheap, but still-expensive hotel when Oz stepped out of the elevator. The sight of her stole his breath. Her dark green dress was a buttery material with a slight sheen that put class on par with sexiness. Like the dress she'd worn on Pretensia, it was slit up the right side to mid-thigh, affording a generous glimpse of her exquisite leg with every step.

The tapered red tendrils on her head were gathered into a shock of cloth that matched her dress, the excess spilling down the back of her elegant neck. Her makeup was light, but the outside corners of her eyes swept up in a feline curve that only made them appear larger and more curious. And she smelled fantastic.

"You look ... otherworldly," Geddy said as she approached.

"You're not so bad yourself, Captain."

"Captain?" He gave a little frown. "You never call me captain."

"You rarely resemble one."

— She makes a strong point.

Oz could always sense when Eli was talking. "Eli agrees, doesn't he?"

A grin tugged at Geddy's lips. "It's almost like you share a brain." He held out an arm. "Shall we?"

Geddy had worn a tuxedo exactly once when he and Kriggy threw a party for the Double A's centennial. It had to be shipped in from Greloria, and it cost him about a week's pay, but he remembered looking like someone far more powerful and respected. Strolling through the balmy evening air beneath the sparkling orange and purple Quaqui Nebula and Xellara's rings with an absolute knockout on his arm reminded him of that time, only way better.

No one ever taught him what love was. Not the romantic sort, anyway. As the one of the only teenagers on Kigantu, the chances of falling for one of the few rough-hewn girls available was nil. Before Jel, his experience was equivalent to two forest animals one-and-done-ing each other in the woods.

But with Oz, he felt the stirrings of something ancient and primal. A deep and abiding sense of potential as real as any electric current. Hotness aside, she was the exact opposite of Tatiana. All they shared was a desire to persevere, but even then, Oz would never sacrifice her principles to do it. Tots wouldn't hesitate.

He drank her in for a long moment.

She reflexively checked herself over. "Why are you staring at me?"

"Would it be corny if I said you were my favorite person ever?"

Oz's head fell back exposing her exquisite neck, her

melodic laughter warming the air around them. "Yes. But don't let that stop you."

— *You sly dog.*

— Yeah, I kinda crushed that one.

They strolled around to the side of the convention center where a private entrance opened in response to the coins in his pocket. A crisply attired Xellaran woman with a robotic eye scanned them in a small room and ushered them into an elevator with no buttons. The door closed, and it hummed upward.

"What's our strategy tonight?" Oz asked.

"I'll make the initial pitch. You agree and bat your eyelashes, maybe flash a little leg."

She looked at him over the tops of her gleaming eyes. "You can't be serious."

"I've been around these kinds of people my whole life. They see a girl like you agreeing with a guy like me, and they'll be intrigued enough to listen, if only to try and steal you away. It sucks, but that's the way it is."

She swished her glossy lips around as she weighed the dignity cost of such an approach. "That's gonna be a challenge for me."

"I know."

The elevator doors opened, and they stepped out onto a literal red carpet flanked by a small army of uniformed workers in stiff, militaristic poses, arms folded behind their backs and eyes straight ahead. Live music played from inside. He and Oz shared a mildly terrified look and continued into the eye-popping event space called the Echodrome.

Where the red carpet ended, a see-through floor began. The vastness of the exhibit area lay so far below that it resembled a city viewed from the air. Overhead, a seamless, optically perfect bubble magnified the dazzling night sky. Sometimes space looked more impressive from the ground.

Geddy and Oz craned their heads upward and turned themselves in a slow circle. It was impossible to take it all in.

"Cocktail?" asked a woman, giving Geddy a start.

His head snapped to level and he came face-to-face with another female android, a fake smile painted on her narrow, angular face. Her robotic arm extension was attached to a tray overflowing with fizzy blue drinks.

"This evening's first featured cocktail is a local twist on an electric lemonade made with Nichuan bardberries."

They both took one and she moved on. Oz gave her head a rueful shake as she looked after her. "That's a universal connector on her arm. She can be whatever they want her to be."

Geddy never gave much thought to Xellara's long history of oppression, but he was starting to understand why Oz fought beside the androids in the failed civil war. Good thing she got out of here.

The drink wasn't his style, but it hit the spot, tasty and strong. Oz took a sip and smacked her lips.

"Oh, that's *good*."

A Zorran band was on a circular stage at the center that slowly rotated, the full brunt of their amplifiers passing like a watchtower spotlight. A thousand people flowed around it, some dancing, some milling around illuminated cocktail tables, or arranged on semicircular couches. Boisterous conversations and laughter filled the festive space, which smelled of hors d'oeuvres and money.

"C'mon, let's see who's here." Geddy wove through the crowd, keeping a tight hold on Oz's hand.

Familiar faces were dotted throughout, so many that it almost felt like being back in the Vault at the Double A. Businesspeople, politicians, warlords, and moneyed puppet masters all in one place. Any number could fund Parmhar's startup, but who to pitch was another matter. The Nads couldn't know he was on to something that could find them. Speaking of which …

— How's that Zelnad detector of yours?

— *They are everywhere.*

— But not every*one.*

— *No. I will tell you if I sense one nearby.*

— Won't they sense you?

— *Perhaps, but they cannot distinguish me.*

— Let's hope so. The last thing I need is to get invited to some Zelnad orgy. I mean, what would I even bring?

Ten meters away, bent over a table and having a hushed conversation, was a Zihnian weapons broker with close ties to Gundrun. A good guy to pitch, maybe. Geddy maneuvered behind whoever he was talking to and eased closer so he wouldn't spot him.

— How about this guy here with the oval green head?

— *Yes.*

Great. A guy who knew Gundrun like the back of his hand was playing for the wrong team. Geddy angled in a new direction. He'd only made it a few steps before someone called out from his left.

"Greetings, Spacefarer!"

His head swiveled toward the voice. It was his old friend Zirhof of Zorr, his bowtie the same cream color as his freshly pressed shirt. At first, it seemed obvious he'd be at the show, but then again, glitz and glamor weren't his things. Antiquities were.

They embraced, and Zirhof whispered, "We have much to discuss."

Geddy kept his hand lightly on Zirhof's shoulder as stepped back to introduce Oz. "Meet my First Officer, Osmiya Nargonis. Oz, this is my old friend, Zirhof."

Like flipping a reliable switch, Zirhof's smile broadened to display his gleaming white teeth. He took a step forward and bend down to plant an appreciative kiss on the back of Oz's extended hand. It was the kind of move Geddy would love to try if he thought he could do it without being creepy as hell.

He half-expected Oz to clamp his throat in that same hand and insist his lips not touch her uninvited, but her cheeks flared red to match her hair and she gave a nervous titter. "Pleased to meet you, Zirhof. Geddy's told me a lot about you."

"All lies, I assure you." His eyes swept up and down her full height. "You're even more radiant than Geddy described you."

Oz' cheeks flushed further, and her hair color deepened. Zirhof was an ace at this high-society stuff. He gestured toward an empty cocktail table nearby and they all grabbed fresh drinks off the tray of a passing server.

"I like him," Oz said to Geddy before they formed a triangle around the table.

— Any Nads within earshot?

— *No. But I am keeping watch.*

"So, what brings you here?" Geddy asked. "Doesn't seem like your scene."

"Business meetings. I'll be on my way after that."

"Any luck with the quantum cubes?" Geddy asked hopefully. "Oz is in the loop."

He'd left the Old Earth storage media with Zirhof in case they contained something useful against the Nads. Zirhof didn't believe the *Project Rearview* transports just stumbled upon a wormhole that led them to this galaxy, and that only advanced jump tech could've gotten them there. But that meant it originated on Old Earth, which almost certainly meant that a scientist named Dr. Birgit Nilsson had the help of a benevolent Sagacean like Eli.

One corner of his mouth curled slyly upward. "It's there, Geddy. Everything we've been looking for. You have no idea how important it is."

He exchanged a meaningful look with Oz, then turned back to Zirhof. "So, where do we go from here?"

"I'm not sure. This Gundrun situation certainly muddies the waters. I must admit, I'm surprised to see you here."

Zirhof wouldn't be interested in Parmhar's startup, but he might know people who would. Plus, it gave them an opportunity to try out their pitch. He explained about the deep-scanning tech as Zirhof listened intently.

After they were done, the man scratched thoughtfully at his prominent, burnt-orange chin. "That is intriguing. But even if you found the Zelnad fleet, what would you do about it?"

He leaned in further and said, "I'd use the evidence to reform the Alliance."

"The Alliance?" Zirhof pulled back, blinking. "That's … ambitious."

"I'm convinced it's the only way."

His friend's eyes swept around them before replying. "I'd be very careful who you mention that to."

"Don't worry — the circle's tight as a Stemiran girl's …" he trailed off at the sight of Oz's cautioning stare. "Yeah, we're being careful."

Zirhof's head tilted to the side. "Something tells me there's a lot more to know."

"There is," Geddy assured him, "some other time. This place is crawling with Nads."

His eyes narrowed. "How do you know that?"

Geddy gave a cockeyed grin. "Like you said, there's much to discuss."

Zirhof sighed and looked apologetic. "I understand. Well, your investment opportunity isn't for me, but I'll keep you in mind as I bend other ears this fine evening. A pleasure to meet you, my dear."

"Likewise," Oz said, offering her hand for another kiss.

"Good seeing you, my boy. I'm sure our paths will cross again soon." He took Geddy's hand and leaned in close. "Until then, you might want to check your six."

"My six?"

— *That means behind you.*

— You do remember I'm a pilot, right?

Geddy spun and drew in a sharp breath. Seated at a high top against the far wall, engaged in conversation with a trio of fawning businessmen, was Tatiana Semenov.

CHAPTER TWENTY-ONE

THREE'S A ... CROWD?

GEDDY IMMEDIATELY SPUN AWAY and stared past Oz as though he'd just seen a ghost. The thought of bumping into Tati here never entered his mind. As long as they were together, she'd never mentioned IASS. Then again, she wasn't in charge back then. Her late father, Ivan, always made it a point to attend. A new ship often appeared on the roof of the penthouse a few weeks later.

— *Did you know she would be here?*

— Obviously not.

— *What are you going to do?*

— I'm leaning toward running.

Sensing his discomfort, Oz leaned sideways to spot whatever had spooked him so suddenly. Of course, she had no idea what Tati looked like, but that hardly mattered. Her slinky gold gown was already burned onto his retinas, and nothing else in the scene could have gotten him so flustered.

"Holy shit. Is that ...?"

His eyes rolled up to the heavens. And the evening had been going so well. "Yeah." The word emerged in a long sigh.

"She's rich, right? We should pitch her."

"Not an option." Geddy downed the last of his drink. He placed his hand in the small of Oz's back and guided her in the opposite direction. "Let's work this side of the room a while."

For the next two hours, Geddy and Oz weaseled their way into conversations with people he recognized, most of whom needed prompting to remember how they knew him. They made their best pitch for Parmhar's startup but were rebuffed at every turn. No one even cared to come by the booth the next day. They all had their own reasons for not being interested, but it boiled down to trust. To them, he and Oz might as well have been flashing fake designer watches from a trench coat.

In the meantime, the crowd began to thin as guests left for other functions or night spots. Eventually, it became harder to avoid Tati. Either they needed to leave or do the unthinkable.

"This is stupid." Oz downed the last of her fourth drink, setting the glass on table with a loud clink. "If you won't talk to her, I will."

"Oz, I don't think that's a ..."

But it was too late. She strode purposefully across the room to Tatiana, who was on her device, presumably lining up her next party. He closed his eyes and finished his own drink, swooning a bit. They called it liquid courage for a reason, right?

— How did it come to this?

— *Perhaps it is fated.*

— I don't believe in fate.

He hurried to catch up to Oz. "Fine, we'll pitch her. But don't say you weren't warned."

They approached Tatiana side-by-side and waited until she looked up. Finally, Geddy cleared his throat. She raised her eyes to him, a self-satisfied grin stretching her pouty lips.

"Well, look who finally grew a pair."

He blinked and cleared his throat again. "Good to see you, too, Tots." When last they spoke, she'd tried to seduce him, erroneously assuming he was there for her. It hadn't ended well, but she gave up Sammo Yann as the man who stole the *Penetrator*, and that led him here. He'd never had empathy for her before but being heiress to the Semenov empire and the steward of her father's complicated legacy clearly weighed on her. By the way she'd been throwing back cocktails, it still was.

He and Oz exchanged a furtive glance. Tatiana's eyes roamed over Oz, and not unappreciatively.

"Who's your new friend?"

"This is ... um ..." Words failed him, as they so often did with Tati.

"Osmiya Nargonis." Oz scowled at him and stuck out her hand.

Tatiana regarded it briefly, then softened and gave it a halfhearted shake. "Tatiana Semenov." Her eyes slid back to Geddy. "I thought you didn't have a pot to piss in, yet here you are at the most exclusive party of the year. Who knew dumpster diving was such good business?"

Oz bristled at the characterization and gritted her teeth. "Says the woman who runs a salvage empire."

— Well, this is off to a rollicking start.

— *She and Jeledine got along just fine.*

— Jel gets along with everyone. Tati's been known to eat other people's young.

— *Compliment her*.

"Actually ..." He flashed his pearly whites. "Tatiana has diversified the business quite a bit. Isn't that right?"

She studied him a moment as though judging his sincerity. "I suppose I like to hedge my bets these days. But how about we skip the foreplay? What do you want?"

"Well, speaking of diversifying, we've got an investment opportunity." Geddy let his eyes travel down the curves of her body and back up. She liked it as much as he did, maybe more. "Might be a good fit. Like your dress."

As soon as the clumsy compliment passed his lips, one of the fragile threads between him and Oz went *plink*. It was the kind of comment Tati would slurp up, but Oz would throw up. Her withering gaze said he'd gone a bit too far.

Tatiana picked up her skinny glass, half full of something white and creamy, and took a sip. She cleared the frothy residue away with a deliberately slow swipe of her tongue.

No one had more possession over her physical gifts than Tati. Every move seemed calculated to entice. Whether it was directed toward him or Oz was an open question.

"Fine. But not here. I've seen enough gray hairs and leers to last a lifetime."

Oz's arms were folded tightly across her chest. She refused to look at him.

"Where?" he asked.

"I know a place." She swept her clutch off the table and started toward the entrance, her hips trying to escape the confines of her dress with each step. She turned back, looking down her sexy nose at Oz. "You coming, sweetie?"

She didn't budge. "Actually, I just got a message from an old friend. You two go ahead without."

The flatness in her voice punched him in the stomach. "Are you sure?"

"Yeah, I'll see you in the morning." She turned and gave a thin-lipped smile at Tatiana. "Lovely meeting you."

Then Oz hurried away before he could say another word.

Tati arched her eyebrows. "You always did like the feisty ones."

Geddy's heart sank as Oz disappeared through the exit. He gave Tatiana a weak smile. "Three's a crowd, I guess."

Tati cocked an eyebrow and smiled. "Oh, I don't know. Sometimes three is a just a good start."

———

IT WAS VERY curious that Tatiana remained at the gala as long as she did, say nothing of her willingness to talk. They'd parted on chilly terms, so much that Geddy doubted their paths would ever cross again. Yet, here they were.

Oz's abrupt departure had him in knots. It was her idea approach Tati in the first place. Was this some kind of girl test? If so, he'd failed.

They caught up as they made their way around the lagoon toward the main cluster of bars and restaurants. The tourism they'd counted on to keep Earth 3 going still hadn't materialized, and cost overruns were widespread. But if it put her in a pinch, she didn't let on, and she clearly wanted to talk about anything else.

They wound up at narrow, trendy bar about a kilometer from the convention center. One of those places where the young and beautiful went to be seen and envied. Though a dozen people waited outside, the doorman spotted Tati and motioned them inside, where a small Xellaran man hurried over to greet them.

"Good evening, Miss Semenov," he said, smoothing his plasticky hair. He didn't have any visible mods, but that didn't mean much. His brain was probably connected to the state network, or his eye was a security camera that identified everyone in the bar on sight. "I have your table right over here."

It always pleased her to be known and catered to, and she enjoyed the double-takes from men and women alike who noticed her sashaying past. Geddy hung back a couple steps as though to emphasize they weren't together.

The man led them to a table along the wall and helped Tati with her chair. "Let me tell you about tonight's wine selection. We have a lovely–"

She cut him off. "Save your breath. We're having Old Earth. One bottle, two glasses."

Old Earth was thusly named because it used to be made on The Deuce, supposedly from Old Earth wheat seeds. But the plug got pulled on that after the accident, meaning an already rare, small-batch whisky was slowly going extinct. Bottles regularly went for six or seven thousand credits. But that was a drop in the bucket for Tatiana.

"Very good, Miss Semenov. Right away." His face lit up at the big-ticket order.

She folded her sleek arms and leaned across the table, so close he got a noseful of her custom perfume. He lacked the vocabulary to describe the scent, but to him, it smelled like sex and power. It had much the same effect as it always had, and he had to shift in his seat.

"So, you spent the whole night striking out with those rich fossils, and now you come crawling to me."

Tots was direct as always. And, as usual, she had his number. "I didn't want to bother you."

She tilted her head doubtfully. "Was that it? Or did you not want your girlfriend to meet me?"

"She's not anyone's girlfriend. Especially mine."

"I wouldn't be so sure."

The owner reappeared with a fresh bottle of Old Earth and proffered it proudly, then set two spotless glasses down. "Our second-to-last bottle." He carefully uncorked it and poured them each a finger, then darted off on another errand.

Tati raised her glass. "To the show."

"To the show."

They clinked glasses and sipped. Truth be told, there were better whiskies, but this one felt like drinking time itself. It always burned going down, but in the best of ways.

"Let's hear it, then." She smacked her plump lips and leaned back.

Geddy gave his best pitch of the night. She listened carefully, nodding and occasionally refreshing their drinks. When he was done, she idly swirled the amber liquid in her glass.

"How much does he need?"

Only one guy had asked that question all night, and he laughed when he heard the answer.

"Seventy."

She flared her eyebrows. "That's a lot."

"It's good tech."

"Can't say I ever imagined Geddy Starheart pitching investors." Her eyes locked with his and she leaned back in. "Why's this so important to you?"

Yet again, he was conflicted about how much to share. Tati hired Sammo Yann, who was clearly connected to the Nads, but that didn't mean she knew anything about what they were doing.

— *She deserves to know the stakes.*

— I'm not sure I trust her. Especially if she's in financial trouble.

He leaned in close and lowered his voice to a near-whisper. "War is coming, Tots. The Zelnads are planning something big. Like, end-of-the-world shit. But we don't know what it is or where they are. We need this to find out what they're up to."

A doubtful look crossed her face like she was about to call bullshit, but she seemed to know from his tone that he wasn't kidding or embellishing.

"An army ... like the ships over Gundrun?"

Clips of the Zelnads' dramatic defense of Gundrun were all over the news. Everyone saw what they were capable of, but because they used their power as they did, public sentiment had swung sharply in their favor. And why wouldn't it? They'd gone from boogeymen to saviors in about ten dramatic seconds.

"Exactly," Geddy continued. "The tukrium shortage is no accident. They've been buying it up for decades, maybe longer. They're well-funded, and they are legion. But right now, no one considers them a threat. If that doesn't change, we're all dead."

"Aren't they just a big cult?"

He gave his head a slow shake. "They're regular people under the influence of an alien consciousness. Like a parasite that's hijacked their minds. And they want us gone."

—I think symbiotic–

—I didn't say *you* were a parasite.

Tati's eyes narrowed incredulously. "How do you know all this? Didn't you just spend the last seven years pulling your pud to the Laguna Mall concierge?"

"First, that was only like once a week or as needed. Second, I know someone who used to run with the Nads a long time ago. He knows what they're up to."

— I never ran with them. Sagaceans do not run.

— Figure of speech.

She leaned back and took another drink as she studied him, evaluating his sincerity. "If I didn't know better, I'd say you just want me to buy you a seventy-million-credit piece of tech. Tech that would give your shitty trawler a huge advantage."

True, if Parmhar's scanning tech worked, it would let them find and identify wrecks and other debris from parsecs away. No more waiting for commercial gigs and no more roaming shipping lanes begging for scraps. But that wouldn't be much use if everyone was space dust.

"More like giving humanity a fighting chance at survival."

Her long, perfectly manicured, cherry-red fingernails drummed on the table a moment. "This is a dog of an investment, Geddy. Hell, it's barely an investment at all. What's in it for me?"

— May I make an observation?

— Only if it helps me convince her.

— How many people at the gala knew her father?

— Are you kidding? Everyone.

— Do they take her as seriously?

— I doubt it. What's your point?

— She wants his respect. His influence. Give it to her and she'll give you the money.

As always, Eli had a point. Tati was still Tati, but while he and Eli labored on their ship, she was dealing with Ivan's death and taking up the reins of his considerable empire with almost zero experience. In a few short years, she'd gone from devil-may-care socialite heiress to effectively running Earth 3, which was now hemorrhaging money. That would never get her into the boys' club. Maybe nothing would, but Geddy could sure give it a go.

"Look, we need that prototype to find out what the Nads are up to. If we don't, losing seventy million will be the least of your problems. But if we do ... Semenov industries will have a massive competitive edge. You could bypass the haystack and go straight to the ... needle."

The front door opened and a young couple entered. Geddy gasped while Tatiana reveled in his discomfort. The man was a handsome young Xellaran in a sport coat, and Oz was on his arm.

CHAPTER TWENTY-TWO

RADER COUNTRY

SEEING OZ WITH ANOTHER MAN, especially one he didn't recognize, filled Geddy with jealousy. Geddy angled himself away from the door of the bar, hunkering down as he flipped up his starchy collar.

"Oooh!" Tati grabbed his forearm and shook it excitedly. "Let's invite them to join us. Remind me of her name."

He pulled his hand away and showed her his palm. "Tots, no. Let them have their–"

"Her name."

He heaved a sigh and closed his eyes, resigned. Tatiana would stop at nothing to make this happen. "Oz."

"Oz!" Tati called, drawing all eyes to her. "Over here!"

She waved her arms, smiling warmly. Oz froze as she contemplated her options. Geddy almost expected her to turn around and walk out, but instead, her heels clicked across the floor as they approached.

"Well, this is *such* a delicious coincidence," Tots said, gesturing toward their drinks. "Pull up a chair."

"We'd love to." The young man checked with Oz. "If it's okay with you, that is."

"Sure, why not?" Oz said stiffly.

The harried manager rushed over with two more chairs. He slid them noisily into place, then left to retrieve two more glasses. As he had with Geddy and Tati, he filled the new glasses before retreating again.

Tati reached her hand toward Oz's friend. Geddy's insides twisted. "Tatiana Semenov."

"Rader."

— *Geddy, he's one of them!*

— *A Zelnad? You're sure?*

— *Very.*

— Should I warn Oz?

— *Perhaps it will not come up.*

When Eli didn't answer, his mind raced. If he played this right, maybe he could get some useful intel off him.

Rader smiled at him. "And you are?"

"Geddy Starheart."

Recognition fell across his face, and he turned to Oz, smiling. "The captain. Of course!"

Rader was blessed with roguish good looks, which, in Geddy's opinion, was rare among Xellarans. He was hollow-cheeked, with an angular bone structure and skin that verged on translucent. Wide-set, inky black eyes peered out from prominent, ridged orbitals that reminded him of an owl.

"And how do you two know each other?" Tatiana continued.

Oz and Rader exchanged a look suggesting the question was fraught.

"We met during the war," said Oz, not elaborating.

Tati finished her drink and poured more. "Freedom fighters. How romantic."

"What about you two?" Rader asked.

"Our stories are almost the same. Geddy made me some bad martinis at a party, then we banged each other 'til sunrise."

Geddy poured the rest of his whiskey straight down his throat and refilled it immediately, avoiding Oz's bemused expression. She wouldn't find it funny once she knew her date played for the away team.

"How romantic," Oz said drolly.

"It wasn't until later that he led me to believe he was dead. Of course, by then, we'd been engaged for almost two years."

That particular detail had never come up in his conversations with Oz. Geddy pulled at his collar and wondered if they needed help in the kitchen.

"So, Rader," he began, a bit too loudly, "what's your story?"

"There's not much to say, really. I joined the resistance when I was sixteen and fought in a pointless and bloody civil war for five years, which is how I met Osmiya. I taught her how to fight, and she taught me how to love."

Geddy's hand formed a fist under the table. Was this really a chance encounter or did Oz want him to feel some of the same jealousy she initially felt toward Jel?

"Our bond flowered, planting seeds of hope in a garden of despair. Alas, it could not take root in such fallow soil."

— *That is a lot of metaphor.*

— More like meta*five*.

Geddy pursed his lips and slid his eyes over to Oz. She

couldn't have looked more uncomfortable if she was sitting on a nail.

"Bummer. Seems you've resolved your issues with the ruling class, though."

"I'm a pilot in the Xellaran Space Corps now. Oz tells me you're pretty good on the stick yourself."

"I've had a lot of practice."

Oz never mentioned her old flame was a pilot, too. In fact, she'd never really mentioned him at all. Were they just catching up, or was this something more.

Tatiana's lips twisted the way they always did when she was sizing someone up. "So, how are you here and not being kept artificially awake in a factory?"

Things didn't work out so hot for the resistance after the war. Most wound up dead or contributing to Xellara's economy in a manner not of their choosing.

His eyes lowered to the table. "You might say I was shown a better way forward."

"Whatever do you mean?" Geddy asked innocently. The guy could only dance around it so long, right?

"I am part of a growing movement that would see an end to all war."

Oz rolled her eyes. "Oh, please. You sound like one of those Zelnad kooks."

A leaden silence descended over the table.

Rader's polite grin flattened. "Is it really that obvious?"

"Wait ..." Oz swallowed hard. "You're a ..."

"A Zelnad, yes."

— *Okay, so maybe it will come up.*

"I'm sorry ... I didn't know," she said.

He gave an aw-shucks shrug. "I didn't think it mattered.

But now I'm curious about your posture toward us. 'Kooks,' was it?"

She shook her head, waving her open palms back and forth. "Rader, no, that's not what I–"

"What happened over Gundrun. Was that ... kooky?" His eyebrows and shoulders shrugged in unison. "If you do, maybe you're the kooky one."

— I think she struck a nerve.

— *Zelnads do not have nerves.*

While Oz fished for a response, Rader turned to Geddy. "Don't you have anything to say in our defense, kindred?"

OF COURSE, Rader thought Geddy was one of them. Eli had the same psychic signature. But Geddy was Geddy, and Eli was Eli. How much of this guy was still Rader, if any?

— *Uh-oh. I really should have seen this coming.*

—What should I do?

— *Play along. Oz knows the truth.*

— Yeah, but Tots doesn't.

Tatiana's eyes flew to Geddy, her eyes droopy. "Kindred? Whazzat mean?"

Geddy glanced at Oz, who seemed resigned to playing along. But Tatiana was a wildcard in every sense of the word. It didn't help that she was on her fifth or sixth drink.

"It's true, Tatiana." Geddy met her quizzical expression with a serious one. "Rader and I are Zelnads."

Her face pinched a moment, then relaxed as she threw her head back and cackled, far too obnoxiously for the muted setting. "Geddy the Zelnad. Can you imagine?" Her laughter tapered off and she dabbed at the corners of her eyes, checking her fingers for mascara residue. "Commitment-phobes need not apply, amiright? Okay, I'm gonna go touch myself ..." She slid out of her chair and shakily stood, steadying herself against the backrest before searching for the restroom. "... up. Touch myself up. BRB."

Rader's brow creased, and he turned to Oz. "Did you know your captain was one of us?"

"Of course, silly." There was a small quiver in her voice. Could Rader tell? Geddy flared his eyes wide at her and gave a small nod toward the restroom. Mercifully, she took the hint and stood, so suddenly that she jostled the table and nearly knocked over the bottle of Old Earth. "I'm going to join Tatiana ... because we girls go to the bathroom together. As you know."

"So true." Geddy gave a nervous laugh and they both watched Oz follow after Tati.

— *Press him for information. Maybe he will reveal something.*

— What do I say?

— *I will guide you.*

— Oh, boy ...

Geddy turned back to Rader and took a fortifying sip of his whisky. "Boy, it sure is great to be a Zelnad, huh?"

"And it will only get better," Rader said conspiratorially. His weirdly unblinking eyes roamed about the bar. "Don't you wonder how it all went wrong? How such promise was so badly squandered?"

"I know. It has more of a coffee-shop feel, right?"

He sighed wistfully. "I must admit, I've enjoyed this body. I will miss it when our final act unfolds."

— Start probing him!

— Really? We just met.

— Geddy!

— Okay, okay!

"What would you say you're looking to most about that final act? I can't pick just one thing."

Rader scowled. "Driving a dagger into the heart of Sagacea, obviously."

"Totally."

"And maybe it's selfish of me, but I hope Osmiya is chosen."

Terror gripped his chest. "Now when you say 'chosen' ..."

"When I took over Rader's consciousness, I found his memories of her ... intriguing."

Geddy was about to ask what memories when Tati and Oz returned from the bathroom. Whether Oz tried to explain what was going on or not, he couldn't be sure, but they both remained standing, which was a very good sign. He wanted out of there immediately.

"Speak of the devil." Rader rose to greet them and pulled out Oz's chair, but she, too, remained standing and gave Geddy a look that indicated the evening should be cut short. Tati half-leaned on her as though she was about to tip over, which may or may not have been an act.

"Where are we often nets?" Tatiana slurred. "Er, off to nest. Next. Where are we going now?"

"How about Geddy and I take you back to your hotel?" Oz suggested.

Tati considered this a moment, her eyes fluttering, and nodded loosely. "Sounds fun."

"Good idea, Oz." Geddy eagerly latched onto the life

preserver she'd just thrown him. "We've got a long day tomorrow."

Rader met each of their eyes in turn before throwing up his hands in mock surrender. "Guess it's an early night for all of us, then. Oz, it's been lovely catching up. Tatiana. Kindred."

"Kindred ... to you as well."

— There better not be a secret handshake you forgot to teach me.

— *We do not have hands.*

Oz threw Tati's arm around the back of her neck and half-dragged her toward the door. When Geddy took a step after them, Rader seized his arm. "See you at the keynote, tomorrow, brother. It's really happening."

"Exciting times. Anyway, thanks for picking up the tab. You should be able to write it off since we talked about work stuff."

Before Rader could protest, Geddy patted him on the shoulder and followed the girls outside.

CHAPTER TWENTY-THREE

THE NO IN KEYNOTE

THE SO-CALLED Grand Salon was an enormous stadium hanging off the back of the convention center. Not as big as the one on Zorr where they watched Sumbakh, but large enough to hold a hundred thousand attendees with room to spare. Voprot found a section nearby for oversized species, which, ominously, hosted a handful of Gundrun military brass. Doc and Parmhar were seated in front of him, Oz, and Denk.

A square stage sat in the middle of the floor under colorful hovering lights. Black steps came up through a hole in the middle, and a projection of "IASS 2427" drifted lazily back and forth.

Parmhar still didn't have his funding. He'd been crest-fallen to learn of Geddy and Oz's unproductive evening but held out hope that Tatiana would come through before the show was over.

The previous night ended with Geddy and Oz helping Tati back to her suite at the Baroness, a luxurious property adjoining the convention center. Her drunkenness wasn't an act, but her willingness to end the night early certainly was. They left her on the bed, promising to return shortly, but she passed out immediately.

They hadn't seen Rader at the keynote, but you couldn't have picked out anyone in a venue this large unless they were nearby. Oz clearly wasn't ready to talk about him yet, and the only information Geddy gleaned from him was that the keynote was somehow significant. Otherwise, they'd still be in bed.

"What did he say to you, exactly?" Oz asked.

"He said, 'See you at the keynote, brother. It's really happening.'"

"What's 'it?' What do they have to do with the keynote?"

"I have no idea."

The house lights dimmed, and a spotlight picked up a sharp-dressed Zihnian as he ascended through the hole in floor of the square platform.

A booming announcer's voice came through the PA. "Please welcome the president of the Intergalactic Association of Ship Suppliers, Meihen Soupadou!"

The small man's ash-gray skin popped against his blue uniform, presumably the sort that IASS leadership wore around the office. He acknowledged the welcoming applause.

"Greetings, attendees, and thank you. Before we begin, I've been asked to make a brief announcement. A gray Nichuan light transport, transponder number 892373Q, has exploded."

A four-armed Nichuan sprung from his seat on the floor and limped hurriedly down the aisle toward the exit, drawing sniggers from the crowd as Soupadou continued.

"Welcome to IASS 2427!" He gestured grandly about

him as the auditorium filled with applause. "On behalf of the association board of trustees, thank you for coming.

"I know you're anxious to hear our top-secret keynote speaker, but first, one of our members has asked for a few minutes of your time to make an important announcement. From Khetaka Central Command on Gundrun, please welcome General Vilguth Arbizander."

— *What is he doing here?*

— I dunno, but I don't like it.

Arbizander appeared through the hole in the stage in full military regalia as supportive applause traveled around the stadium. Above him, projectors formed a large hologram of Gundrun.

"Thank you, president Soupadou. As you all know, Gundrun came within a hair's breadth of destruction recently when a massive asteroid collided with one of our moons. The debris overwhelmed our planetary defense system, the khetaka, and all seemed lost. I, along with billions of you, watched helplessly, expecting to witness the end of our world.

"But that's not what happened."

The animation re-created the asteroid's collision with Valniuq and the overwhelming cloud of rock that punched through the khetaka. Then, the schnozzes just appeared in a blink and assembled themselves into the Zelnad supership, blowing the planetoid-sized pieces to smithereens.

"Gundrun asked for help, and help came. The Zelnads appeared like the hand of god, and they saved our world."

That last sentence echoed ominously through the arena. Oz and Geddy exchanged a worried look. There was no mention of the broader effort to help Gundrun.

"But what if Gundrun had been Zihnia, or Aku, or Eicreon? Who would answer the call? If a giant asteroid or invading force threatened your world, who would defend you? The time has come to pick up the pieces of the failed Alliance and build something that truly serves all our worlds. Which is why, today, I am proud to announce the formation of a new Coalition of Independent Worlds, starting with Gundrun and the Zelnad Nation!"

Geddy's jaw fell open. Zelnad *Nation*? How were they supposed to reform the Alliance if Gundrun and the Nads were building their own?

Murmurs of surprise and confusion rippled through the audience. Meanwhile, the Gundrun leaders seated near Voprot in the oversized-alien section remained stone-faced.

The Nads planned all this. Knocking a rock out of the Elenian Belt just so. Jumping in front of it at the last moment like a heroic cop taking a bullet. And, now, forming a new coalition with a powerful ally. It was strategic, and it was smart.

But there was one glaring problem with their plan. Nobody knew who the Zelnads were, where they were, or what they wanted. Even with Gundrun on board, a coalition would be a tough sell.

Apparently, the Nads realized that, too.

"Until now, the Zelnads have largely stayed out of galactic affairs. Today, all that changes. Representing the Zelnad Nation, please welcome my good friend, Colonel Zarymid Pritchard."

The name hit Geddy like a cartoon sledgehammer. Pritchard was his father's commanding officer in the Planetary Defense Force back on Earth 2. He hadn't thought of him in years and figured he'd ridden off into the sunset. Apparently not.

He emerged from the center, waving and smiling warmly. He was bald, with an avuncular white goatee, probably in his late sixties — the perfect age for screwing over future generations.

No one here had a reason to know who Pritchard was. Earth 2 never fought in the Ring War, and even there, he was just another humorless PDF officer.

Oz was just as shocked and turned to him, her empathic abilities clearly attuned to the churn in his stomach. "You know him, don't you?"

"Unfortunately."

When Geddy was thirteen, his father, a captain in Earth 2's Planetary Defense Force, took a joyride with his mother to the Ice Castles in the north and never came back. Col. Pritchard was his commanding officer, and it was he who showed up in his classroom that day to break the terrible news. Later that same year, not long before Geddy stowed away on a ship bound for Kigantu, Pritchard abruptly retired and disappeared. Apparently, his post-retirement plan was to become a Zelnad.

The restless audience was buzzing by this point, presumably along the lines of, *Is that what they look like?* or, *Does that mean Zelnads are all human, or that all humans are Zelnads?* or, *What the hell is happening right now?* and a million other excellent questions.

Pritchard quieted the room with a calming pump of his hands. "Please ... all your questions are about to be answered."

— *I do not understand. That cannot be the same Colonel Pritchard who—*

— Told me my parents were dead? That's him, all right.

Geddy's brain, which was only running about seventy percent on account of his moderate hangover, labored to make sense of this baffling development. But no threads were connecting.

The crowd noise faded, and Pritchard continued.

"Thank you. Now, I realize you won't trust anything I say until you know who I am." He touched his splayed fingers to his chest. "I am Zarymid Pritchard, formerly a colonel in the Planetary Defense Force on Earth 2.

"But 'human' is not my highest, or even my most important identity. I am Zelnad. Is that a religion? No. Is it a ..." he gave exaggerated air quotes, "... 'cult?'" Again, no. What unites Zelnads is an unwavering belief that things can be better. That they *should be* better. In fact, the word 'Zelnad' means 'evolve' in one ancient tongue, and this coalition is not a revolution, my friends. Rather, it is an *evo*-lution.

— *He is not lying.*

— Not yet.

— *He doesn't have to. Anything can sound appealing to anyone if it is delivered right.*

— Fucking politics.

"Self-interest has only brought us war, strife, and greed. We are sick of it. Gundrun ..." he pointed a shaking finger at Arbizander, who stood off to the side with Soupadou, "... is sick of it. We fight war after war and stab each other in the backs again ..." he pounded his fist into his open palm, "... and again ... and again, and all we learn is how to fight better the next time. How to kill more. Never, ever, do we say, "You know what? Maybe this isn't the way to go."

Geddy turned and studied the faces behind them hoping to find signs that the crowd wasn't buying this bullshit, but that was naïvely optimistic. They were slurping it up.

Pritchard knew everyone would agree about the end, but few would question the means. The manufactured drama over Gundrun was like a shrill whistle that seizes everyone's attention in a crowd. Now that he had it, he was delivering the exact right message at the right time and in the right way to a sizable cross-section of the galaxy. The Nads weren't just strategic geniuses, but marketing geniuses, as well.

He jabbed his finger emphatically at his feet, his face grave. "This coalition is about stepping out of our forefathers' shadows. Even in the full light of truth, we will have nothing to fear from each other, because fear will no longer exist." He raised the same finger next to his head as he shook it. "But as they say in sales, *that's not all*. Joining us on the path to peace are some worlds who know all too well the costs of war. Please welcome the leaders of Ghruk, Kailoria, and Aku, the former Triad planets!"

Geddy drew in a sharp breath, sinking as deeply into his chair as he could possibly go. This just kept getting worse and worse, yet it sounded good even to him, and he knew the truth.

The Screvari Circle, the president of Kailoria, and the Ghruk Grand Senate all marched onstage to thundering applause like bygones were bygones. The people behind them were getting teary-eyed. Worse, this crap was being simulcast everywhere.

The leaders of all four worlds — about twenty in all —

lined up shoulder to shoulder and locked arms in a show of solidarity. Pritchard took a couple steps back and joined the lineup at the middle, laughing and having a grand old time.

"A new tide is rising, IASS. A tide ... that truly will raise all ships!"

In a bit of clumsy, contrived choreography, the new Coalition of Independent Worlds gestured skyward.

As they did, banks of lights in the murk overhead turned on, and a handful of very cool-looking starships instantly materialized under the dome.

Gasps exploded through the crowd, which teetered between awe and fear.

"Ladies, gentlemen, and genders yet to be categorized, it is my honor to introduce the 2428 Hovensby Starship lineup, featuring the all-new Insta-Jump Bubble Universe Drive powered by Zelnad Technology!"

CHAPTER TWENTY-FOUR

HANG OUT HERE OFTEN?

Until that moment, Geddy had felt like they were getting closer to unraveling the Zelnad plot. But in the space of a few minutes, that long and winding road had become an impasse and Pritchard's led to a false paradise.

It really was masterful. Create a mystique. Let the theories spread. Then, stage a dramatic entrance. Once you've seized everyone's attention, give them something big. The only thing more powerful than inspiration was relief, and now that everyone thought they had nothing to fear from the Nads, the matter was settled. Maybe not forever, but long enough.

The court of public opinion had rendered its verdict. Making allies got the Zelnads further, faster, than making enemies. Eli and Morpho were right. Why meet your enemies in battle when you can earn their trust and slit their throats in the night?

Every world that signed on to their so-called coalition made them stronger, and they wouldn't see they'd been duped until it was too late.

The partnership with Hovensby, the luxury starship brand, was just the cream in their Twinkie. Until now, Zelnad tech only came through the Double A, and rarely. People with money knew what that tech was capable of, and now they could all get their hands on a little piece. The very advocates the Nads needed.

Once Pritchard and the Coalition began descending into the stage, the house lights came up and the Gundrun brass got up and left. Geddy wasn't entirely sure if they were there out of obligation or in support of Arbizander, but it hardly mattered. The deal was done, and the ball was rolling faster than ever.

None of Geddy's balls were rolling.

They collected Voprot and filed out with the rest of the crowd, most of whom went straight back to the show floor or hurried off to one of the many educational sessions scheduled next. There were nerdy ones aimed at engineers like, "Cracks in Your Warp Shell: Boosting Field Integrity Through Dynamic Boson Regulator Throttling" or ones for captains like, "Leveling Up: Motivating Long-Haul Crews Through Gamification."

"What now?" asked Oz, her voice heavy with despair.

He shook his head and muttered, "I don't know."

When they finally emerged onto the show floor, they discovered that the area overhead had already been taken over by the new Hovensby ships for test flights, and attendees were lining up for their opportunity. The Nads' dog and pony show onstage had won some converts, and now test rides would keep the energy going.

He hadn't seen Tatiana, but that hardly meant anything. If she'd come for the keynote, which wasn't likely, she, too, would've been hard to spot in the teeming crowd. Realistically, he didn't expect to see her again until mid-afternoon, if he saw her at all. If she passed on Parmhar's company, he didn't know what they would do.

Tatiana Semenov, who was probably in her room trying to drown her hangover with a tray of room-service Bloody Marys, somehow was their only hope. Not an ideal situation.

"Hey, Cap, can Voprot and I try a Hovensby?" Denk asked hopefully. "Y'know, for research?"

For the first time, Geddy noticed that Voprot was carrying at least half a dozen of the fancy bags vendors handed out, all filled to capacity and hanging off his scaly right arm like fish on a stringer.

"You don't have to ask permission," replied Geddy, who was fixated on Voprot's loot. "What's all that for?"

"Voprot like swag. Look!" he reached into one bag near his elbow and withdrew a bunched-up piece of rubberized black fabric resembling a swim cap. It bore the logo of Kemik, the engine manufacturer.

"What is it?"

"Protector for bike seat," Voprot said, grinning.

As was so often the case with the Kigantean, so many questions filled Geddy's mind that he opted out. "Is that the only color?"

Voprot's face fell. "You not like?"

Denk elbowed the big lizard in the thigh, which was as high as his elbow reached. "C'mon, V, he's just jealous. See you guys later!"

They trundled off through the crowd like two little kids, one of whom was pushing three meters tall.

"I feel like they should be leashed to each other," Oz mused.

"Listen, I'm gonna hit the head. Meet you at the booth?"

"I've got nowhere else to be."

He threw her a wave and joined the crush of people headed toward the bathrooms.

— *It seems the Zelnads have been playing a long game.*

— Meanwhile, we can't even get the box open.

— *You cannot lose heart.*

— Easy for you to say. You don't have one.

Geddy entered the bathroom and waited for a Napnap to do his business at the multi-species urinal, then bellied up to relieve himself. Who were they kidding, reforming the Alliance? The Nads built a whole brand in the space of a week. All he had was the counsel of an ancient alien who could never be as guileful as their foe, a barely viable trawler, and a well-meaning but mostly powerless crew.

"How was the gala?" asked a familiar voice at the next stall.

Geddy turned to find Zereth-Tinn peeing beside him. How was he so adept at running into him?

He scanned the area. Plenty of aliens were waiting in line behind them, but between their polite observations about the keynote and the constant flushing, no one was listening. Maybe that was why Zereth-Tinn followed him here.

"Let's just say it was the start of an interesting night. Thanks for the opportunity."

"Did you get your funding?"

"We've got a few good leads," he lied.

This awkward encounter couldn't be accidental. How did he not see Zereth-Tinn while he was waiting? Did he bribe whoever was next in line? This cat worked in mysterious ways.

"Look, maybe this is a terrible question to ask at a urinal, but can I help you with something?" He finished and zipped up his pants.

Zereth-Tinn did the same and gave a quick look around him. "I gather you watched the keynote."

"Yeah, why?"

"Let's take a walk."

They washed their hands and headed for the exit with Geddy trailing just behind his cryptic acquaintance.

— Whaddya think?

— *What do you have to lose?*

He followed Zereth-Tinn down the concourse and up two sets of fire stairs, then down a hallway lined with administrative offices. By then, no one was around besides the odd Xellaran worker. Nobody paid them any mind, and the hubbub on the show floor was muffled.

"Where the hell are we?" Geddy asked.

The hallway ended at an unmarked door. Zereth-Tinn paused in front of it and squared up to him.

The tops of his steel-blue eyes locked on. "This is going to change things for you. Once I open the door, there's no turning back."

With the Nads taking control, there was no back to turn to. He still didn't know whether he could trust Zereth-Tinn, but what choice did he have?

"Surprise me."

Zereth-Tinn gave the door three sharp raps. A few seconds later, it slid open, only revealing a privacy wall. He stepped back and gestured for Geddy to come through.

Inside, a meeting was underway. Fifteen people were seated around a large U-shaped table. Geddy recognized half of them. One was Zirhof, who he'd just seen at the gala. There was also Smegmo Eilgars, his very rich young friend from the planet Ceonia, whom he hadn't seen in at least a decade. Seated next to him was Everett Hau, the flamboyant trillionaire who ran Caloth. But there was also a Ghruk, a Kailorian, and his old pal Balzac, the leader of the Screvari underground on Aku.

Seated across from him at the middle of the U was a face he'd sincerely hoped never to see again. Confusion, anger, and fear collided inside him, and his palms began to sweat. His impulse was to turn around and run.

"Hello, Geddy," Tretiak Bouche said stiffly. "We're the Committee."

CHAPTER TWENTY-FIVE

THE COMMITTEE

For a pregnant moment, Geddy stood at the top of the U in the boardroom staring dumbly at Tretiak. No one spoke.

"Good to see you again, old friend," said Smegmo.

"You, too, kid."

"Have a seat," Tretiak said.

Before Geddy could say he preferred to stand, Zereth-Tinn retrieved a chair from a stack in the corner and placed it beside Geddy. If he didn't sit, he'd seem like a douchebag. That normally wouldn't have stopped him, but he still didn't know what this was.

"Is this an intervention? Because I've been trying to cut back. I mean, not last night, but that was ..." When no one so much as allowed a grin, he trailed off. "Wow. Tough room."

— Are they Zelnads? That would explain why they didn't laugh.

— No. There may be another explanation.

At least that was something. Tretiak leaned back and looked imperiously down his long, thin nose. "This body has no official capacity. You are free to leave whenever you wish. But we're hopeful you'll indulge us."

The only woman at the table was an older Xellaran. Geddy and Tretiak represented humanity, unfortunately.

Geddy pretended to check his nonexistent watch. "There's a noon presentation I'd like to catch about cleaning nutrimush tanks, but I'm free until then."

"I suppose you're wondering why you're here."

He gave an exaggerated shrug. "Seems clear enough." Again, not so much as a smirk, which made him even more nervous.

"Some of us believe you may know a great deal more about the Zelnads than we do. If so, we'd like to know what you know."

Geddy's impulse was to crack another joke, but he thought better of it. All eyes were on him, and they were dead serious.

He leaned back and crossed his right leg over his knee. "How about you start by telling me what this 'Committee' is. If it's the itty-bitty-titty one, I'm out."

Before Tretiak could reply, Zirhof leaned forward with his finger raised. "If I may, Mr. Chairman ..."

Tretiak gestured him to proceed.

"Geddy, various iterations of this group have met in secret since the Ring War to learn as much about the Zelnads as possible. Frankly, we don't know a whole lot more than we did back then."

He wouldn't have put it past Tretiak to stage something like this just to blow a hole in his chest. But Zirhof? Smegmo? They'd earned his trust.

"Why do you think I know something?"

"Your actions at the Double A got me wondering about Sammo Yann," Tretiak said. "I knew he was working with the Zelnads, but I couldn't imagine what he'd want with your little ship. Plus, your dedication to getting it back was rather ... out of character."

— How dare he? I've been dedicated to all kinds of stuff!

— *He does not mean serial masturbation.*

"Which is why," he continued, "we asked our intrepid friend here to test you."

He jutted his chin toward the door. Zereth-Tinn was propped against the wall with his hands in his pockets.

"The Zelnads didn't ask me to put a tracker on your ship," he explained. "I just wanted you to think they did. Only you didn't seem too surprised."

Tretiak picked up the baton. "And his successful blackmail proved you had some reason to fear the Zelnads. We'd love to know what that reason is."

"Especially in light of their big coming-out party," added Zirhof.

Geddy's eyes roamed the faces in the room, weighing his options. Everyone had vast wealth and influence, certainly, and it seemed none of them were Nads, but he couldn't imagine Tretiak being in charge of anything legit or well-intended.

"If the blackmail was just a test, then I want my money back."

"Even though it led you to Old Earth and the quantum cubes?" Tretiak asked, missing the point while making a better one.

It wasn't just Zirhof who knew about the cubes. It was all of them. Only they assumed the Nads came up with the jump tech, and Eli felt certain it was a Sagacean who helped Dr. Nilsson invent it. They might never know for sure.

"You'll have to forgive me for being a bit skeptical," Geddy said to Tretiak. "Considering our history and all."

Tretiak's eyes briefly flashed anger, but when they met Geddy's, there was only resignation. "The time for personal vendettas has passed. We're about to lose the war before a single shot's been fired because we don't know what we're dealing with."

— Whaddya think, Eli? Is he on the level?

— *We cannot know for sure. You may have to trust him.*

— Trust Tretiak. Hmph. Those words don't belong together.

Reforming the Alliance was always going to be border-line impossible, but there was fresh urgency to it now, and the people in this room likely offered the shortest path to that goal. As usual, the Nads were several steps ahead.

He heaved a sigh and stood. "You got a comfier chair?"

GEDDY TOLD THE COMMITTEE EVERYTHING.

Not the part about causing the accident that ruined The Deuce, but pretty much everything else. Eli. Sagacea. Tukrium. Shinium. That the war to come that may not be a war at all. He ended by explaining why he was at IASS in the first place, which was to find an investor in Parmhar's tech.

"This is the technology we need to find the Zelnads."

"Does it work?" Zirhof shifted forward in his high-backed chair.

"On paper. But he can't make a prototype without working capital, and–"

"How much?" Smegmo had evolved from a dopey, mopey, sesehlu-practicing teen to a self-possessed business-man. Geddy hoped he'd made a small, but lasting impression.

"Seventy million."

Smegmo laughed and shared an, *isn't that cute* look with Everett Hau, who basically owned Caloth. Not surprising since they probably made that in the time it took to say it.

"I think we can manage that. How fast can he get the prototype built?"

And just like that, Parmhar had his funding. It felt a little anticlimactic. Soon, the focus returned to Geddy.

"Just to be clear, you're telling us that one of these ... Sagaceans lives inside you and is listening to us right now?" Tretiak face held a grave expression.

"Yes, but as I said, he's not a Zelnad. Same world, two opposing philosophies. The only other Sagacean we know about is Morpho, our mechanic."

Tretiak paused to absorb this information. "But the Zelnads are legion. Where are all the Sagaceans?"

"The Zelnads are mostly, if not entirely, copies of the same consciousness."

"Like a virus?" Zirhof asked.

"Yeah, but it's not random. They have some way of choosing who they take over."

"And what do Eli and Morpho say about all this?" continued Tretiak.

Geddy blinked, his eyes meeting both the Ghruk's and Kailorian's. "That our best shot at stopping them is to reform the Alliance."

It might've been his imagination, but the whole Committee took a collective breath. The words hung in the air between them.

Balzac broke the silence with a hearty laugh. "You've got to be kidding."

"I wish I were. They've been holding court in my head."

Zirhof leaned forward, his face knotted in confusion. "They communicate telepathically?"

"Yeah, but they need to be very close. The point is, they've worked through every scenario, and they think it's our best bet."

"The Alliance fell apart eighty years ago," complained the Xellaran woman. "Rebuilding is as practical as raising the dead."

"Otaro Verveik would disagree."

Everyone stiffened in their chairs, exchanging incredulous looks and assuming Geddy was joking. Everyone but Tretiak, whose eyes remained uncomfortably fixed on him.

"Who's that?" asked Smegmo, by far the youngest among them.

"Otaro Verveik," Geddy replied. "Last supreme commander of the Alliance."

"Verveik is dead," stated Tretiak with finality. "Murdered years ago by Triad assassins."

Horror and hopelessness pierced Geddy's heart.

Apparently, this was news to everyone, including Zirhof, who gasped and turned to Tretiak. "Are you sure? I never heard anything of the sort."

"A senior Gundrun official confirmed as much when he was at the Double A years ago. They never released it to the public."

Geddy deflated like an untied balloon. His long-shot plan had just gone from exceedingly difficult to impossible. Without Verveik, there could be no Alliance. Especially after the Nads' brilliantly branded debut.

Of course, now that Gundrun and the former Triad planets were playing for the away team, it might not matter anyway. His seemingly immortal childhood hero was dead, and so, it seemed, was the Alliance.

"It doesn't change anything," affirmed Smegmo. "We still need to find the Zelnad fleet and prepare a defense."

A grim determination built in Geddy's gut. "This isn't about defense. It's about offense."

"What do you mean?"

"The Nads want to end civilization now and forever. That means wiping out all intelligent life in the universe *and* destroying Sagacea so it never starts again. War doesn't get that done."

"Why have they been hoarding tukrium if not to build ships?" asked Tretiak.

"They have been building ships, but they've been looking for trace amounts of shinium, too. Whatever weapon they're building to take out Sagacea needs a lot of it."

"They would destroy their own home world?" Zirhof asked, incredulous.

"Yes. But whatever they're planning for the rest of us, they need to do at scale. All I know for sure is that Gundrun, this Coalition BS, the Hovensby deal ... it's all part of a plan. They've probably been laying the groundwork for millennia."

By the looks on their faces, all their assumptions about the Nads had just been upended.

"Don't forget about novaspheres," said the Xellaran

woman, whose role on the Committee apparently was wet blanket. "The Zelnads have a stranglehold on the supply."

"If I've said it once, I've said it a thousand times." Geddy was unable to pass up the softball she just tossed at him. "Blue balls are everyone's problem."

— *Surely, you've always wanted to say that.*

— I figured I might not have many more chances.

"Can we replicate their jump technology in time?" Tretiak asked Zirhof.

"I'm not sure. My team is reviewing the data on the cubes as we speak."

A shellshocked pallor blanched their faces. Tretiak cleared his throat and rose. "Clearly, there is much to discuss. Geddy, your insights have been invaluable."

"That's it?" Geddy's despair morphed into irritation. These were some of the most powerful people in the galaxy.

"Return here at eight tomorrow," Tretiak instructed. "Tell no one."

The only ones Geddy trusted on the whole Committee were Zirhof, Smegmo, and maybe Balzac. Good guys, but not alphas. He'd feel a lot better about all this if he had another staunch ally. Somebody with a low tolerance for bullshit who would have the common courtesy to stab him in the heart and not his back.

He knew just the woman.

CHAPTER TWENTY-SIX

A SUITE OPPORTUNITY

GEDDY'S CONSTERNATION over his objective only grew as he made the long walk out of the convention center's labyrinthine offices and back to the show floor. He must've appeared troubled because a uniformed employee stopped to ask if he was lost.

— *Your blood pressure is elevated. Is something bothering you?*

— I don't trust Tretiak. Someone needs to keep him honest.

— *Someone like Tatiana.*

— Yup.

— *But you're not sure you can trust her, either.*

— Nope. But I don't think she wants me dead, which is more than I can say for Tretiak and Hau.

Even Eli couldn't argue with his logic. Geddy checked his comm device and found a couple messages from Oz regarding his whereabouts. He messaged that he'd secured funding for Parmhar's company and had some details to work out. She said she looked forward to hearing more.

After a few wrong turns, he finally spotted a sign pointing to Tatiana's hotel, the Baroness, and followed it to a wide, completely empty skybridge that connected it to the convention center. The afternoon sun blazed through the windows as he crossed into the dimly lit hotel, whose rich decor boasted conspicuous luxury.

The dark gray marble floor was polished to a mirror finish, reflecting tasteful lights set flat to the wall. Silky fabric adorned the arched ceiling, gathered into slender pleats that ran its entire length. The faint lilt of piano music drifted through the air like a wandering ghost.

A handful of Temerurians and Xellarans were gathered in a corner of the lounge area near the front desk, reclined in plush leather couches and having a hushed conversation over dainty cups of coffee.

This was definitely Tatiana's kind of place.

The front desk attendant glanced up and pushed aside a holographic readout as he approached.

"How may I help you, sir?" Her voice was pleasant but mechanical, as Xellaran androids tended to sound.

"I'm looking for Tatiana Semenov."

"Ah, yes, Miss Semenov." The whole guest database was probably on a chip in her head. "Who may I say is calling?"

"Geddy Starheart."

"One moment." Her eyes fluttered briefly, then without moving a muscle, she rang Tatiana's room. "Yes, good afternoon, Miss Semenov. A Mr. Geddy Starheart is here to see you." A moment later, she gave a thin smile. "Very good. I will send him up."

She reached underneath the counter and withdrew a flat crystal with the Baroness' logo etched inside, then held it up to her eye. A red laser from her pupil briefly passed over it, then she dropped it in his hand.

"Place this in the key port on the elevator. It will take you to her suite. The elevators are right behind this wall." She gestured behind her.

"Thanks."

He tucked it in his pocket and followed the edge of the reception desk around the wall to a bank of eight elevators. The one nearest him opened, and he placed the crystal key in the glowing slot. It sucked it in, and the doors silently closed.

— *You think she will want to join the Committee?*

— *I know she will. But will they want her?*

The elevator whisked him to the top floor in a few seconds, and the door opened straight into Tatiana's suite. A huge living area with plush furniture narrowed to a hallway with an open door from which light spilled out. Beyond it lay the dim bedroom.

He ventured a few steps further in. "Tots?"

Tatiana leaned out of the open door with her hair wrapped in a towel, wearing a silky peach robe fastened haphazardly about her slender waist, ending midway up her thighs. One flick of her hand and it would fall open. It might anyway, if she leaned a bit. She'd clearly just thrown it on.

He hadn't seen her without full makeup in a very long time. Even when they were together, she usually completed her morning regimen before he woke up. Apparently, her hangover had other plans.

"To what do I owe the pleasure?"

The remains of a green smoothie had dried to the inside of a tall glass on a tray beside the elevator door.

"Figured I'd see how you were feeling after last night."

"I'll live."

He could only see her when she stepped away from the mirror. Otherwise, he was just talking to the ginormous shower behind her.

"What do you remember from last night?" he asked.

"I remember Rader thinking you were a Zelnad. And then your girlfriend told me we needed to go back to the hotel. I didn't think that meant tucking me in."

"She's not my ... never mind. Before we left, Rader said something about this morning's keynote, so we went."

"And?"

He caught her up on the morning's bombshell events. She was intrigued but didn't appear to grasp the implications, suggesting she might not recall all the details from the evening before.

"Colonel Pritchard." She dabbed on foundation then leaned in to smooth it. "As in, my dad's old crony from the PDF?"

"One and the same."

"He's seriously their leader now?"

He'd wondered about that, too. He spoke like he was, but then again, the Zelnads were all of the same mind. Maybe they didn't have any use for hierarchy, or maybe Pritchard was chosen for his charisma.

"I don't know. But after that, I got pulled into a *very* interesting meeting. A secret cabal concerned about the Nads."

She stuck her head back out, roughly halfway through her lengthy process. "Secret cabal?"

"They call it the Committee. It's been around since the Ring War, but it only convenes at IASS."

Tati rolled her eyes and leaned back out of view. "I'm

sure my father was on it. It would explain why he came to this ridiculous show every year."

"Probably, but I don't know whose side he would've been on."

She had no particular love for her father. Ivan could be warm and ebullient or distant and brooding. With her, it was generally the latter.

"No offense, but what would a secret cabal want with you?"

"To know what I know about the Nads."

She leaned fully out the door like a prairie dog from its hole, and eyes narrowed. "You mean the war you say is coming."

For a long moment, he stared back at her, torn about what he should or shouldn't reveal.

"Tots, there's a lot you don't know. Can I trust you?"

The gravity in his tone held her there, and her face softened. "Yeah …"

She walked out and took a seat in the facing chair, concern filling her azure eyes. Even without mascara, they could pierce his soul.

He repeated what he told the Committee, again omitting the part about turning Earth 2 into The Deuce. Never in a million years did he think he would be telling Tatiana about Eli, but he had to. In a way, it came as a relief. He really had broken her heart, but at least now she understood why.

"Wow." Her unfinished eyes gave a rapid blink. "You're actually serious."

He shrugged. "It was bound to happen eventually."

"Thank you for telling me."

"The fact that there's an alien in my head doesn't freak you out?"

She shrugged, and her pouty lips curled into a smirk. "Sounds like you both get something out of the deal. You get good advice, he gets plenty of room to stretch his little spore legs."

"Cute, but he already made that joke."

She got up and returned to the bathroom. "And you believe these people can help rebuild the Alliance?"

"All I know is, we can't do it alone."

"Who's on this Committee, anyway?"

He ticked off the names he knew. The only one she recognized was the Xellaran woman, Geminaya, and not very well.

Tati had made him feel a lot of things over the years, but until now, never empathy. She had an overindulged childhood and a turbulent, carefree young adulthood. Until Ivan died, she hadn't worked a single day in her life. The only thing she knew how to be was beautiful and conspicuously wealthy. Ivan's holdings were vast and diverse, and she inherited all his problems but none of his network. Through no fault of her own, she was an island unto herself now — literally and figuratively.

"Sounds like a real who's who of the galaxy." She carefully drew dark lines across her eyelids.

"Which is why you should be on it."

"What makes you think I'd want to?"

He rolled his eyes. "Please. A top-secret meeting of power brokers? You're still a Semenov. They're reconvening at eight tomorrow. I'll get you in the door."

"Fuck that. You're not the only one with useful information."

"What does that mean?"

"Get me in the door and you'll find out."

Not knowing what bomb Tati might drop on the Committee gave him pause. What could she know that he didn't?

"You're really gonna make me wait?"

"Aww, poor Geddy." She leaned out and playfully pouted her lips. "You used to like it when I made you wait."

She had him there. He got up and shoved his hands in his pockets. "Fine. I'll meet you downstairs at a quarter to eight."

"I hate that I need your help to get in the boys' club."

"Oh, I know."

CHAPTER TWENTY-SEVEN

AD-HOC

Geddy arrived in the lobby the next morning to find Tatiana already waiting. She wore a dark gray business suit with one of her signature tight skirts, her long, blond hair gathered into a ponytail that curled behind her neck and spilled over the front of her tailored jacket like a silken waterfall.

"You look ready to slay."

She narrowed her steely gaze. "I'm always ready to slay."

They walked through the skybridge, her shiny black heels click-clacking across the polished floor. She'd met with a group of Earth 3 contractors the previous evening to express her displeasure about the endless cost overruns in the Bubbles and was in bed by ten. A full night's sleep looked good on her.

At precisely eight o'clock, Geddy gave the door to the conference room a soft rap.

Zereth-Tinn opened the door and frowned upon seeing Tatiana. "What's this?"

"Zereth-Tinn, I'd like you to meet–"

"I know who she is," he said flatly. "What's she doing here?"

With heels on, she already towered over him, but he seemed to shrink under her murderous glare.

"The sausage party's over, little man. You want information, I've got it. Now move."

Tretiak came into the doorway, his eyes roaming appreciatively over her lithe body. "Miss Semenov. What a lovely surprise. I don't believe we've met."

She drew herself even taller. "You'd remember if you did. You must be Tretiak."

He gave Geddy an acidic glare. "How can I help you?"

"I'm the CEO of Semenov Trans-fucking-galactic, and you need to know what I know. Besides, someone's got to keep you shit-for-brains men from screwing the pooch. I think we all know how it plays out when they don't."

Tretiak grinned broadly. "Consider me charmed."

He stepped aside and gestured for her to enter. Zereth-Tinn scowled at Geddy as he came in behind her. Zirhof was the first to introduce himself to Tati, followed by the others.

Tretiak nodded for Zereth-Tinn to close the door, then briefly took Geddy aside. "This had better be good."

Tati took the plush chair Geddy was going to sit in, leaving him to fetch one of the stiff banquet chairs from a nested stack in the corner. He slid it over at the end of one table, suddenly feeling like a tagalong.

"You have the floor, Miss Semenov." Tretiak returned to his spot at the bottom of the U. Murmurs traveled around the table.

— *You have no idea what she's going to say?*

— *She keeps her cards tight to that gorgeous chest of hers.*

Tretiak gestured to Tati, who cleared her throat and leaned into the table.

"As you know, Earth 3 has a bit of a ... mogorodon problem." Everyone nodded, as this was common knowledge. "What you may not know is, there's a thriving market in culinary circles for their ..."

— Don't say polyps, don't say polyps ...

" ... parts. A while back, a Myadani broker offered me an obscene amount of money for a breeding pair. He said it was for commercial farming, but I did some digging. Turns out this guy wasn't remotely connected to the food industry."

Tretiak leaned back and shrugged. "Perhaps he knew about your financial problems."

Tati stiffened and shifted uncomfortably in her chair. "That's why I was suspicious. Turns out this guy went missing a couple years ago."

"A Zelnad," mumbled Zirhof.

Tatiana nodded. "It's a safe bet."

"What do Zelnads want with a breeding pair of mogorodons?" Zirhof asked the group.

"I don't know, but it can't be g–"

"Oh, *shit*." Geddy's popped wide as he sat fully upright. All heads swiveled to him.

— *Did you just figure something out on your own?*

— Maybe you're rubbing off a little.

The Zelnads' strategy was nuanced and clever. Yesterday's announcement proved it. The right creatures could take out entire worlds for them, and it would explain a lingering mystery from his first day on the *Fiz*.

"A while back, my ship ran across a disabled Xellaran vessel headed for Myadan. Some kind of biotransport. It had a hole in the side made by a ranse. Now, for various reasons I won't go into, we didn't get to look inside, but I'm willing to bet it was half of a breeding pair."

"What was the name of the ship?" asked the Xellaran woman.

"*Sirwin.*"

Her recognition was instant. "She was one of ours. The *Sirwin* got hijacked. We assumed pirates took her."

"Are you saying what I think you're saying?" Tretiak asked Geddy.

"These things could take out whole worlds. You want to wipe everyone out, that's a real time-saver."

Mogorodons in the water and ranses on land. What would fill the skies? Surely there were some deadly ptero-dactyls or flesh-eating insects. Thinking about it now, it sounded like old-school, end-of-the-world stuff. A thousand plagues and what not.

"You refused this man's offer, I hope?" asked Zirhof.

"Yeah, but I won't lie. It was tempting. As he clearly knew it would be."

"We still know almost nothing about them," Smegmo pointed out. "How do we know any of us aren't Zelnad?"

"You're not," Geddy assured him. "Eli can sense others of his kind."

That intrigued Tretiak immediately. "Can he, now?"

"Don't get too excited. He has to be close."

"Can the ability be synthesized?" asked Everett Hau.

— Eli?

— *Possibly, but it is far too late for that. Proving the Zelnad threat will be hard enough.*

"Eli says it's too late for that. We need to prove the threat."

Tretiak's face hardened. "How can you be sure your invisible friend isn't a Zelnad? Say nothing of this ... synthetic organism of yours?"

He'd wondered that himself from time to time, but if he couldn't trust in Eli and Morpho's fundamental goodness, then what was the point of it all?

"Eli's been in my head for almost eight years. I'm sure. As for Morpho, he's done some very unsavory things to keep me alive. They're on our side."

"All right." Tretiak's voice was loud and authoritative. Everyone stopped talking and looked at him. "It seems we are long on problems and short on solutions. Our work is cut out for us." He locked eyes with Smegmo. "Mr. Eilgars, help this Ornean inventor finish his long-range scanner. We need something actionable."

Smegmo nodded, and Tretiak pivoted to Zirhof.

"Mr. Zirhof, keep working on your jump tech. Maybe we can level the playing field."

Zirhof nodded, and Tretiak's eyes found Tatiana. "Ms. Semenov, work with Geminaya to find out why the *Sirwin* was headed to Myadan. If they're looking to breed dangerous creatures, we need to know."

Tati gave the Xellaran a tight-lipped grin. Two strong personalities working together would be interesting, though Geddy was glad for it. Of everyone on the Committee, it was Geminaya he trusted least. But next to Gundrun, Xellara's android army was the largest. If the Zelnads got to them, it might be game over.

"Mr. Hau, if we can't control the narrative, then let's

muddy it up. I want the rumor mill humming about who the Zelnads are and what they want. I want to see stories about abandoned families and shattered lives. Let's also hit novasphere prices, the scarcity of tukrium, and galactic inflation. Every dirty PR trick there is."

Everett Hau's spaceport on Caloth was the busiest in the galaxy. A rumor that started there would be everywhere in days. And no one was better at seizing media attention than the flamboyant trillionaire.

When Tretiak was done, everyone had their marching orders. Geddy had always admired his command presence. In one form or another, he'd earned the fear and respect of everyone at the table except Geddy. Seizing the reins of a shadowy cabal was right in his wheelhouse.

"What's Starheart gonna do?" asked Hau with a taunting sneer. "Drink all their beer?"

"My priority is to stop them from destroying Sagacea. Only then will I drink all their beer."

CHAPTER TWENTY-EIGHT

ESTRUS FOLLIES

THE STREET in front of the bar formed the outer edge of the vast retail and entertainment district surrounding the Donglan convention center. It wasn't especially busy, and most of the patrons looked like they just wanted to be alone. Maybe the conference hadn't gone well for them so far.

Geddy and the crew, Parmhar, and Smegmo Eilgars had pushed a couple tables together in the game area and exhorted the android server to keep them coming. Thanks to Smegmo, Parmhar had his funding. Orneans were rarely exposed to wealth like his, so when Smegmo offered to transfer the seventy million on the spot, he was suspicious.

Once he was convinced Smegmo had no interest in meddling with his company, the deal was made, and they got along famously. The time had come to eat, drink, and be merry.

After a couple beers, Denk suggested a dart game pitting him and Voprot against Geddy and Oz. Geddy agreed, foolishly not expecting he'd have to teach Voprot how to play first.

In the lizard's thick, scaly fingers, a bar dart looked like the kind that came out of a pygmy blowgun.

"This is weapon?"

"No, it's for the game." Geddy mimed throwing a dart at the board.

"Game?" He shook his giant head.

Denk waddled up with a fresh mug of Xellaran ale. It tasted less like a draft and more like a first draft, but maybe the androids who made it weren't equipped with taste buds.

"Yeah, a game. Don't they play games on Kigantu?"

"Voprot once play stare-at-sun game. First to blink is loser."

Geddy's impulse was to say that this game was less likely to end in total blindness, but he couldn't know if that was true. He took a sip of his drink, a very good Ceonian whisky Smegmo recommended, and crossed the distance between them and the dusty dartboard hanging on the wall.

He ran his hands along the edge of the board. "This is your target, okay?"

"Target is threat?"

Geddy blinked. "Threat? No, it's a damned dart board. You throw the dart into the middle of it, like this." He returned to the line and tossed one with a flick of his wrist, just wide of the bullseye. He removed it from the board and returned to the line. "You get three tries, then it's someone else's turn."

Voprot cocked his head. "Throw too weak to kill."

"I was just ..." Geddy sighed. "This isn't a ranse hunt, V. It's just for fun."

"Tell him about the rings and points." Denk's eyes drooped, and a silly smile coated his face.

Considering Voprot's tenuous grasp on the very concept of a game, and the fact that they were leaving first thing in the morning, he opted to skip all that. "Let's keep scoring out of it for now. Voprot, you ready to try?"

"Okay."

The Committee left Geddy with more hope than he came with, which had to be a first as far as committees went. It didn't change the odds against them all that much, but at least now, they weren't alone. Powerful, deeply connected people were in the fight now. The kind you needed to get shit done.

Having Tatiana on board was more reassuring than he expected. She begged off their little celebration, which was probably for the best, but Tretiak promised to keep the Committee posted on everyone's activities through its encrypted private frequency. Since the Nads were on a different level in terms of tech, they couldn't be too safe.

Geddy and Denk took a couple big steps back. Behind them, the rest of the crew, along with Parmhar and Smegmo, paused their conversation to watch.

"Voprot stand on line?" His arm stretched nearly halfway to the board when extended, flaps of dead skin hanging off the underside like weathered tapestries.

"Yes," Geddy replied.

— How do I get stuck teaching Voprot stuff? I shouldn't teach anyone anything.

— *Maybe he will surprise you.*

— That's what I'm worried about.

Voprot's enormous tongue shot out and licked both his eyes clean. They narrowed at the target and Geddy held his breath.

The dart shot from his giant hand with such velocity that it punched right through the board and embedded so deeply in the wall that only the fins still poked out. But damned if it wasn't dead center.

Voprot turned to them with his big, dumb, toothy grin, terribly pleased with himself, and a tack of dead skin drifted from his elbow to the floor like the first leaf of autumn. He thrust his arms in the air.

"Voprot wins!"

"Nice throw," cooed a sultry voice from the darkened corner of the bar.

A lithe Nurithean female stepped out the shadows, her long tail snaking behind her. She had shiny blue-gray skin, four arms, and a bony head like an inverted pyramid. Nurithea was a small planet with weak gravity, and its people were rail-thin and tall. She came slinking up to Voprot, their eyes nearly level. If anything, she had a few centimeters on him.

He froze like a statue. She circled around him, appraising him like she was at a bachelor auction. One arm held a bright yellow cocktail, another a thin, smoldering pipe that smelled like the psychedelic called castanea. That left the other two hands free to trace lines down Voprot's muscled arms.

Geddy couldn't catch Oz's attention because she, too, was held rapt. As far as this Nurithean was concerned, they weren't even there. She only had eyes for the lizard, which was batshit.

— I feel like I'm watching the nature channel.

— *It is beautiful.*

— She's not a Nad, right?

— *No.*

"Voprot hit center and win game."

— *Let it go.*

— Already gone. I'm not spoiling this for anything.

"I like a man who can find a small target," she cooed. "Your name is what again?"

He nodded. "Voprot called Voprot." Panic crossed his eyes as though he didn't know what should come next. Geddy gestured that he should reciprocate. "You have name?"

"Militanda." Her slender, clawed fingers peeled a long strip of epidermis from his bicep like a piece of bacon. She held it up to the light, a faint grin decorating her small, oval mouth. "Looks like somebody's ready to ... shed his skin."

Denk leaned over and whispered, "I'm growing uncomfortable."

Geddy gave his head a slow shake, wishing he had popcorn. "Are you kidding? This is solid gold."

"Voprot from Kigantu." He hesitated, then added, "Where you from?"

"Nurithea." She took a long pull from her pipe through a tiny mouth hole at the bottom of her long face, then expelled the acrid smoke through gill-like flaps in her neck. "Kigantu ... Is it as ... big as I've heard?"

"Bigger," said Voprot, somehow stumbling into the only appropriate reply.

One slender finger poked Voprot's upper chest and slowly worked its way down. "You know what, Voprot of Kigantu? It's my last night in town. How about we go back to my room for a little cultural exchange?"

— *Well,* that *developed quickly.*

— Not like he had to talk her into it.

"Voprot have two more throws. Then someone else's turn."

Geddy smacked his palm against his forehead, muttering, "My god, it's like teaching quantum mechanics to a single-celled organism."

Who could've imagined Voprot would get laid before him? Assuming he didn't screw it up, of course. He finally exchanged a delighted smile with Oz, who was enjoying this little scene at least as much as he was.

"Are you sure this is in the best interest of evolution?" she asked.

He shrugged. "The world might be ending soon, which means this may never happen again. Doc, what do you think?"

"It's fascinating to observe." Doc had left the table to join them on the side of this little scene, his expression dead serious. "Female Nuritheans are only in estrus once per year."

"In other words, you like to watch," quipped Oz.

"Oh, very much," said Doc, not getting the joke.

Geddy started to laugh but stopped when Denk punched his arm. He whirled to find Voprot had come up right behind him. Desperation and fear colored his expression.

"Words fail Voprot," whispered the lizard, as though this was unexpected. His eyes darted between them. "What Voprot say?"

Geddy flared his eyebrows suggestively. "Remember what Doc told you to say to an attractive female? Try that."

The memory washed over Voprot, who nodded excitedly and returned to the patient Nurithean woman. "Voprot ... *lick* you."

She leaned in, popped the strip of dead skin into her mouth, and chewed, purring, "Militanda lick you, too."

A horrified silence descended over the room. Militanda took Voprot's clawed hand and led him toward the door, hips swaying suggestively. He followed reluctantly after her, his expression a mix of terror and excitement as he looked anxiously over his shoulder.

"Eight o'clock in the lobby," Geddy called after him. "Don't be late. And use protection!" Muttering, he added, "For all our sakes."

Denk leaned dreamily on his knuckles as he watched them leave. "I guess he really did win, huh, Cap?"

Geddy gave him an avuncular pat on the back. "We all won tonight, buddy."

The moment the door closed behind Voprot and his date, the whole table exploded with laughter.

CHAPTER TWENTY-NINE

JUST IN CASE

A SHARP RAP on the door jolted Geddy awake — no small feat considering how much fun they'd had at the bar. He lifted his head off the pillow just enough that both ears were engaged in listening, but when it didn't repeat, he dismissed it and instantly rejoined his sleep-in-progress.

Of course, the knock came again a moment later.

He checked the time and heaved a sigh. Three thirteen. No good news came that early, or late, or whatever you wanted to call it. Eyes half closed, he flicked on the night-stand light, grabbed his blaster, and shuffled to the door. The little screen revealed Tretiak waiting outside holding a hard case.

— *What could he want?*

— I dunno, but I'm leery.

Geddy opened the door a crack and peered at his old boss with one bleary eye. "This can't be good."

"Only one way to know for sure." Tretiak pushed past him, noticing the blaster in his hand. He arched a bushy eyebrow.

"Still paranoid as ever, I see."

"At least the reasons are different." He checked both ways down the hall and closed the door. "What do you want? What time is it?"

Tretiak meandered into the room, taking note of its no-frills appointments. It had a nice holoscreen, but only a smallish bed and a cramped bathroom. They definitely got less than they paid for. He set the case down on the foot of the bed. It was a meter long with a beefy handle on one side and thick buckles all around. Geddy handled hundreds of similar containers at the Double A and noted the auction's nondescript symbol stamped on the front.

"Aren't you going to put on pants?" asked Tretiak.

"Why?" Geddy glanced down as though he didn't know he was buck naked, and a shrug rolled over his shoulders. "Are we going somewhere?"

He gave a sly smirk. "I have a parting gift for you."

Tretiak undid the buckles on the indestructible case and opened the lid. When Geddy saw what the foam interior cradled, he audibly exhaled.

It was Otaro Verveik's Screvari-made tukrium and skolthil blaster, the Scimitar.

Seven years earlier, prior to stealing Tretiak's ship, the *Auctionaut,* and fleeing to Earth 2, Geddy packed a duffle with some personal effects, five hundred grand in cash, and this, his most valuable possession. Not even Tretiak knew he had it, and that was a good thing because its value was staggering. He'd stowed it in a hidden compartment on the ship the night before he left. After he jumped away, he went to retrieve it, but it wasn't there.

He never knew exactly what happened, but one way or

another, Tretiak got ahold of it. Geddy always wondered if he'd kept it for himself or sold it directly to a private collector. That mystery, at least, had been solved.

The weapon wasn't the reason he and Smegmo Eilgars were friends, but it endeared the kid to him in a way that no other gift ever could've. Smegmo couldn't have known what it would mean to Geddy to own it. He merely wanted to replace Geddy's own custom blaster after it was taken by a vengeful Ceonian prostitute.

The Scimitar was a long blaster pistol, exquisitely balanced and light for its size. But it was made for a giant Gundrun hand. In his, it was closer to a rifle with a pistol grip. At close range, he figured it could bring down a small ship, but he'd never actually fired it. Whether out of fear or respect, he couldn't have said.

He set down his Exeter and lifted the Scimitar free of the cutout. Its tukrium barrel glinted like onyx in the dim light of the bedside lamp. Gold skolthil accents encircled the dual interphasic coupling and were inlaid into the giant handle like filigree, wrapping around the Alliance insignia in a way that suggested flames. Engraved on the underside of the barrel were the initials OKV.

"Geddy, it pains me to say this, but I agree with you. Reforming the Alliance is our best option, but it will take time. Coordination. Politicking. These, the Committee can handle. But Verveik is another matter."

Geddy's sagging spirits gave a twitch like an awakening zombie. "Verveik? But you said he was ..."

He swatted it away. "No, no. I just had to get them off that idea."

"Why?" Geddy blinked, disbelieving. In one moment, the switch flipped from despair back to hope.

"Because I still don't know who I can trust. And, frankly, neither do you."

He had a point. Just because Eli didn't detect any Zelnads among them didn't mean they couldn't shield themselves somehow, or that someone on the Committee wasn't playing both sides like he thought Zereth-Tinn was.

"So Verveik's alive?"

"As far as I know. He's been incommunicado for a year now, which worries me. I need you to find him and tell him what you told us."

"Where is he?"

"A world called Verdithea."

It was pretty rare to hear the name of a planet he didn't recognize at all. "Verdithea? Sounds like a skin condition. Maybe an ugly cousin."

He held out a small storage device, a shiny metal disc called a cryp. They barely existed anymore outside Tretiak's world of money, crime, and secrecy.

"This is a dossier compiled by Verveik and his team, including their last known location."

Geddy turned it over in his fingers. He hadn't handled one in a while. Usually, they contained account details or other super-secret information. "Where has he been all this time?"

He pursed his lips. "After the War, he went into exile in the south desert of Kigantu for sixty-six years."

Geddy gasped. If that was true, then he and Verveik were actually on the same planet for *fourteen years*. If you knew how to survive in the desert, you could completely disappear.

But for that long? Gundrun sometimes lived to two hundred, but still. A long weekend on Kigantu was plenty.

Tretiak continued. "A year or two after you left, he came to me in Aquebba. I don't know how he knew I was on the Committee, but he proposed a partnership. He said if he had the resources and absolute secrecy, he could work out a way to stop the Zelnads. I was frustrated by the Committee's lack of progress, so I agreed. That was almost five years ago."

Geddy chewed on this as he walked over to his pants, which were hanging from a hook on the closet door. He dropped the cryp in a zippered pocket, giving it a pat for good measure.

"How'd you get the gun?"

"The boys brought it to me."

Geddy couldn't have guessed at the gun's worth, but it had to be pushing seven figures. The notion that Tretiak would've knowingly sat on it for this long struck him as ludicrous.

"But it never went on the block. Why?" Geddy asked. "It's got to be worth high seven figures at least."

Tretiak shrugged as though the answer was obvious. "Because I didn't know how you came by it or what it might mean to you."

— That's the most human thing he's ever said.

— *Which makes it suspicious?*

"Why give it to me now?"

"Because I don't know Verveik's state of mind. It might be the only real bargaining chip you have."

This was all a bit much. Between Zelnad tech and their influence on tukrium prices, the Double A had flourished. It was hard to believe a man like Tretiak would see the bigger picture.

"You'll forgive my skepticism."

Tretiak's eyes narrowed. "You think I'm a monster, don't you?"

"I was a scared, dumb kid who stowed away on the wrong ship. Of all the things you could've done, you put me to work for the goddamned Double A."

His face softened. "I made mistakes, Geddy. I can admit that. But I never betrayed your trust."

"You imprisoned me. And then you tried to kill me."

"You stole from me. It was never personal."

"It felt personal when you stole my ship."

Understanding fell over him. "So *that's* what this is about." He closed the distance between them and sighed. "Sammo Yann brought me a small ship that looked like it might be tukrium. I had no idea it was yours. All I knew — all I *ever* knew — was that you took the *Auctionaut* and left me with your debts. Then you turned your ship into a missile and blew up *Auctionaut* 2. I didn't find out Tompanov took it until much later."

That seemed like years ago, yet it had only been a few months. He'd really jumped out of a spaceship with nothing between him and the void but a Morpho-balloon. Thinking back at the sight of the *Auctionaut* 2 being ripped apart by the *Penetrator* always made him feel warm inside.

"Bullshit."

"Geddy, if I wanted you and your friends dead, you would be. Why do you think I never came looking for you on Earth 2?"

Geddy paused, blinking. "You knew where I was?"

"You made a choice, and I respected it. And, frankly, the Scimitar was probably worth more than the *Auctionaut* by that point. I figured we were even."

Having your most cherished assumptions upended was never easy, even when it was for the best. Yes, he'd done many unsavory things for Tretiak, but it was his own choices that put him in that situation. Tretiak could've sold him as a slave or done any number of terrible things, but he didn't. He and Kriggy taught Geddy how to do business and stay alive, which was all they ever knew.

But back on Kigantu, Tretiak indicated he had an especially important piece of information.

"You said you knew what happened to my parents."

Tretiak gave a pained smile. "I only know pieces. Verveik's pieced together the whole story. You want real answers, you find him." He headed for the door.

"How do I know you're on the level?"

He paused with his hand on the latch. "You don't. Good night, Geddy. And good luck."

CHAPTER THIRTY

ROLL CALL

TRETIAK's unexpected visit in the dead of night left Geddy in knots, his mind racing with questions. Why was Verveik hiding on a planet he'd never heard of? What did he know about his parents? And were the stories he'd told himself for so long about Tretiak really not true?

Sleep came in fits and starts after that, and by six a.m. he was already showered and dressed. He almost took the case with the Scimitar down to breakfast, but figured it was probably safer in his room. He slid the case under the bed and activated the do-not-disturb sign before heading down for breakfast.

A continental breakfast in a galaxy comprising more than a hundred worlds and countless species was a challenge for any hotel, especially one as economical as the Miniprice Hotel, although nobody stayed here for the food.

A meager assortment of pastries and weird Xellaran fruits were arrayed on large serving plates beside two carafes of unidentifiable liquid. One had separated, leaving the top bluish white and the bottom the same sickly yellow as the water aboard the *Fiz* before they replaced the recycler. Ranse milk straight from the teat seemed like a better choice.

And so, as it had been since the dawn of man, coffee and a couple stale rolls were the only safe choice. Geddy loaded his flimsy plastic plate with a croissant and what he could only hope was a danish, then got his coffee and sat at one of the little tables. It was only six thirty, so the rest of the crew wouldn't be down for a while, but that was fine. He hadn't given himself many quiet moments like this since they arrived, and he wanted to relish it.

In a few hours, he'd be back in space, and with any luck, the next world his boots touched would be Verdithea, a planet he knew nothing about. Who or what would try to kill him there, he wondered?

He was halfway through his croissant when Doc entered through the lobby.

"Good morning, Captain."

"'Morning, Doc. Good night's sleep?"

"Adequate, thank you."

Doc only slept a couple hours per day, which he claimed was typical for Orneans. Every moment he wasn't watching the long-range scanners or patching wounds, he was reading various studies or ancient texts on the net. Lifelong learner, that guy. He passed Geddy and investigated the morning's offering, such as it was.

"I opted for strong rolls and weak coffee," Geddy said. "You might want to do the same."

"And pass up a perfectly ripe Xellaran fighting fruit? Certainly not!" he reached into the fruit bowl and withdrew a knotted, dark green fruit a bit smaller than a novasphere. Geddy watched with great interest as he held it in the light. "The fighting fruit is home to a worm ancient Xellarans called *udrith'nai* — the guardian — which lives its entire life inside. It must be disoriented first, or it will defend its home, sometimes to deadly effect."

Doc gave it a sharp rap on the table, then dug his thumbs into the fruit to crack it open. The fibrous, pale-yellow flesh resembled an overripe melon but didn't seem to have much juice. Sure enough, a bright orange worm was in the middle, flailing angrily about amid a cluster of brown seeds. Both ends of the worm came to needle-sharp points. Doc casually dumped it out onto the table, prompting Geddy to shove his chair back.

"Dude!"

"Don't worry," Doc said, amused by his reaction. "It cannot survive outside the fruit for more than a few seconds. See?"

The wriggling worm's neon color dulled as its frantic motion slowed. Not ten seconds passed before it shriveled, turned roughly the same dark green as the fruit's outer skin, and stopped moving.

"The worm can survive through adulthood as long as there is moisture," Doc continued with a cautioning look. "More than one careless soul has ingested the worm or seen it burrow into his skin like a hypodermic needle. Once inside a host, it will grow fat on blood and lay thousands of eggs."

"You'd think there'd be a sign or something." Geddy felt very good about his pastries.

— See? You could have it worse.

— That's why you're a finalist in the symbiote awards.

Doc gathered the dead worm into a napkin, then took a bite of the fruit as Geddy grimaced. Just then, the hotel doors parted, and Voprot appeared, his chest heaving from exertion. The fearful front-desk attendant pressed himself tightly to the wall as Voprot spotted them in the breakfast nook. As he lumbered over, Oz and Denk came out of the elevator.

"Hi Oz! Hi Denk!" panted Voprot. "Hi guys! Hi Eli!"

— *Aww, nobody says hi to me. Please say hi back.*

Geddy sprang to his feet, his mind racing to imagine why Voprot would be out of breath the morning after his first romantic encounter. Was Militanda a Zelnad after all? Would their hail-Mary effort to stop the Nads end before it even began?

"What happened to you?"

"Voprot need fluids," he rasped.

— *A Kigantean should not be this thirsty.*

— He must've got worked over like a new ball glove by that horned-out Nurithean chick and forgot to hydrate.

— *Oh?* Oh.

Nothing had ever taken this kind of toll on him, suggesting he'd been at it for hours. An image of him and the Nurithean mashing their alien parts together flashed through his mind too quickly to stop.

His tail knocked one of the tables over on his way to the juice station and went straight for the carafe of disgusting, separated liquid. But instead of pouring it straight down his gullet like Geddy expected, he dutifully took a little cup and filled it. He threw it back, refilled it, and repeated over and over like he was doing shots until it was almost empty.

Literally everybody had won in this scenario. Ah, the things that passed for entertainment anymore.

"What'd I miss?" Oz asked, wisely remaining near the door.

"An absolutely perfect confluence of events."

Despite being physically spent, Voprot's scaly skin had turned bright green and lustrous. The papery sheath that had covered his body was entirely gone.

"Wait. Did she ...?" Oz asked Geddy.

He gave a slow nod, remembering how Militanda treated Voprot's molting skin as an amuse bouche. "She ate the whooole thing."

Behind them in the lobby, the terrified android attendant pointed at a little comm device in one hand as though asking whether he should contact authorities.

Geddy waved him off and approached the hulking Kigantean where he stood in front of the counter. "Hey, ah, you feel okay there, big fella?"

Voprot threw away his little cup and sank down onto his haunches with the biggest, dumbest grin Geddy had ever seen.

"Voprot in love."

"Aww ..." said Denk.

Geddy gave a hard roll of his eyes. "Oh, for fuck's sake."

— *He is an adolescent. It is only natural.*

— Yeah but come on.

He turned to the rest of the crew. "Grab something to eat and let's hit the road. I'd steer clear of the fruit." Turning back to Voprot, he added, "Can I assume you're staying on Xellara with the love of your life?"

"No." Voprot made a scuffling noise as he rose from the floor. "Voprot have responsibilities."

"I'm curious to learn what those are, exactly." Geddy shook his head at Denk and beckoned for Voprot to join them, then patted his back.

"C'mon, Loverboy. You can't break a thousand hearts until you break the first one."

CHAPTER THIRTY-ONE

PASSION PROJECT

DENK SAID he knew a natural wormhole that would get them close-ish to Verdithea's coordinates, at least in interstellar terms, but it still would take a couple days to reach the entrance and another four or five on the far end. Since they'd need at least two novaspheres to get there otherwise, it seemed like the prudent choice.

As good as it felt to clear the orbital traffic jam over Xellara, the next two days saw Geddy grow increasingly anxious about the mission. Tracking down Verveik was a concrete step toward reforming the Alliance and getting a handle on the Zelnad situation, but there was no way to know if they were within weeks of executing their plan or years. That wasn't the kind of uncertainty he could live with much longer. Adding a completely unknown planet to the mix had him on edge.

In addition, Tretiak said Verveik might know what happened to his parents. If he was being honest, he wasn't sure he still wanted to know.

"Wormhole's looking clear," Denk reported. "No ships within scanning range."

Standard wormholes were stable and reliable, but in a way, that also made them dangerous. If you weren't vigilant, you could be ambushed by pirates lying in wait on the other side. Back in the Double A days, on the rare occasion he used a wormhole, he'd hover his hands over the controls, ready to fight the moment he came through.

"Be ready for anything." Geddy moved to the jump seat next to Oz and buckled in.

"How do you do with wormholes?" she asked, referring to his body's adverse reaction to multiple jumps.

"Never had a problem. Mr. Junt, proceed when ready."

"Aye aye, Cap."

Wormholes didn't look like anything. No shimmery gate, no bending of light. Just a steady stream of gamma rays that showed up on scans as a bright green doughnut.

Denk lined them up and pushed through. There was a compression, like ears popping at altitude followed by intense vertigo, and then nothing. The screen displayed an identical-looking ocean of stars as always.

"Are we through?" Geddy asked with his eyes closed, riding a wave of nausea.

"Hang on," said Denk. "The sensors are recalibrating."

Geddy kept his eyes closed and drummed his fingers on the armrests as he focused on his breathing, trying his best to exhale positivity.

Thirty seconds later, Denk slapped his hand on the control panel. "Hot diggity, we made it! Point two-four parsecs from Verdithea! Three or four days and we'll be there."

"Sweet." Geddy opened his eyes and let the room settle before he unbuckled himself and stretched his hands to the ceiling. "Who's up for some sesehlu?"

"Me!" said Denk, who already had the ship set to autopilot.

Just then, Morpho, who he hadn't seen since Jel was on board, came swinging along from the ceiling and plopped onto his shoulder.

"Well, look who decided to join us. I wish I knew what the hell you did all day." Morpho formed an arrow and jutted it toward the back of the bridge. "You want to do seseluh with us?"

"I think he wants us to follow him," Denk offered.

"Is there something wrong with the ship?"

Morpho jiggled back and forth. *No.*

"All right. Lead the way, I guess."

Morpho slung a tendril back to the conduit in the ceiling and stickily followed it out of the bridge. Just before reaching the internal airlock, he turned right and disappeared up the ladder toward the empty escape pod hatches.

"Hey Morph, if this is a dime tour of the *Fiz,* I can spare you the trouble. There's not much we haven't seen."

Morpho only continued up. Geddy's anxiousness to find Verveik flared in his gut. Voprot stopped at the ladder. He'd tried to ascend it once and got stuck in the opening at the top. It took two liters of nutrimush to make him slippery enough to back out.

The maintenance crawlspace over the port side of the hold was too low to stand in but high enough that crawling felt infantile, not to mention hard on the knees with the stupid steel grating. The only way to do it was to sort of chicken-walk at a half crouch. But that was nothing compared to his deep hatred of confined spaces. Morpho knew that, which meant this had to be important.

Worry gripped him. He was *so close*. What would Morph say they needed now, and where the hell would they get it?

Morpho paused at the end of the cramped passageway and waited for them to catch up. Once they did, Geddy gave him an expectant look, but he only hung inertly from the roof.

"Are we letting the suspense build, or–"

Like bursting flak, five slender threads shot out of Morpho's center and into their ears. Biosynthetic fibers snaked through their auditory organs and latched on to their cerebral cortices. It was neither welcome nor unwelcome, like a visit from a stranger who intrigues you.

Having Morpho join him and Eli was weird enough. Now there was Oz ... and Denk ... and Doc ... and ...

— Oh my god, Voprot's in my head.

— *Hi, Voprot!*

— HI GUYS! said Voprot.

— Morpho, what the hell's going on?

— **We are sharing a psychic room. Think of it as, 'my space.'**

— Umm, not to sidetrack us, but ...

— *I think it is a fine name.*

— Wait — how did you reach Voprot from here? That has to be twelve meters at least.

— **Length is not a problem for me.**

— Must be nice.

— **Please listen. This is not easy.**

— You mean entering our minds?

— **No. What I have to say. I do not … handle emotions well.**

— Totally relate. Please continue.

— **What I want to say is, I have failed you all in the past. Like with the pirates. You were injured.**

—Morph, hold that thought. I just have to say, do you know how long it's been since there was another voice in my head besides mine and the Sagaceans? This is nice, isn't it?

— It really is, agreed Oz. Effortless.

— Guess we all know how bad it feels to be lonely, said Denk at last.

A hush fell over the nonexistent room that Morpho had every damn right to call, "my space." Sharing your mind with people you cared for was amazeballs. No artifice, no hiding. Leave it to Denk to cut through the bullshit and speak the truth.

This, right now, was the least alone that any of them had ever felt, and it was fucking glorious.

— **Sorry to interrupt, but …**

— Oh, shit. Morpho!

— **This is sort of the big finish.**

— You have our undivided attention.

— **Push the button.**

— Button? Hold up — is there a 2014 Mitsubishi Galant behind this door?

— **PUSH THE DAMN BUTTON, YOU DIMWIT!**

— Okay, okay. What button?

He shot a tendril over to a very discreet metal button,

inset and nearly seamless. A deeply unpleasant thought shot through Geddy's reverie like a barroom dart.

What if Morpho really was a Zelnad about to float them all? They were far aft, practically the back of the ship. It would be so easy. Earn their trust, then spring a trap just before a potential breakthrough in their fight against the Nads? They still didn't *really* know where he came from.

Morpho finally pressed the button for him, and Geddy hated himself for flinching. What was on the other side of the door stole his breath, but in a good way.

He had built them an outer airlock with a lot of space inside. And ... controls?

— What is this?

— **This has been my passion project these past few months. Ever since our run-in with the pirates.**

— What is it?

— **It is a combination escape pod and outer airlock, with room for the entire crew and supplies. I improvised a link with the NIMSOC system on most ships so it has gyro-sync with the *Fiz*. The wiring was tricky.**

— When did you do all this?

— **I worked on it every night while you were on Xellara.**

— Morph ... I don't know what to say.

— **If the only way to save all of you is to sacrifice myself, I will not hesitate.**

— I would die for you.

— **Thank you, Geddy.**

— No, I mean, 'I would die for you' is a cleaner way to say that. But also, I would, too.

Me, too, said Oz and Denk and Doc.

— Voprot die, too, said the lizard.

— **I will do whatever is necessary to keep you safe.**

— Thank you, Morpho.

Thank you, they all echoed. And then Morpho's tendrils retracted, and they were alone again, but alone together wasn't so bad.

CHAPTER THIRTY-TWO

CREATURE TEACHER

It took three days from the wormhole exit to reach Verdithea, though it had no markers and therefore no detailed atmospheric or gravitational data. The *Fiz's* scans of terrestrial conditions would've been fatally wrong if they even bothered to try, which they didn't. But this world was completely foreign to them, and the cryp that Tretiak had given Geddy was all they had to go on.

The data had been compiled by Verveik's team, mostly a scientist who was always behind the camera. It was a pastiche of archives and notes that Doc was happy to review and distill over the course of their journey.

The crew gathered in the hold to hear Tardigan's briefing. He'd set a holobar on the workbench to run his presentation, which displayed a slowly rotating image of the planet.

"Verdithea," he intoned. "Class three exoplanet orbiting two suns. Breathable atmosphere, but dense and intensely humid. Eighty percent of the surface is jungle. The canopy is so dense that little light can break through, and the leaves are infused with nickel, making orbital scans of the surface impossible.

"The rest is liquid water, primarily rivers and lakes," Doc continued. "It has no spaceport and no cities. Only small villages under the canopy populated by the most advanced species, Verditheans."

"That's an easy one to remember!" offered Denk.

"They're largely an arboreal species. They have evolved six arms in order to live amongst the trees while simultaneously fending off the planet's innumerable predators and caring for their young. While they only have–"

"Sorry, Doc, when you say, 'innumerable predators,' do you mean no one's put a number on it or there are too many to count?" Geddy asked.

After living most of his life with giant centipedes called ranses just outside the city walls of Aquebba, Geddy had developed a low tolerance for terrifying creatures.

"Yes, and I am getting to that. The Verditheans have also evolved extensive bioluminescent markings, likely to distinguish one another in near darkness."

The camera on the display followed a group of Verditheans as they scrambled effortlessly through the trees, more like spiders than any humanoid race. Their hairless heads were small and raked back in sort of a teardrop shape. Thick, leathery webbing stretched between all six limbs, allowing them to glide or check their descent.

"Now let's find out what's gonna try to kill us," Geddy said to no one in particular.

The display changed to a slowly rotating animated creature with little stats displayed by it. "As you might imagine, such biodiversity over millions of years has evolved a very effective predator, dubbed *luftrithides virans*. Essentially, it is a sky snake."

Denk's eyebrows upturned hopefully. "That doesn't sound so bad."

"It's pure nightmare fuel," said Doc grimly. Denk's face fell.

He zoomed in on the creature. It had a distinctly snake-like body about the thickness of Geddy's calf and was three to five meters long, with hundreds of spiny rays running down both sides. Translucent webbing similar to the long dorsal fins of some fish connected them. A scale beside it indicated that these "wings" extended nearly a meter to either side.

Next, the display pushed in close on the creature's mouth, a lengthwise slit under its head so packed with teeth that it couldn't close all the way.

"The creature can propel itself through the heavy atmosphere with shocking speed and attacks from above. It cannot fly far, but it doesn't have to because it, too, spends most of its time in or around the canopy."

The display pulled back to show a skinny quadruped resembling a four-eyed hairless deer, grazing innocently near the edge of the jungle. The camera operator was hidden behind a tree a healthy distance away.

"The skysnake has a very unique way of hunting." As he spoke, a green streak pierced the upper left part of the frame and wrapped up the little deer like a barber pole. "First, it wraps around its victim as a constrictor would, its fins over-lapping like plastic wrap. It then releases a flood of chemicals in an exothermic reaction that essentially cooks the outer layer of flesh. The creature's jaws then expand to consume it starting with the head, during which time its victim is almost certainly conscious. Of course, that is just the male of the species."

Denk's prominent cheeks sucked inward as he huffed to calm himself. Oz's eyebrows pinched together, and they exchanged a worried look. Voprot didn't react either way. Maybe these things were distant cousins.

A seed of panic sprouted deep in Geddy's gut. After all they'd endured to get to this point, and with Verveik so close, he'd hoped finding him would be the easy part. Now, he worried for his crew's safety.

"Lemme guess," Geddy said. "The female does the same thing but lays eggs inside you then dies so you're trapped in a snake-husk while a bajillion baby skysnakes eat their way out."

Tardigan flared his eyebrows, impressed. "How did you know?"

The foul energy in his stomach spontaneously released. "I didn't have to. Know why? Because everything in fucking space wants to lay eggs in you! Can't aliens just dig a damn hole in the sand? At least ranses and mogorodons have the common courtesy to rip you to pieces!" Realizing his insensitivity, he softly added, "No disrespect to the late Captain Bykite."

The whole crew had turned to stare at him, their faces knotted with deep concern.

"Are you okay?" Oz asked.

It wasn't like him to lose his cool, but everything Doc said about Verdithea made it sound like a horror show. Charging into the unknown sounded romantic until it endangered the lives of people he cared about.

"Yeah. Yeah, sorry. I just got a little fired up there."

"Do they have any weaknesses?" Oz asked.

"I had the same question." Doc zoomed in tight on one of the skysnakes' noses, which tapered down to a ridged white point. "This is a sensory organ similar to a bat. It probably uses echolocation to hunt under the canopy. A sharp blow would likely stun the creature for a few moments."

Waves of panic kept crashing over Geddy, but he shoved them away, took a deep breath, and combed through his hair with his fingers. "Enough about the skysnakes. Where's Verveik?"

The hologram highlighted a mountain range in the far south bisected by a river valley. "The coordinates cover an area of about fifty square kilometers. Here." Doc traced the valley with his finger. "The valley is near the upper limits of skysnake habitat so it should be relatively safe."

"So what — we wander around playing Marco Polo with the guy?"

"Essentially."

Geddy threw up his hands. Fifty clicks was a big area to cover, even with all of them fanned out. But splitting up in such a foreign and dangerous place wasn't an option. If something happened to one of his crew, he'd never forgive himself.

"Okay, how much room is under the canopy? Could the *Dom* squeeze through the trees?"

"Hmm ..." Tardigan scratched his chin. "Perhaps. The river that runs through this stretch of jungle is at least as wide as the *Dom*. But it would be very difficult flying. Arguably, the ground is the safest, but it is mostly swamp."

Difficult flying, he could handle, but who the hell knew what was in those trees? And where would they land? Every way he turned it over, he only saw peril. Rebuilding the

Alliance was never going to be easy, but the odds against them loomed like a cresting tsunami. Geddy's heart thumped in his chest and sweat beaded on his forehead. He undid his shirt halfway, finding it suddenly difficult to catch his breath.

"What about the Verditheans?" Oz's eyes darted back and forth between Doc and Geddy. "Could they help us?"

"Unlikely. They are deeply distrustful of outsiders, if not outright hostile, and translator implants cannot parse their language."

Geddy abruptly stood and bolted toward the door. They couldn't see him like this, his heart racing out of control, darkness inching into his peripheral vision.

Without looking back, he said, "Thanks, Doc. Anything else?"

"No, Captain."

"Great. Let's, uh ... mull this over and come up with a plan." He was out the door before he even finished.

— *Geddy, are you okay?*

— Yep, great.

He hurried to his quarters and shut the door. The sound of his huffing filled his ears as he pressed his back to the wall and slid to the floor.

— *Deep breaths. In ... out ...*

He closed his eyes and tried to slow his breathing.

— What's happening?

— *You are having a panic attack. Focus on the breath.*

A rap came at the door. "Ged?" Oz said softly. "You okay?"

"Fine." His mouth had gone dry, causing his voice to crack.

"I'm an empath, remember? You are not fine."

— How do I make her go away without being an asshole?

— *Just open the door.*

He got up and placed his hand on the cold handle, taking a couple seconds to center himself. When he finally slid it aside, Oz's big, caring eyes practically lit up the darkened hallway.

Turning away from her, he sat on his bed and stared at the floor. "Don't look at me like that."

"Like what?"

"Like I'm losing it."

"Are you?"

"I don't know."

She plunked down on the bed beside him. "You know what your problem is?"

"There's only one?"

"You have this ... rich inner life, but you only share it with Eli. Never anyone else. I may not know what you're thinking, but I can usually tell what you're feeling."

Oz could always tell when he and Eli were talking, and he hadn't been very successful at lying to her. But he didn't understand what came over him at Doc's briefing, either.

"That makes one of us."

"Tell you what — I'll guess what you're feeling, and you stop me when I get it wrong."

His instinct was to say no, but if she could help him feel better, he was willing to indulge her. "Okay, sure."

"You've never had a purpose you believed in. Now that you do, it feels impossible. You've never had people you truly cared about, either, but now you do, which complicates your choices. This planet's like a maze you can't see your way through, it's full of unknowns, and maybe for the first time in your life, you're genuinely scared. And not just for yourself."

Scared? Geddy Starheart didn't get scared. He got even. He got shit done. But only for himself or at the whims of people with money and influence. Now that it really mattered, he doubted his ability to deliver. Doubt was just another word for fear. As usual, Oz had him pegged.

"You could tell all that just by sitting next to me?" She said she didn't read minds, but sometimes it sure seemed that way. Was understanding emotions like that a gift or a curse?

"I don't have to be human to understand the human condition." She placed her slender hand on his shoulder and gave it a tender rub. "I get it. But you don't have to carry it all anymore. We're a team, but more than that, we're family. We're here for you. *I'm* here for you."

Their eyes locked, her pupils wide as an owl's to drink in the dim light of his quarters. Through them, he felt like he could see straight into to her soul. It was open to him. In that moment, he'd never felt closer to anyone besides Eli. His heart rate slowed, and the tightness in his chest eased.

Before he could change his mind, he cupped her pale, smooth face in his hands, warm and soft against his calloused hands. Her own hands closed gently around his wrists, and he pulled her lips to his.

CHAPTER THIRTY-THREE

SOLTERO

THE LAST DREGS of panic that had seized Geddy earlier evaporated the moment he kissed Oz, as though she somehow absorbed it. They sat there for a few long silent seconds deciding what it meant.

Geddy thought no one could ever know him as well as Eli, but then Oz came along. Since his mother died, no woman had ever lowered his guard like that. Not only was she the glue that held the crew together, but at the time being, she was holding him together as well. Maybe someday, when all this was over, they could be a thing. With the future as clouded as it was, he needed something to hold on to.

"Right." Oz stood and took a deep breath. "I'll, um, think through our situation and we'll, um ... hash it out in the morning. You should get some sleep."

Geddy stood and fidgeted nervously with his hands. "Yeah, we'll come up with a plan. We always do, right?"

Knowing sleep would be impossible after that kiss, and that there was no plan that didn't put everyone in grave danger, Geddy had gotten to work prepping the *Dom* and taking inventory of the dry bags where the survival gear was kept.

The next night, while the others slept, he retrieved the Exeter from the weapons locker and secured the holster to his hip. Even that light rustling was enough to summon Morpho from whatever dark corner of the ship he'd been hiding. He dropped onto Geddy's shoulder and formed a little cone shape that twisted back and forth between him and the locker as though to say, *So ... whatcha doin'?*

"It's too dangerous. This is a solo mission."

Morpho elongated into a flat snake shape, then formed into a tight coil, making it look like someone was wriggling inside.

"You heard all that, huh? Well, then you know why it has to be this way."

— *This is unwise.*

— Nobody asked you.

— *The crew is committed to our goal. The decision to accompany you should be theirs.*

He closed the door to the locker and pressed his forehead against it with a sigh.

— I know. But I'd rather have them pissed at me than cooked alive.

— *Oz and Voprot are skilled fighters. They can hold their own.*

Geddy pulled his forehead away from the locker.

— This is not a discussion.

— *Then at least take Morpho.*

In his determination to go alone to Verdithea, he hadn't even considered the wisdom of bringing Morpho. He was as much a part of the crew as anyone, but outside the *Fiz,* he had no family or friends. No one to miss him. And, he'd proven himself to be pretty damned good at keeping Geddy alive.

"Morph, I think you've babysat this rust bucket long enough. You ready to visit Skysnakia?"

Morpho gave a thumbs-up. Geddy tiptoed out of the bridge and opened the hatch that led to their dropship bay. It clanked as he turned the wheel, sending a jolt of adrenaline through him. He waited a few seconds, but no sound came from the crew quarters. Heaving a sigh of relief, he descended the ladder into the bay where the *Dom* awaited and the motion lights activated.

"Do me a solid and give her a quick once-over. Attitude control felt a little sluggish leaving Xellara."

Morpho dutifully slung a sticky tendril out, grabbed the *Dom's* left rear fin, and swooped into the thruster to begin his inspection. Meanwhile, Geddy popped open the belly hatch and climbed up into the ship. He got all the way inside and intended to double-check that the Scimitar was still there, but he didn't need to bother.

Oz was holding it in her lap.

She looked over the tops of her eyes at him and said, "We need to talk."

Oz HELD up the blaster like a mother who'd just found his stash. "Tell me about this."

"It's not mine. My boy Ray Ray asked me to watch it for the weekend."

"I think we're beyond jokes, don't you?"

Morpho briefly poked out from the side of an inset panel, noticed the two of them, and sucked back inside.

Geddy heaved a sigh. His plan had just gotten a bit muddled.

"Is OKV who I think it is?" He nodded. "So why do you have it?"

"That's a very long story."

She looked at her watch. "I've got time."

He shook his head. "I don't."

"Everything we've been through, and you still haven't figured it out. Do I really need to explain that we all have a stake in this?"

"I know that! But this ..." he shook his head, unable to put words to it. "Look, Oz, you wanted me to take the damn reins, well, here you go. I'm the captain and finding Verveik was my idea. If anyone dies, it's gonna be me."

Oz leaned forward in her chair, her eyes just wide enough for the daggers to shoot through. "This isn't about protecting us. This is about your childish need to be the hero."

Was that true? It didn't sound true. "Really? What kind of hero turns Earth 2 into a damned Dutch oven then spends the next seven years alone, literally pulling his pud to a hologram while an ancient alien tells him how to build a ship?"

Her eyes widened. "Whoa, whoa, hold up. Are you saying you *caused* the accident?"

Geddy gave his eyes a tired roll. "You already knew that."

Oz's finger wagged at him. "No, no, you just said 'Earth 2 happened.' You didn't say *you* did it."

— Oz is right.

— You both are. It's so annoying.

Shaking his head to clear it, he blinked and said, "Technically, it was half Eli's fault."

— Hey!

"I don't want to be the hero." When her head tilted sideways and her mouth flattened even further, he corrected the lie. "Okay, I *do* want to be the hero, but that's not what this is, okay? This is about me not wanting my crew to become alien fucking egg sacs. It's that simple."

Everything Oz told Geddy about himself to this point had been right on the money. This wasn't about machismo or any of that crap. "You're right, Oz. I'm scared. Verdithea scares me." The words felt unnatural from his mouth. "I dragged you into all this."

Oz looked to the heavens, exasperated, as she so often did with him. "Geddy, we have a shot at saving all intelligent life in the fucking universe. Hundreds of billions of lives. Trillions, probably. You don't get to take that shot away. Certainly not from me."

He leaned his elbows on his knees and heaved a long sigh. "Denk and Doc can't come."

"Obviously. They'd die immediately."

"Voprot?"

She swished her lips back and forth, considering this, then shook her head. "Too young. And he doesn't know the jungle."

"Neither do we. But ... I agree. Denk's young, too, but Voprot's ... "

"A kid," she finished. "Which, now that I think about it, means we did nothing to stop a child from having sex with a stranger."

He shrugged. "Meh. My conscience is clear."

"Anyway, back to this ridiculously large blaster."

"Is it, you know ..."

She cocked her eyebrow. "Too big for me to handle? Yes, Geddy. But I don't really care how you got it. I care what you're planning to do with it."

"It's a bargaining chip. In case he needs convincing."

Her long fingers ran up and down the barrel and she smirked. "A man and his gun ... like a binary star."

"What else could possibly fill our lives?"

She held out the weapon for him. He took it, again admiring how beautiful it appeared in the dimmed lights of the cabin. Oz reached over her shoulders and withdrew her energy blades, igniting them with a crackle that split the air like pink lightning.

"Skysnakes are a small target flying at high speed. Melee weapons are the way to go."

He curled his hands into a comical, old-timey pair of fighting fists and circled them in front of his face. "My mama gave me the only melee weapons I need."

"Then I'll try not to damage them when I'm cutting your ass out of a skysnake." She flicked off the blades and returned them to their magnetic sheaths behind her shoulders.

Morpho reappeared, this time through a vent at the back of the cabin. He swung back and forth as though taking the room's temperature. They both turned to him.

"How we looking, Morph?"

He formed his customary thumbs-up, and Geddy nodded. His eyes pivoted back to Oz. "Will Denk understand?"

"He'll be hurt. You're not the only one who wants to be a hero. But he'll get over it."

Denk helped out back on Aku, but otherwise hadn't really gotten his shot. Geddy spared him from racing at Ponley Point, and now he was sparing him from this.

Geddy heaved a sigh. "I hope so."

"How's our gear?" she asked.

"Squared away. The energy bars expired six years ago, but they're probably fine."

"All right, then."

He powered on the *Dom*, switched pilot control to his chair, and tightened the harness about himself. Oz returned the gun to its cubby beneath the floor and got strapped in herself. They shared a heavy look, and he extended his hand to her. She took it tenderly and gave him a tight nod.

Morpho came swinging up behind him and landed on his shoulder as he dropped Oz's hand to open the bay doors. He then reached for the glowing holo-switch that would release the dropouts.

"Verdithea, here we come."

He hit the button, and they dropped into space.

CHAPTER THIRTY-FOUR

VERDITHEA

VERDITHEA'S DENSE, moist atmosphere cradled their descent like colossal hands, so much that he didn't even need to fire the retros. Hull temperature spiked and didn't come down as fast as he would've liked, but otherwise it was about the easiest entry he could imagine.

He couldn't help but think of Tatiana.

They descended through opaque clouds stacked on each other like pancakes, sporadically catching glimpses of the endless carpet of green below. The planet's two suns cast it in a disorienting mix of orange and purple, making it difficult to tell what color anything actually was.

"The flora is crazy," said Oz, shaking her head. "Not so much as a bare rock."

"I know. Talk about your big-bush energy."

The topography was a mix of short mountains and wide, flat basins and crisscrossed by rivers that occasionally widened into lakes or petered out into swamps like a burst aneurysm. Over the canopy, clouds of pale green creatures wound sinuously through the air like clusters of sperm hunting an egg.

"There they are," Geddy muttered, his heart rate increasing.

Even from five thousand meters up, their abundance was obvious. Occasionally a cluster would drop out of the winding, roiling murmuration and plunge through the canopy to visit their horrors on some hapless creature. Others came to rest atop the leaves.

The heads-up display flashed red, meaning they were being hailed. Geddy swallowed hard.

"Guess we know who that is," Oz said. "You want me to do the talking?"

"No, no, it should be me." He accepted the call, and a bleary-eyed Denk came onscreen. "Hey, Denk."

"Hey, Cap. The dropouts kinda woke me up, so I got up and saw you took the *Dom* down. You and Oz doing some recon? I sure do hope those skysnake things aren't as scary as Doc made 'em sound, because I'm not sure if I–"

"It's not recon, Denk." Geddy cut him off. He looked guiltily at Oz. "It's the mission. We're going to find Verveik."

"Oh."

The hurt in his voice matched the look on his face. The little guy had been psyching himself up for this.

"I'm sorry, Denk, but this place is no joke. Someone's got to stay with the *Fiz*. Someone dependable."

His tired eyes drifted down and he forced a smile. "Dependable ... yeah, that's ol' Denk. All day long."

"Hell yeah, it is." He tried to make it sound punchy, but it rang hollow in his ears.

"Cap, I know I'm not much of a fighter, but I've got

plenty of fight *in* me. Doc, too. And Voprot? He's the strongest of us all."

That point was hard to dispute. But his childlike naïveté aside, there was a bigger problem.

"He weighs like eight hundred kilos, Denk. You felt how the *Dom* handled with him in it. I need to be nimble if I'm gonna maneuver under the canopy."

First and foremost, Denk was a pilot. It was where his heart was, and he took it seriously. He knew the rationale was sound, but he couldn't be expected to like it.

"Yeah, totally. It's better to be light."

"Something tells me this won't be your last shot at saving the universe, pal."

Denk's gigantic front teeth beamed, and he squared his jaw. "I hope you're right."

"Now get some rest but be ready for anything. And make sure Doc is on comms. We'll contact you as soon as we find Verveik."

"Aye aye, Cap. You guys be careful down there, okay?"

"Roger that." He closed the channel to find Oz regarding him warmly. "What?"

"Once in a while, Starheart, you surprise me in a good way."

He threw a wink her way and returned his attention to the display. The mountains began abruptly as though they shot out of the ground with speed. Somewhere beyond lay the swatch of jungle his hero called home.

He leveled out and skimmed over the mountaintops, only a handful of which weren't completely covered in trees. Rivers split the canopy like cracks. They still spotted some small flocks of snakes in low-lying areas, but fewer than where they came in.

A translucent blue boundary onscreen outlined Tretiak's coordinates. Fifty square kilometers wasn't *that* big an area, but considering they'd be stumbling through the dark, it might as well have been five hundred.

Oz pointed at a blue expanse in the upper right corner of the screen. "There. That must be where the river empties."

"I see it."

He banked right and descended to just above the long, reedy grass and scrubby trees of the lake, hoping there wasn't some giant piranha waiting to bite the ship in half. A massive bird with skinny wings and four eyes glided beside them, checking them out and squawking its disapproval.

He waved at it, prompting a chuckle from Oz, and it peeled away. "What's up, big bird?"

"At least the snakes aren't the only thing in the skies," she offered.

Part of him was glad Oz forced her way into this mission. Another wished she'd stayed aboard with the others where she was safe. But still another worried how the crew would function with both of them gone, especially in an emergency. Technically, Doc had the conn, but Geddy wasn't sure how he'd handle real pressure.

"All we need now is an open mouth." He gave Oz a moment to react. "Of course, I'm referring to the river."

"As soon as we get back, we're meeting with HR," she said, badly hiding her grin.

The closer they got to where the jungle began, the slower he went, scanning for the place where the river emptied into the lake. At two o'clock, some white streaks caught his eye. The white streaks of a waterfall poured over a domed rock formation, leaving a hollow between the water and the trees overhead.

Oz spotted it, too. "That looks like it. Can we fit in the mouth, or are we too big?"

He gave a laugh and winked. "Only one way to know for sure."

The gap was short but relatively wide, and the overhanging branches didn't look too substantial. They crept along until they were just a few meters from the waterfall, so close that its mist beaded on the windshield. Geddy eased the *Dom* into the maw of the jungle, and darkness swallowed them whole.

"Well, it's been nice knowin' ya," Geddy said.

GEDDY NEVER SPENT any time in a forest. The few trees to speak of on The Deuce were planted by the original *Rearview* colonists, and then it was straight to Kigantu, which of course had no vegetation whatsoever. He'd been in virtual forests but didn't see one for real until Zirhof practically made him.

On his first visit to Zorr, Zirhof was dismayed to learn of this gap in Geddy's experience and suggested he take a few hours to visit the northern forests before heading back to Kigantu. Sightseeing never interested Geddy much, but Zirhof insisted. After leaving Nova Auris, he headed north about a hundred kilometers and discovered a vast and unspoiled wilderness of rolling hills, frothing rivers, glassy blue lakes, and trees beyond reckoning.

He set the *Auctionaut* down in a meadow and took a wide, looping trail through the woods, marveling at the towering evergreens and the spectrum of wildlife it sustained. It filled him with awe.

This forest had the opposite effect.

For starters, it was shockingly dark. The enormous, football-shaped leaves of the trees drank in all the light just like Doc said, leaving little for the thick blanket of moss covering the forest floor. The roots originated around twenty meters up, forming knotted bases half as wide as they were tall. And holy shit, were they tall — a hundred meters, he figured. Only tiny shafts of the weird light pierced the nearly opaque canopy.

He switched on all the *Dom's* landing lights, forming a bubble of weak light around them as he crept along over the shallow stream. The area between the roots and the canopy afforded the most room, though that wasn't saying much. In places, he only had a couple meters to play with on either side.

Oz's big eyes took it all in, roaming anxiously over the forest so he could concentrate on staying between the trees. Deep shadows draped everything beyond the reach of the lights.

"What's that?" Oz pointed down to the left.

Geddy squinted. A pig-like creature about the size of a large dog rooted in the muck, its entire body studded with spikes. It looked curiously up at them, its eyes covered in papery skin.

"What's up with its eyes?"

— *I believe they are vestigial.*

— Come again?

— The forest likely grew darker and darker to the point where its eyes became useless. The same happens to cave dwellers.

"Eli says it must've stopped needing eyes at some point."

"Doc would love this."

Guilt stabbed him. "Yeah. At least he'll enjoy watching the video."

Movement to his right. Just a flash. He sucked in a sharp breath and tightened his grip on the controls.

"What's wrong?" Oz asked.

"I saw something."

They hovered there for a moment, the only sound the soft hum of the engine. Morpho tensed on his shoulder.

Another movement, this time from the left. Oz spun her head, but not in time. On the ground, the spiky, blind pig froze and sniffed at the air.

A shape shot from the darkness like a bullet and was on the pig in milliseconds. It coiled around it in a tight spiral like Doc described, but when it hit the spikes, it loosened its grip just long enough for the pig to buck it off and sprint deeper into the forest, well beyond the reach of the lights.

"Guess he got away."

No sooner did he say it than the same animal came bounding back, this time covered in multiple skysnakes that squeezed it tighter and tighter until it lurched forward onto the mossy ground. A heartbeat later, dozens more swooped in, a dull orange light emanating from beneath their spiny wings as the creature was cooked in its own juices.

While their attention was on the pig, a sharp knock at the top of the *Dom* gave them both a start. Their eyes rolled up to the roof. *Thunk. Thunk. Thunkthunkthunk.*

"Time to go!" Geddy accelerated as much as he dared.

His impulse was to try and shake them off, but he couldn't get going fast enough. The impacts came faster and faster now as he wound between the trees, plunging deeper into the jungle.

The front display went black save for the overlays.

"Shit, they're covering the camera! I've gotta drop the shield."

Most ships had retractable shields of Gundrun steel or tukrium so a bird or space debris couldn't damage the windshield. But you could drop it in an emergency, which this now was.

The shield quickly retracted into its hood, and they could see again, but what they saw was a tree trunk twice as wide as the *Dom*.

"Shit!" Geddy banked hard left. Six skysnakes flopped onto the windshield.

They continued dropping from overhead, the sound growing muffled as they piled up. Geddy leveled out and centered them over the river, but the *Dom's* controls were already getting sluggish. These things had to weigh four or five kilos each, and there were hundreds. A few seconds later, more had crept their way onto the windshield and started closing their field of vision like a living, writhing aperture.

"They're gonna wrap us up like that creature! Do something!" Oz shouted, reflexively pulling her legs up into herself.

This may have been the upper range of their habitat, but these things seemed to be doing just fine. He hadn't figured on them attacking the ship like this. The *Dom* didn't have some fancy shock weapon, and even if it did, he never got around to learning enough Kailorian to know. You'd think they'd include a multilingual tutorial or something.

At any rate, they were probably going to die.

— Please tell me you know a way out of this.

— *You have to go back or ditch.*

As always, Eli was right. Ditching got them out of the sky, at least, and arguably it would take out a few of the bastards in the process. But after that?

"I've got to put in the river!"

Oz's eyes widened into plates, her lithe frame tightening into a ball. He'd never seen her scared, but this was breathless terror.

"What?!"

"Trust me. I've got a hunch."

At the merest tap downward, they dropped like a stone. They were carrying an extra two thousand kilos at least, maybe three. He nosed down and fired the retros just before they slammed into the river, sending a sharp torrent of water up the sides.

Oz screamed. Skysnakes tumbled off the fuselage like rain. Hundreds splashed down in a seething knot.

Geddy kept the nose pointed at the water, illuminated only by a shrinking cone of light from just beneath the windshield.

"What're you doing?" cried Oz.

"Seeing how they feel about water."

"Do we know that's water?"

The skysnakes thrashed about in the river, frothing the otherwise placid — and therefore deep — water. But the spiny wings that ran their full length clung stubbornly to the water's surface. The ones that landed with their toothy mouth slits up were still writhing frantically as they floated downstream because they could breathe. The ones that landed mouth down stopped moving altogether.

— *Geddy! That was actually smart!*

— Um, thanks?

In nearly perfect unison, Geddy and Oz turned to each other and exclaimed, "They can't swim!"

CHAPTER THIRTY-FIVE

JUMP FOR MY LUFTRITHIDES

"As soon as we hit, I'll get the Scimitar, and you get the hatch open," said Geddy, the *Dom's* fuselage again growing heavy with more skysnakes as they piled on. "She'll fill with water fast, so we need to be quick."

"Are you insane?! We can't ditch!"

"Oz, we have to. It'll take those things downstream and get hung up somewhere. We'll circle back."

"But it'll be waterlogged. It'll take days to fix, if it doesn't sink!"

She was right. It solved one problem but created an even worse one. Namely, being stuck on this planet. But Geddy came to find Verveik, and that's what he was going to do.

In his panic to come up with a plan, Geddy hadn't noticed Morpho frantically tapping his left cheek until he inserted a tendril and gave him a tiny shock.

"Ah! What was that f ...?" Before finishing the question, he thought of a better one. "Wait — can you fly?"

What a dumb question. Morpho knew every rivet and relay on the *Fiz*, and the Zelnads designed him as a weapon for disabling, but not destroying ships. Of course, he could fly!

Morpho withdrew the tendril, slung out another behind him and sprang to the controls, taking over for Geddy.

"Take care of her. We'll call once we find Verveik."

Morpho gave a thumbs-up and held their hover better than Geddy had, which was growing increasingly wobbly with the weight. Geddy popped out of his harness and threw open the storage compartment behind them. He yanked out the Scimitar case while Oz got the two dry bags full of survival gear and fished out the headlamps. They threw on the backpacks, fixed their headlamps, and stood over the hatch. It was a two-meter drop.

"We've gotta go quick or they'll get inside. Morph, get ready to close the hatch behind us."

He worked the lever. As soon as the hatch fell open, Oz crossed her arms over her chest, took a deep breath, and dropped down into the water. Geddy waited two seconds, then followed her.

Water filled his ears as he plunged in, the dancing shafts of light from the *Dom* like angels in the root beer-colored water. But between the watertight pack and the Scimitar case, he didn't stay down long.

When his head burst through, he came face to face with a skysnake as it swooped low over the river. Its eyes were narrow, inky triangles set to either side of its pointy nose.

Instinctively, he swung the gun case in front of him and the snake smashed into it. It emitted a high-pitched *scree*, flailing helplessly as the current swallowed it.

"Oz!" he called, twisting frantically around in search of her.

"Here!" she called from behind him.

He whirled. She'd grabbed a submerged root on the bank and stretched her arm out to him as the current tugged him downstream. He frog-kicked himself across and hooked her outstretched hand. When the current swung him under her, his feet found purchase in the muck, and he grabbed a root of his own.

"You okay?" Geddy pulled himself upstream so he was next to her.

"Yeah, you?"

"I think so."

His relief was quickly swept away by the chilling realization that Morpho would take the big lights with him. Their headlamps already seemed woefully inadequate, though they made it very clear how many skysnakes were whistling through the air just overhead.

Morph spun the *Dom* around and punched it, sending another shower of skysnakes splashing into the river downstream.

Instantly, they were plunged into near darkness, the canopy only allowing starlike pinpoints of light to penetrate the murk. Before long, the thrashing downriver faded, and the only sounds that remained were the soft gurgle of the river and the *whoosh whoosh* of skysnakes overhead, so close at times that Geddy could feel their wind on his wet skin. The air here was so heavy that it took some extra effort to exhale. His ears kept popping, and his head felt leaden.

"Ugh, the atmosphere's so thick, you could chew it."

"Tell me about it," Oz said. "My head is pounding."

"Think we can wait them out?"

"Not likely."

He angled his headlamp upward. There were still a couple dozen skysnakes circling overhead. Not as many as before, but even one seemed like too many. The whoosh of wings filled the silence.

— *Try being very quiet.*

He thought back to what Doc said about the sensory organ at the tip of their nose. Being quiet wouldn't matter for echolocation, but they probably used movement and sound, too.

"Stay still and don't make a sound," he whispered.

They held very still in the surprisingly cold water for several minutes, during which the sound of flying snakes began to fade. The next time he raised his headlamp to the trees, he only saw a couple, and none near the river.

"Are they gone?" Oz asked.

"They're not swarming anymore. I guess that passes for good news."

The skysnakes seemed drawn to movement, so if they stayed low and slow, maybe they could start their sweep. But knowing they were relatively safe in the water made it hard to leave.

What began as a faint tingle on the backs of his hands quickly turned into pain. "Ah! What now?!" He hauled the gun case onto the bank, then moved his hand in front of the light to see what the hell was munching on his arm.

Tiny aquatic creatures resembling baby tadpoles had latched onto him by the dozens, biting like underwater mosquitoes. He angrily swiped them off into the water, leaving tiny red welts behind.

"They're on me, too!" cried Oz, doing her best to clear them.

— And it was so charming to this point.

— *Get out of there!*

As much as he wanted to scramble away, Geddy eased himself quietly onto the bank, staying as flat to the ground as possible. As soon as he was clear, he reached out a hand to Oz and hoisted her free of the water. They both lay prone in the moss for a few moments listening for the whoosh as they wiped the slimy, black, diamond-shaped little biters off their skin.

Oz's head flicked up at something behind him, and she gasped. "I just saw something."

"Where?"

"Behind you."

From the murk of the forest came a faint blue light, quickly becoming brighter and clambering like an animal. That light was joined by another, and another, winding between the cage-like roots of the colossal trees. As they neared, their shapes resolved into what could only be described as giant spiders with glowing, bluish green veins.

Verditheans.

They didn't move like spiders so much as multi-limbed acrobats. The chaotic air around them shifted and gathered like a breath as the skysnakes formed a column and punched toward these fresh targets with a collective *screeeee*. There were so many that the Verditheans briefly disappeared behind the attacking cloud.

Next came the unmistakable sound of metal singing through the air and cleaving flesh. Faster and faster they came, slice after slice, accompanied by a staccato series of whistled communications. Before long, the natives appeared again through the roiling cluster, and skysnakes retreated into the canopy. Streaks of light painted the darkness as they slipped between the leaves, creating an unsettling strobe effect as they fanned out, trapping Geddy and Oz between them and the river.

They were only a bit taller than Denk and walked upright except for when they scrambled between the roots like monkeys.

The streaks of bioluminescence were not veins, but rather some kind of viny growths on their skin. Four of their six arms held long, thin swords similar to katanas, dripping with pale green blood. Their webbed feet kept them from sinking into the soft ground as they strode over the still-twitching bodies of diced-up skysnakes.

They came right up to the edge of the stream and stared up at Geddy and Oz through big, glassy eyes the size and color of eight balls. The one nearest them whistled something between a birdsong and Morse code.

As Dr. Tardigan had warned, their translator chips were useless.

"What do you think he said?" Geddy asked.

"How do you know it's a 'he?'"

"Want me to ask what its pronouns are?"

The Verditheans engaged in a heated chorus of whistling that could only be about them.

Geddy scanned the ground for the Scimitar case, but one of the Verditheans had already snatched it up. Two of them skittered up, their long, three-fingered hands roaming over their dripping clothes. They found the Exeter in its holster and Oz's blades in their sheaths and removed them, then made them remove their packs. It felt odd to get patted down by such an animal-like alien, but it meant they were intelligent.

"What now?" Oz asked.

Before he could reply, three of the seven Verditheans sheathed their blades, and headed back whence they came. The one nearest them gestured that they should follow.

"Looks like we're going with them."

Geddy and Oz hesitantly fell in. The four remaining natives with all their gear dropped in behind them, and they marched into the jungle in a line, the carpet of dead skys-nakes gently crunching under their feet.

CHAPTER THIRTY-SIX

WELCOME TO THE JUNGLE

Not that it was ever a consideration, but the notion of getting out of the river and running from the skysnakes grew even more absurd as Geddy and Oz trudged across the jungle floor.

It comprised a thick layer of moss essentially floating on an ocean of foot-sucking muck that stank like a loamy version of The Deuce. They hadn't gone a hundred meters before Geddy had to stop and catch his breath. Each labored step made his muscles burn. The smaller, lighter Verdithean, with their wide, flat feet, stayed on top of it with ease.

Aside from being heavy with humidity, the air was also utterly stagnant, allowing clouds of insects to simply float in place, sticking to their clothes and skin like burs as they passed. As with the tadpoles, brushing them off required constant vigilance. Legions of other, larger bugs skittered across their path.

They quickly learned to avoid breaking through moss by taking quick, dainty steps. It killed your legs after a while, but it was better than pulling your feet from the muck with each step.

The Verditheans chirped back and forth frequently during this death march. Geddy didn't need a translator chip to understand they were irritated by their glacial pace.

"What do you think lots go for around here?" He again paused to catch his breath.

"Probably out of our price range, considering the view," responded Oz.

Up ahead, the leaders stopped. One of them leapt up onto a root and grabbed a thick vine, which it cut with its blade. Water practically poured out of it. It held its mouth under the stream and slaked its thirst, and the rest followed suit. Then it cut two more and held them out for Geddy and Oz to take.

He turned to her. "You think it's safe?"

In lieu of a reply, she lurched forward and drank deeply. "It's delicious."

That was good enough for him. He snatched the vine out of the Verdithean's hand and held it over his open mouth. It had a green, vegetable taste but was pleasantly cool and clean. Even after drinking his fill, it kept coming out. A bit of energy returned to his muscles.

They continued in this way for nearly two hours, winding through so many colossal roots it was impossible to tell whether they were headed out or deeper inside. At any rate, the thought of them searching fifty square kilometers in these conditions was comical.

The Verdithean camp appeared so suddenly that it seemed to materialize out of the darkness. Half a dozen colossal trees formed the perimeter with an open space in between. Roots and vines were knotted into a web of suspended walkways and huts that clung to the sides of the smooth-skinned trees like mushrooms two meters off the swampy forest floor.

Dozens of natives emerged from the huts with excited chirps and whistles, their bioluminescent bodies creating a dazzling scene of lively neon shapes that could've passed for performance art.

In the faint blue light, Geddy discerned the shape of a distinctly un-Verdithean individual waiting for them in the middle of the clearing. Specifically, a Ghruk carrying a rifle.

———

THE GHRUK ACTIVATED his own headlamp and slithered toward them on a trail of slime, its eyestalks fixed on them. The males were about as long as Geddy was tall and most closely resembled a giant snail. A thick, segmented shell ran most of its length, with two thick, boneless arms in front and two vestigial ones in back. In full light, they were dark green, but here, everything was a shade of black.

Between them and the Verditheans, the award for Weirdest Species would've been a dead heat. You didn't see many Ghruk these days, not even at busy spaceports, which made finding one here that much more surprising.

The Ghruk chirped something in the natives' language, and the leader let forth a stream of whistles that received a tepid response. Their rescuers used lengths of vine to strap their weapons, packs, and the Scimitar case to the Ghruk's thick shell and stepped back, still surrounding them.

He made a slow circle around them. "Who are you?"

"We're the band." Geddy's eyes roamed around the camp. "This is the Abramowitz bar mitzvah, right?"

His face lit up with joy, slapping his four-fingered hands together. "A sense of humor. How fun! But seriously, who are you?"

Geddy and Oz exchanged a very confused look. The Ghruk weren't known exactly known for their flamboyant personalities, but there were always exceptions.

"We're looking for Verveik," Oz said.

"What a coincidence!" He leaned forward with a conspiratorial smile. "*I work for Verveik.* It's so lucky we ran into each other."

Apparently, they had an arrangement with the Verditheans, who couldn't possibly have crafted such fine skysnake-slicing blades themselves. Such a peace offering likely bought the occasional favor.

"That belongs to him." Geddy nodded at the gun case. "We're here to give it back."

The Ghruk studied the case in the dim technicolor light. "Must be important to come all this way. What is it?"

"It's for his eyes only." Geddy took a step forward, but the Verditheans instantly tightened their circle, blades raised, and he stopped.

"Yeah, yeah, of course." He pursed his flabby lips, then opened it anyway.

Apparently, Geddy was in no position to make demands of the Ghruk.

He gave a low whistle. "Now that's a big gun. And fancy!" Satisfied, he re-closed it. "Well, you two seem like a hoot. Whaddya say we bounce?"

"You know where Verveik is?" Oz exchanged a quizzical look with Geddy.

The Ghruk began sliding away, and the Verditheans parted. "I'm pretty sure I said I worked for him, so ..."

"We're supposed to just trust you?"

He stopped and turned his upper body nearly a hundred eighty degrees. "I am merely offering the *chance* to see Commander Verveik. You're welcome to hang out with the Verditheans until you're red in the face. Or until you have no faces at all. We have an arrangement with them, but this was a big ask. Now, chop, chop. Because that is the sound you will hear if we don't skedaddle."

He slithered away from the camp, leaving them no choice but to follow. They picked up their gear and hurried to catch the Ghruk, his slime trail sparking in the light of their headlamps.

"So, what's your handle?" Geddy had to hustle to keep up, sidestepping to avoid the slippery trail left by their guide.

"Glarry," he said cheerfully over his shoulder.

— Glarry?

— *He seems nice.*

— You say that about everyone.

"Just to be super clear, your boss is former Supreme Commander of the Alliance Otaro Verveik?"

"Ooohhh, *Otaro* Verveik. No, no, I work for *Otto* Verveik. Common mistake. We get, like, a *ton* of his mail. I mean, why'd he have to build right across the street?"

— Is he trying out material?

— *Maybe you could be his opening act.*

"Yes, *that* Otaro Verveik, dummies!"

Oz threw a *WTF* look back at him, to which Geddy could only shrug.

"What kind of work do you do for him, exactly?" Oz asked.

"It's not work if you love it," he winked. "Me and the other mercs provide security for Commander Verveik and Dr. D. Hey, try to keep up, would ya? We're losing the light. Ha!"

Geddy and Oz both gave a patronizing smile. Glarry's goofy charm, amusing though it was, made real answers hard to come by.

"Who's Dr. D?"

"Dr. Denimore. You'll meet him, too."

That must be the scientist who provided the data on the cryp.

"I guess we should thank you for saving us," Geddy said.

"I'm just glad the luftrithides didn't get you."

"You mean the skysnakes?" Oz asked.

His eyes twisted around each other and popped wide. "Did you say *skysnakes*? That is *way* better than *luftrithides*. Not to mention easier to spell. Anyway, yes, them. But circling back to this message you're here to deliver ... can I get a hint?"

"No."

"Category?"

"No."

"First word starts with ..."

"No!"

Oz's body shook with laughter. Great. Not only was this guy pushing all his buttons, but now his comic stylings were working on Oz.

"Ugh, fine." Glarry gave his head a vigorous shake, flinging off bits of slimy sweat. "We'll let the suspense build. Not that our camp needs any more *drama*!"

Tiptoeing along for hours on end had set Geddy's quads aflame. Wherever they were going, they'd better get there soon.

"How many are you?" asked Oz.

"Let's see, there's me, the old man, Dr. D ..." He mumbled inaudibly as he ticked off names on his tapered fingers. It went on like this for a full minute. "Six. No, five."

"You're a funny guy, Glarry."

"Aww, you're just trying to butter me up because you'd be lost without me."

— Would this be a bad time to make an escargot joke?

— *Is there ever a good time?*

"No, I mean it. It really makes the time pass."

He patted his chest. "Thank you for saying that. Compliments are among Verdithea's scarcest resources."

Light appeared up ahead, and not courtesy of glowing Verditheans. The forest had begun to thin, and the ground solidified under their feet. As they covered the next few kilometers, the moss gave way to bare soil, then sand, and then loose rock. The terrain turned uphill, and they emerged into clear air and a fully lit sky, immensely glad to be bathed in the weird blue-orange light and not wrapped in darkness.

They ascended the steep slope in a series of short switchbacks. Between their heavy legs and packs, the going was slow. Panting, Geddy threw a look back over his shoulder to find that they were now above the endless sea of shiny, faintly metallic leaves of the canopy.

Glarry noticed him looking back. "This river basin used

to be an ancient freshwater lake. In a few hundred years, the trees will consume what's left of the water and die." He barked a laugh. "Listen to me getting all science-y. I sound like Dr. D."

The loose sedimentary rock slid away beneath their feet if they veered off the well-worn, zigzagging path up the embankment. Hard to believe it had all been underwater once.

"You must go to the jungle a lot," Geddy said.

"Sometimes for water, mostly for the muck. We can't grow food without it up here."

"The skysnakes don't come up this high?" asked Oz.

"They still need the trees, but they venture higher every year, the buggers. It's only a matter of time before they take over the highlands, too. Hopefully, we'll be long gone by then."

They reached what might once have been a beach on the ancient lake's pristine shores, and the ground mercifully leveled out. They rounded a giant battlement of sandstone and came upon a flat area well-protected on all sides by rock. In the middle was a ring of geodesic terraforming habitats, the kind colonists and researchers used. They were circular and seven or eight meters across, made of a dull silver fabric stretched over a carbon frame raised half a meter off the ground.

Whatever this was, Tretiak's money made it happen.

"Welcome to ZIP," said Glarry.

"ZIP?"

"The Zelnad Identification Project."

CHAPTER THIRTY-SEVEN

A MERC-Y PAST

As they entered the camp, a couple of Glarry's colleagues came out of their habs. One was a shark-like Sarak, his face badly scarred and sporting an eye patch. The other was a musclebound Screvari holding two blades like the ones Glarry and the Verditheans carried.

"That's Mantwin and Torkin. I forget which is which." The Sarak grunted a greeting and the Screvari lifted his chin. Glarry slithered toward the largest of the five habs. The door opened as they approached, and a Kailorian stepped out.

"A Ghruk, a Screvari, and a Kailorian walk into a clearing ..." Geddy whispered.

"Is this a setup?" Oz quipped.

— My god, this woman so gets me.

— *I agree, but this is most curious. The whole Triad is represented.*

"Greetings!" The Kailorian smiled and extended his hand to each of them. "I am Dr. Denimore. I sent Glarry here to find you before the Verditheans decided you were worth more as food than bargaining chips."

"They saved us from the skysnakes," Oz said.

"Skysnakes?" A smile crept across his lips.

"It's good, right?" Glarry asked. "Why didn't we think of that? I mean, *luftrithides virans* is fine, but the fewer syllables the better, I always say."

Geddy shrugged. "Our gift to you. I'm Geddy Starheart and this is Osmiya Nargonis. We're here to see Commander Verveik."

The Kailorian's smile faded, his eyes darting suspiciously between them. "Who sent you?"

"Tretiak."

He gave a little gasp. "The Committee?"

Geddy shook his head. "Just Tretiak. The others don't know we're here."

His long face furrowed with concern. "Trust is hard to come by these days. What of the Zelnad situation? The commander hasn't exactly been forthcoming with news."

Not that long ago, Zelnad-related news was slow or nonexistent. You could go a year or three and not miss anything. But it had been a monumental week, and these guys didn't know shit. Neither did Verveik.

"I'll tell you everything as soon as I'm standing in front of him."

Torkin took a couple quick steps toward them and removed the case from Glarry's back while Mantwin took their packs and weapons.

"What's this?" He unbuckled the lid, then removed the Scimitar from its foam cradle. "My stars ..." He marveled at it, running his fingers lovingly over the skolthil. "This is my grandfather's work. I'd know it anywhere. Where did you get this?"

"Long story," Geddy said.

"We rarely have guests," came a deep, booming voice from the middle hab. "Take all the time you need."

Verveik had to crouch and turn sideways to get through the narrow door. He was brawny like any other Gundrun, but not as big as Arbizander and certainly not as imposing as he seemed in old footage. He looked great for being a hundred and thirty, but some of his greatness had faded. The years had diminished him.

Even so, Geddy was awestruck. He'd heard stories about Verveik and the Alliance since he was little. His dad and the other PDF officers weren't even born yet when the Ring War still raged, but tales of his exploits inspired many to serve. Verveik built the Alliance into something great, but its rise heralded a precipitous fall.

Geddy took a couple nervous steps toward him, his palms sweating. "Commander Verveik, meeting you is one of the greatest honors of my life."

Verveik grunted and approached Torkin, who still held the Scimitar. He took it from the Screvari and closed his hand around the grip. In his giant, viselike hand, it looked as it should — a long, scoped pistol.

He hefted it a moment, one corner of his mouth turning wistfully upward.

Just as fast, the look disappeared, and she shoved the weapon back into the Screvari's hands.

"The safety's off. You should be more careful." Turning to the Kailorian, he jerked his head toward Geddy and Oz and said, "Doc, test them. Then we'll gather around to hear this 'long story' of theirs."

Verveik returned to his hab without another word. Geddy and Oz exchanged a confused look.

"Well, that was anticlimactic," Oz muttered.

"Please, join me in the lab." Dr. Denimore gestured toward the larger hab.

"What test was he talking about?" asked Geddy.

"Right this way, please."

While Dr. Denimore was talking, Glarry slithered closer to Torkin and Mantwin, and they engaged in hushed conversation around the Scimitar. Geddy and Oz hesitated.

"Please," he said, more firmly this time.

Geddy reluctantly stepped into the hab, followed by Oz.

The lab was ringed with computer equipment and devices, a simple cot tucked into one corner. The soft hum of fans filled the space.

Denimore closed the door behind him. "Welcome to my humble laboratory." He strode to a table and picked up a small, handheld device.

"What is all this?" asked Geddy.

"This," Denimore began, futzing with the device, "will test for what I call the Zelnad harmonic." He returned to them holding the device, which featured a prominent circular antenna. "Hold still, please."

"Are you saying it's a Zelnad detector?"

"If you'd like."

— Is he bluffing?

— *It is theoretically possible. You should warn him.*

"I could've saved you the trouble. If it works, she'll test negative. I'll test positive. But I swear I'm not a Zelnad."

"Let's see what the science tells us, hm?" He pressed the antenna to Oz's forehead and the ring turned green.

"So far, so good. Now you."

He repeated the procedure with Geddy, and it turned red, as they knew it would. Denimore's pleasant smile vanished, and he took a step back.

"Torkin!"

"Easy, pal, I told you this would happen. There's a lot you don't know. If I could just speak to Verveik …"

Torkin burst through the door, weapon at the ready. "What's wrong?"

"He has the harmonic. Just him, not the woman."

Torkin leveled his rifle at Geddy. "You're certain?"

"Yes. Take him outside, please."

Before Geddy could react, Torkin grabbed his shirt and shoved him backwards through the door. He backpedaled into the courtyard between the habs, almost falling on his ass.

"Hey!" Oz moved to intervene.

"It's okay." Geddy steadied himself and held up his hands. "I'll clear this up in no time."

Torkin strode toward him with the rifle pointed at his face. "I had a bad feeling about you, Zelnad."

Verveik emerged from his hab, arms crossed and jaw set. Dr. Denimore led Oz out of the lab and held the device up for him to see.

"He's one of them."

"No, I'm not!" Geddy protested. "Just let me explain."

Unamused, Verveik brought his giant face level with Geddy and narrowed his crinkly, hawklike eyes. "How did you find this place?"

"He claims Tretiak sent them," Glarry chimed in.

"If this one knows where we are, then they all do," Verveik growled. "Get packing."

"It's not what you think," Geddy pleaded. "Just give me five minutes. Five to ten. Let's say eight-ish minutes."

Verveik drew himself back up and sneered. "You have one."

Geddy breathlessly spilled everything he knew, a tale that began with Eli and ended with the Committee and Tretiak. By then, the Sarak and Mantwin had drawn closer to listen.

When Geddy was finished, Verveik's eyes met with each of his men, gauging their take.

"That's a pretty specific story," Denimore noted.

"It's too late for your test anyway," Geddy said. "They already had their coming-out party over Gundrun, and they were the darlings of the ship show."

Denimore's face fell, and he turned away with his head in his hands. "All my work ... wasted."

"Only the Zelnad identification part," offered Mantwin.

Denimore turned on the Sarak. "This is the Zelnad Identification *Project*, you imbecile!"

Now Geddy was really confused. "Wait ... that's all you're doing here?"

"Guess we've both got stories to tell," said Verveik. "Let's take a walk."

CHAPTER THIRTY-EIGHT

THE HEAVY STUFF

Oz and Geddy followed Verveik away from the jungle and deeper into the sandstone hills. The trees here were short and scrubby, the soil rocky and poor. A couple hundred meters in, they came upon a surprisingly large field sown with neat rows of root vegetables, bean-laden vines crawling up handmade trellises, and a couple small fruit trees. Considering the other flora, it was surprising to see, but as Glarry said, the topsoil came from the swamp.

Verveik set his giant hands on his hips and gestured proudly at his garden. "It used to be a lot harder to grow things up here. But add enough swamp muck, and you've got a garden."

"Tretiak said you've been here about five years?" Geddy asked.

"Yes, and we've made good progress, but as you said, it's insufficient."

Verveik traced a defined path along the edge of the field. It turned right and zigzagged up between two pillars of sandstone.

"Tretiak said he hasn't heard from you in over a year. His coordinates put us in the middle of the damn jungle."

He gave an exaggerated shrug. "There hasn't been much to report. As for the coordinates, we baked in time to size up any uninvited guests. I'm sure you understand."

As they climbed the path between the pillars, they reached a ledge with a nearly 360-degree view of the jungle-choked basin. The lake they'd flown over on the far side stretched all the way to the mountains. It had a stark, unspoiled beauty further enhanced by the peculiar quality of the light.

"How'd you come by my old gun?"

Geddy related a heavily abridged version of the story, starting with Smegmo Eilgars gifting it to him on Ceonia years ago and ending with Tretiak bringing it to his hotel room on Xellara.

"I don't know how Old Man Eilgars came by it," he finished.

Verveik's eyes drifted from the horizon to the ground. "I had to rid myself of everything to do with the Alliance. Starting with that ridiculous weapon."

At last, they'd hit upon the magic word.

Oz flared her eyebrows at Geddy, out of Verveik's sight. He was still staring out over the unbroken canopy.

"How come?" she asked.

His fierce, crinkled eyes turned glassy as they peered across the basin, his voice low and dark. "Because it only reminded me of my failure. And my hubris."

Geddy blinked. "What do you mean?"

"The Zelnads bought up all the tukrium. They knew

we'd go to war over it eventually. They've had eons to learn our patterns."

The implications hit Geddy so hard, he grew dizzy. What if the Ring War was a test? The final opportunity for civilization to learn from eons of conflict and make different choices? What if the Alliance was the closest they'd ever get to a unified galaxy? The Nads easily could've engineered a war. Maybe they were doing it again.

They'd all failed the final exam, and the Nads were getting ready to expel them. Civilization would hang from its own rope.

The weight of it had rounded Verveik's shoulders, perhaps even crushed his spirits. The way he saw it, he'd presided over the beginning of the end.

"There's still time to stop them," Geddy asserted, trying to get Verveik to look at him. "We know what they want, and we're close to finding out where they are. That's a helluva lot more than we've ever had before."

Verveik gave a bemused snort. "Do you know how to stop the inevitable? Because I certainly don't."

Geddy gulped. Oz gave him an encouraging nod. He'd fantasized about this moment for weeks. "We reassemble the Alliance."

The way Verveik looked down at him, you'd think he'd have grown an extra head. For a long moment, neither of them spoke.

"You're serious." Incredulity colored his expression. "And how, exactly, do you see that playing out? They've already got Gundrun and the Triad. Xellara can't be far behind. Nothing can stem this tide now. Nothing!"

The words struck Geddy dumb. Maybe he was naïve, but he expected more from his childhood hero. The Otaro Verveik he'd grown up hearing about would never be so fatalistic.

Righteous anger gathered in his core. "So, what, we just throw up our hands? Run out the clock munching carrots on Skysnakia??"

The big Gundrun grunted and brushed past them back down the trail. "My advice is to do whatever you want for as long as you can. Like I said, they've been at this for thousands of years. They know how it all plays out."

Geddy stared after Verveik, dumbfounded. "What are you talking about?"

Verveik stopped and about-faced. "Humans spent centuries searching for evidence of intelligent life. So have we. Gundrun, Ornea, Temeruria ... Only we found it. Thousands of other worlds in other galaxies. Know what they all had in common?"

Geddy and Oz shook their heads.

"They're gone. Wiped out. Some for so long, their cities have returned to dust."

Verveik continued down the path, leaving Geddy to grapple with this new revelation. It meant their galaxy was only the latest to come up for extermination. Maybe even the last.

Oz huffed and hurried after him. Geddy caught up in time to see her pass Verveik and plant her feet in front of him like a child jumping in front of a tank.

"Move, girl, or I'll move you," he growled.

Geddy came up beside her.

"No!" Oz stomped her foot and pointed a shaking finger skyward. "This is *our* world. *Our* families. *Our* civilization. Once everyone knows what's at stake here, they *will* fight."

"Then you don't need me." He marched right between them, forcing them both to jump out of the way.

This was not how either of them saw things going. There was no plan B.

A distant thunderclap echoed from the mountains.

"That'll hit us in twenty minutes, maybe less," Verveik said, looking over his shoulder. "You'll want to be inside when it does."

———

EVERY PLANET HAD its own brand of severe weather, and Geddy had either flown through or been caught in some wild situations, such as the acid showers on The Deuce and weeks-long sandstorms on Kigantu. But a storm on Verdithea was in a class by itself.

The lighting was incessant, the metal-infused trees sucking in electrons as fast as the sodden, low-hanging clouds could dish it out. The wind came in violent gusts, sometimes throwing so much water at the habs it felt like they might be ripped apart, but they were made to withstand much worse.

Verveik's hab was the second largest of the five and the only one with a common area. They sat in a circle around a folding table playing uguinok and had been for hours. Geddy was up a hundred credits, but his heart wasn't in it.

He drew two fresh cards and took a peek. A pair of fives. He slid them over to Mantwin. "Pair of threes."

Mantwin hemmed and hawed, then passed it to Verveik. "He's got it. He's always got it."

"Not this time," said Verveik, and flipped the cards to discover the fives. If your opponent thought you were lying on the high side, they'd call your bluff and flip. If you lied on the low side, they lost. He groaned and slid a square across the table as Geddy beamed. "I'll hand it to you, Starheart. You're hard to read."

"And I find reading hard. Pretty sure that makes me a double threat."

Verveik drew his own cards, coinciding perfectly with a roll of thunder that shook the hab. Not looking, he passed them to Torkin. "Sixty-four."

"Bullshit." Torkin lifted it. Sixty-two. Oh well. Now it was his turn to pay. No one had any actual credits on them, so they were using stones.

Wind gave the hab a sustained battering. He couldn't imagine the forces needed to push such heavy air around like that.

"I've gotta know," said Geddy. "How do a Ghruk, a Screvari, and a Kailorian wind up playing uguinok together with the former leader of the Alliance on this little slice of heaven?"

The mercs all looked to Verveik. "I wanted my team to come from the Triad."

"How come?" Geddy inquired.

"Because I figured if the former commander of the Alliance and guys from the Triad could agree on a common purpose, there might still be hope. C'mon, Torkin, you're up."

"And?"

"And what?" asked Verveik.

"Is there hope?"

The mercs and Dr. D swiveled their heads to Verveik,

curious what he might say, but he said nothing.

Torkin's already furrowed face pinched further as he drew cards. "It's all been a waste of time of you ask me. Too little, too late."

"Which is why we need to rebuild the Alliance," Oz said.

Torkin and Mantwin gave rueful laughs, while Glarry and Denimore shared a significant look.

"And how might that happen, exactly?" asked Denimore.

Geddy locked eyes with Verveik, who was growing impatient by the turn of conversation. "It all starts with the right leader."

Verveik's nose wrinkled, his upper lip curled as he stared murderously at him.

Meanwhile, Denimore had snapped out of his funk. "Is it possible, Otaro? Could the Alliance be rebuilt?"

"No."

"But Commander, what if we—"

Verveik's giant fist smashed down on the steel table, denting it. "I said no!! The Alliance didn't collapse — it shattered. There's nothing to rebuild." He grimaced and shook his head. "We couldn't get out of our own way, and we never will."

The mercs, who had spent every day and night with Verveik for however long, stared at him incredulously. Geddy's hero had lost all hope.

"You're all relieved of duty." Verveik finished his swamp scotch and rose. "Get some sleep. I'll arrange for your return first thing tomorrow." His sad eyes met Geddy's and Oz's. "You two are on your own."

He lumbered into his personal quarters adjacent to the common room and shut the door behind him.

CHAPTER THIRTY-NINE

GREAT EXPECTATIONS

EARLIER IN THE EVENING, Mantwin and Torkin agreed to bunk together so Oz and Geddy could share Torkin's hab for the night. In spite of nearly unlimited funding, the habs were pretty no-frills. Empty crates from resupply runs were pushed along the right side. Torkin's cot was flush with the back, and his clothes and other gear were neatly folded and stacked on shelves to the left. A fan in the center of the ceiling mostly failed to circulate air.

Terraforming habitats were made to withstand extreme conditions, but the lashing gusts still made the frame groan in protest.

Dehumidifiers inside produced the bulk of their drinking water, but Torkin's couldn't stay ahead of the storm's moisture. It might as well have been a steam room inside, so they stripped down to their underwear. Oz took the cot, and Geddy a bedroll on the floor. It was too hot to do much but sweat.

He tried multiple times to hail Morpho or Denk from the hab, but the storm was causing too much interference. The moment it cleared, he'd get to higher ground and try again. The storm had weakened a great deal in the last hour, so hopefully it was breaking apart.

Under other circumstances, being alone in private with a half-naked Oz might have turned his thoughts toward the romantic, but their bodies were covered in ugly red welts from the biting tadpoles, especially their hands and feet, and their BO would've given Voprot a run for his money.

Their final interaction with Verveik had left them deflated. It was a hard thing to reconcile. Geddy had played the moment out in his head a million times. Bringing him the Scimitar would be like that part in *Lord of the Rings*, one of his favorite Old Earth books. Gandalf the wizard brings old, bewitched King Theoden his sword and breaks the spell that has kept him out of the fight. Verveik was supposed to regard it with wonder, say something like, *I've missed you, old friend.* Then he'd put a hand on his shoulder and add, *Well, Captain Starheart? Whaddya say we blow those Zelnads straight to hell?*

It didn't go like that. Not remotely.

"He can't really believe that, can he?" Geddy stared at the curved ceiling, tinged green by the indicator light on the dehumidifier.

Oz turned onto her side to face him, her right arm dangling to the floor. "He's probably just cynical. From Supreme Commander of the Alliance to camping on Verdithea is kind of a long fall."

"Tretiak told me he exiled himself to Kigantu for sixty-six years."

"That's a long time to think."

Knowing that Verveik blamed himself for the collapse of

the Alliance cast his self-exile in a whole different light. He pictured the old man in a cave, clearing out whatever sand had blown in during the night only to spend the entire day second-guessing every decision he ever made. Hell, he probably came to believe the War itself was his fault.

It reminded him a lot of the book Doc told him about. Was Verveik broken like Melpf Lowderthistle, the victim of his own unhelpful ruminations?

"He couldn't even say he had hope."

"No, but I could sense it."

If Oz detected it, then Geddy had to trust it was there, but he sure hadn't shown it.

She couldn't see him flare his eyebrows, but for his part, Geddy didn't get a real hope-y vibe from the old man. What would he do after sending everyone away? Live out his days here? Commit ritual suicide? Write a memoir? He'd already gotten into gardening. Making birdhouses couldn't be far behind.

"What if he won't help us?"

Oz heaved a long sigh. "I dunno. Then I guess it'll be up to us."

— *Commander Verveik could be forgiven for losing hope, but you can't, Geddy. You just can't.*

Putting up a credible defense against the Zelnads would've felt like a long shot even with the Alliance at full strength. But finding the Nads and destroying their Sagacea-killing weapon without *any* military support? That was impossible. Even warning the Sagaceans was impossible. A cargo hold full of blue balls still wouldn't get anywhere near the center of the universe.

— *You should tell her now.*

— As soon as we're off this shitty planet. There might not be much time.

— I will hold you to it.

"What does Eli have to say about it?"

"That we can't give up even if Verveik has."

As they talked, the itch to contact Denk grew more insistent. The endless patter of fat raindrops had largely tapered off, and fifteen or twenty minutes had passed since the last blast of wind shook the small building. Between the cloying humidity, his troubled mind, and Oz's glistening body, sleep was impossible.

Geddy got up and strapped on his headlamp.

"What are you doing?"

"I'm gonna try Morph and Denk again."

"You're going out in your underwear, in the dark, with just a headlamp?"

"It's called camping," he said with a wink. "Be right back."

CHAPTER FORTY

DARK SIDE OF THE RAINBOW

The camp had been turned into a lake that came halfway up the habs' raised platforms. If it rained any more, they'd be swamped. It was still dark out when Geddy slipped on his still-wet boots and splashed into the muddy water. Hopefully the tadpole things, or something worse, hadn't come down with the rain. That would really be the capstone on this house of horrors.

He waded across camp and back inland, past the swamp-muck garden and up the trail between the spires where they'd walked with Verveik earlier. The flashes of distant lightning were the only light other than his headlamp. The storm clouds were well off in the distance now, drenching the mountains on the other side of the jungle. Low-hanging clouds had taken their place, the underside as smooth and defined as a blanket.

When he reached the top, he raised the comm device to his lips. "Morph, we're ready to dust off from our current position. Over."

Geddy stared anxiously at the screen, his heart clanging

in his chest. He spoke a wish into the universe that Morpho and the crew were okay. Morph couldn't speak aloud, but he could use universal distress code, as he had done to warn them about the tardigrades over Old Earth.

Finally, one letter appeared.

K

Elation flooded his soul. They were getting off this shithole. He let out a small whoop that ricocheted off the sandstone.

Again, he spoke into the device. "I'm gonna try the *Fiz* now, but you might want to do the same. See you soon." He switched to the *Fizmo's* hailing frequency. "Doc? Denk? It's me. Come in."

Several seconds passed with no reply.

"Listen, if you can hear me, Morph is on his way to pick us up. We should be on our way back by ..."

A flashing light at the bottom of the screen indicated he was being contacted on another frequency, well outside their usual spectrum. The band of thieves.

— *Who could that be?*

— Probably a telemarketer. I'll get rid of them.

"New phone. Who 'dis?"

"Geddy! Thank the stars, I've been scanning frequencies for hours!"

He blinked and shook his head. "Jeledine? How did you ...?"

"Shut up and listen for once!" Her voice was frantic. Jel didn't get frantic. "Xellaran fighters just entered your atmosphere. I don't know w–"

Her transmission abruptly cut off. Xellarans? What would they want with Verdithea?

"How many?"

No reply.

"How long ago? Jel, come in!"

Still nothing.

"Shit!"

Frantic, he half-slid down the trail and sprinted back toward camp. He bounded down the hill and splashed back into the shallow, muddy water, high-stepping it through the camp like some water-walking gecko.

— *What happened? Where'd she go?*

— They're jamming her.

"Oz! Verveik! Glarry! Wake up!" Geddy yelled as loud as he could from the center of camp. "We've got company!"

Oz was the first to poke her head out, followed closely by Verveik, then the rest.

"What are you talking about?" demanded Verveik.

"Xellaran fighters inbound!!"

Verveik and the mercs sprang into action.

"Code red, people! Let's move!" They were back in their habs retrieving their emergency gear before the order was fully given.

Oz was still staring at him from under the vestibule. He was about to yell at her to grab her shit when five Xellaran Darkstar PK-5s plunged through the cloud layer over the jungle and leveled out, heading straight for them.

They'd be there in seconds. Verveik said Xellara would be next to cast their lot with the Nads, but maybe they already had. Did they already know about Verdithea and its skysnakes or had they followed the *Fiz* here? Rader must have something to do with this. Hell, he might even be piloting one.

"Oz, let's go!"

She spun and grabbed their sodden clothes from where they hung under the vestibule and tossed Geddy's at him as he burst through the door, his boots overflowing with water. They struggled to pull them on, then shoved the rest of their gear into their packs.

Oz finished before him and threw on her blades. "How did you–"

A sharp explosion cut her off, the shockwave blasting a spray of muddy water through the open door. Geddy whirled to see Dr. Denimore's lab reduced to ribbons, a black scorch mark etched into the rock behind it. He was gone.

The jungle canopy had the best cover, but that wasn't an option. One of the nearby rock formations was their best bet.

He jumped off the platform into the mini lake. Mantwin and Torkin came bounding out of their hab, rifles in hand.

Their feet had just touched the water when another disruptor volley slammed into Mantwin's hab. The blast arched their backs and sent them flying halfway across camp, both landing face-down in the water.

Geddy ran toward their motionless forms, checking over his shoulder to make sure Oz was on his heels. She'd skipped her boots, her bare feet bounding through the turbulent pond.

Verveik emerged from his hab like an angry god carrying the Scimitar in his right hand and a satchel slung over his shoulder. But the squadron had already disappeared into the low clouds. Total snipe hunt. His eyes briefly scanned the clouds, then he and Glarry joined Geddy beside the fallen mercs.

Geddy rolled Mantwin over to find his lifeless shark eyes staring back up at him. "Shit."

Torkin coughed up muddy water as Verveik rolled him over, but a streak of blue blood was leaking from the corner of his mouth and left ear. He didn't look good.

Without hesitation, Verveik scooped up Torkin, wrapping him around his neck like a scarf as though he'd done it a hundred times before. Torkin cried out in pain.

"There's a small cave nearby. Let's move."

He took off at a trot toward the hills, his strides so large, it was a challenge to keep up. Following Glarry, they darted through the creases between hills until they reached a small clearing. Verveik was motoring toward a jagged overhang on the far side with a dark space beneath that Geddy took to be the cave. It was only seventy meters away.

Glarry, unfortunately, could only move at a snail's pace.

Geddy grabbed Oz's hand and they passed him, gaining on Verveik. As they opened more distance between them and Glarry, a muffled rumble came from their eight o'clock. The Darkstars dropped back out of the clouds, the glowing tips of the disruptors brightening as they bore down on them.

"Glarry, slither faster!" Geddy called over his shoulder, ignoring the fire consuming his weary legs.

They weren't going to make it. Verveik pulled up short of the cave, pivoted back, and took a few big strides back toward them. What the hell was he doing?

"Get behind me," he growled, leveling the Scimitar at the fighters. Geddy and Oz skidded to a stop behind him, twenty yards from the cave. "Zelnads identified." He pulled the trigger.

For various sentimental reasons, Geddy couldn't bring

himself to shoot the Scimitar himself. It seemed like sleeping with your best friend's girl. Good thing he hadn't because its recoil would've knocked him flat on his ass. A ringed purple beam shot from the barrel and blasted off half the fighter's down-swept left wing.

The shockwave slammed into him and Oz like a medicine ball and pinned his hair back. The lead fighter flamed out and went into a hard spin before smashing into the hill behind the cave, black smoke billowing into the sky as it flaming husk tumbled off the side.

The other three split and vanished into the clouds again. Geddy's ears still rang from the blast.

"Move, soldier!" Verveik shouted at Glarry, then spun back around. He hurried to the overhang and gently rolled Torkin off his shoulders onto the ground, then crawled underneath to pull him in. Unfortunately, the opening was small, and there was only room for one of them to enter at a time.

The skies had fallen silent, the ships' location impossible to know. Glarry was almost there.

"I'm pretty sure that's your boyfriend," Geddy panted.

"Wha ... you mean *Rader*?"

He shrugged. "We did leave him to pay a five-figure bar tab."

"How could he possibly know we were here?"

"He must've followed us through the wormhole."

"Oh, no." Horror filled Oz's eyes. "The *Fiz*!"

Geddy didn't have time to reply before the fighters reappeared, this time right on Glarry's six. They dropped low to the ground and lined up to fire. Behind them, Verveik was still trying to ease Torkin into the cave. A few well-placed shots would bring the overhang down on top of them, but there was no other cover nearby and no way for Verveik to take a shot without hitting Glarry. Geddy's Exeter was useless against them.

He and Oz could only hit the dirt. Geddy peered through his fingers. It was down to luck now.

The Darkstars unleashed a torrent of bolts that punched holes in the earth behind Glarry, launching a spray of wet sand and rock into the air. His eyestalks straightened as his whole body raised up, and he curled into a ball that rolled toward them just ahead of the blasts. When he reached them, he unfurled across him and Oz with his thick shell facing out.

"That's how I roll!" He winked.

But the next blasts hit him square in the back with sickening force, showering them with bits of shell as he bellowed in pain. It was a miracle he wasn't torn to pieces. Ghruk shells must be stronger than Geddy thought.

The fighters stopped firing and broke away, boring a hole through the wall of smoke from the downed one as they passed.

Glarry coughed up green blood, his eyes dimming, the acrid smoke from his blasted shell like burning hair.

"Come on, let's get him inside!" Geddy urged, trying to figure out which part of him to grab. But he was never going to fit through the opening.

Oz gave him a heavy look and shook her head.

"First to die in the ... last war," Glarry sputtered. "Maybe they'll write songs about me."

"Not just songs." Geddy clutched his slimy hand. "A whole fucking musical."

Glarry gasped and smiled, and a black curtain closed over his eyes. "A musical ..."

"Let's get him inside!" Verveik yelled.

But it was too late. Geddy looked over his shoulder with a grave expression, his eyes meeting Verveik's as he was about to come help. The big man grimaced and looked away.

Geddy swallowed his own grief and scrambled to the overhang, then knelt at the entrance, motioning for Oz as she lingered over Glarry. A fresh rumble came from the clouds, bigger this time. "Oz, come on, get inside!"

She sprang to her feet and sprinted toward him as he reached for her hand. He almost had her when she froze in place, her eyes widened in shock. An invisible force yanked her violently backward and into the opaque clouds like she'd reached the end of some invisible bungie cord. An unseen ship rumbled as it accelerated away.

"Oz!!" he screamed. "Ozzzzzzz!"

A heartbeat later, the remaining fighters dropped back out of the clouds and bore down on them. Only this time, their missile ports opened. Even one would turn the rocky spire over the cave to gravel, and he saw dozens. This was it.

A familiar whine from behind shocked his heart back into rhythm.

As the Darkstars lined up to fire, a bright yellow stream of antimatter pierced the sky and turned another one into a fireball that plowed into the ground to their left, the heat so great it singed Geddy's eyebrows.

Morpho!

CHAPTER FORTY-ONE

I'LL SHOW YOU MINE

THE DOMINIC WHIZZED past as the two remaining fighters split and vanished again, apparently too surprised to even return fire.

"Yeah, Morph! Woo hoo!" Geddy cried.

Morpho swung her around and settled into a hover, then lowered the ladder, the jets whipping the stiff shrubs in the clearing.

"Friend of yours?" Verveik shouted over the engines.

"All you need are a few good ones. Let's go!"

Geddy was focused on the point in the sky where Oz had flown as though that would help. He bolted to the ladder and pulled himself into the ship, then threw off his pack. Verveik would be a tight fit.

But the Commander hadn't yet emerged from the cave. He was still kneeling over Torkin in the shadows and gently placed a hand on the Screvari's chest with his head lowered. Geddy closed his eyes and swallowed the lump in his throat. He hated rushing the man after he'd just lost his whole crew, but the fighters would return any moment and Oz, wherever she went, was getting further away.

His mind raced. Who took her? Was it Rader? Were they going to send her to Zelnad conversion camp like he wanted? Was it really the Xellarans or just their ships?

Verveik crawled out from the cave and covered the distance between him and the *Dom* in a few mighty strides, them up the ladder he went. He had to turn sideways to fit through the opening, grunting with effort, but soon worked his way inside and closed the hatch behind him as Geddy buckled in.

"Torkin didn't make it." Verveik's voice was heavy.

Geddy raised the ladder and spun her around. "I'm sorry about your crew, Commander. But we have to go after Oz."

Before he could punch it skyward, Morpho latched on to his hand.

— **Geddy.**

— Thanks for the assist. Did you see the ship that took Oz?

— **What ship? What happened?**

— You must've seen it was just here.

— **The scans are clear. Whoever took her has jumped away. We have to go.**

Geddy glanced at the screen to verify. There were no ships within range. None.

That's not possible. The *Fiz*–

— **The *Fiz* is gone.**

Fear and guilt stabbed his heart. Losing Oz was bad enough, but the *Fiz*, too?

— Whaddya mean, gone?

A million scenarios raced through Geddy's head. They must have been forced to jump away. Or maybe they dropped out of orbit and were on the other side of the planet. Were they hiding from the Xellarans? It could've been just about anything.

Verveik strapped himself in the copilot's chair, the top of which only reached halfway up his back. He bent down and squinted at Geddy. "Starheart, you need an invitation?"

Morpho unplugged from him, but he felt paralyzed. His mind was being pulled in so many directions, he couldn't do anything.

— *You have to trust they're okay. This is bigger than you now.*

Eli was always right, but nothing seemed right about this. In the space of two minutes, he'd become a captain without a crew and Verveik a commander without his troops. The difference was, Geddy could still get his people back. In theory.

"Hey! Do I need to get out and push??"

"My ship is gone," he said dumbly. "My crew. Oz. I don't know what to do."

The two remaining Darkstars reappeared on the scanner like they'd been there all along. Verveik reached for the switch that would give him the control. "That's it. I'm flying."

Geddy stayed his hand and grimaced. "No. I've got it."

He hit the lifters, kicking up wet, clumpy sand, and spun them around. The *Dom* might be able to outrun them, but every neuron was screaming at him to crawfish back, duke it out with the Darkstars, and go after Oz.

But Eli, as always, was right. This really was bigger than him now. The key to the Alliance was sitting in the copilot's chair. A person he'd admired his entire life. If he said they needed to go, they really did.

Geddy nosed her into the clouds and punched it.

It wasn't that he didn't believe Morpho, but he had to see for himself. If the Darkstars caught up, they'd be outgunned. Even trying to look was a needless risk, but he did it anyway.

He visually scanned the space over Verdithea where the *Fiz* should've been. It really wasn't there.

"They must've followed you through the wormhole." The gravity of what just happened playing on Verveik's chiseled face.

Guilt descended over Geddy. "Your men ... your camp ... This is my fault."

"Don't start down that road," Verveik cautioned. "Trust me, it never ends."

Knowing the *Fiz* was really gone hurt his heart, but it also helped return him to the present. The glowing blue sphere on the readout flashed to warn him of the approaching fighters, which were actually gaining though he had it floored. He'd burned through his missiles dealing with Tretiak's mercs, leaving only the wing-mounted blasters and the anti-matter cannon in the nose. No way to fire behind him.

The missile warning sounded, and four red streaks shot out of the diamond-shaped contacts on the screen. Thanks to Denk, he knew that the countermeasures button inexplicably resembled a stick man taking a dump. He pushed it, and ...

Nothing. A flashing box at the lower left indicated they were gone. At least he'd learned something new.

Ahead, a brief flash met his eyes, the glint of a knife in a dark room, and the two Darkstars appeared in front of them, disruptors blazing.

"What the hell?!"

There was no time to react. A barrage of bolts slammed into the front shield, and the level plunged to sixty percent. Another barrage, and they were down to forty. Each impact jolted them in their seats. They were trapped between blasters and missiles fired in opposite directions from the same ships, courtesy of Zelnad jump tech. The *Dom* wasn't jump-capable at all.

Geddy fired the cannon and the disruptors at once, but the Darkstars disappeared before the shots could land.

But for a moment, he only had one thing left to worry about. He spun the ship around and unleashed a cloud of bolts at the incoming missiles. He managed to hit two, but the others dodged the blasts and kept coming.

"Shit! I don't know how to fight this way!"

Verveik picked his satchel up off the floor. As he did, the Darkstars reappeared, this time from nine o'clock high. Another barrage slammed into them, and the shields were down to twenty percent. One more hit and they were toast.

From off to the right came a shower of red bolts, and the last two missiles flashed out.

"Ha! Found you!" said Jeledine over the comm.

The *Bogart* swooped past, then circled back in front of him close enough that he could see her at the controls.

"Jel, you've gotta get out of here!"

"Is that your way of thanking me? Where are the fighters?"

Verveik calmly removed a small device from his satchel a little thicker than a tablet.

"What's that?" Geddy asked.

"We're outmatched. Make your friend jump away or she's

dead."

Under any other conditions, Geddy would've questioned the order, but hearing it from his hero's lips was all he needed. "Jel, you have to jump now! Anywhere! Trust me!"

Up ahead, a flicker of light and the fighters appeared at twelve o'clock high. A fresh cluster of missiles flashed red as they released and blazed toward them like a wall of death.

"Commander ..."

Verveik tapped the device, and nothing happened.

Or so it seemed. A blink earlier, there had been nothing in front of them but open space. Now, there was a pale gray moon half again as large as Old Earth's. He didn't recognize it, but there probably weren't ten moons in the whole galaxy he could've identified on sight.

But apart from the moon, there was a nebula in the distance. It hadn't been there a moment ago either. And yet, he'd felt nothing.

Verveik gave an appreciative nod. "I'll be damned. It really works." He tucked the device back in its satchel and stowed it back under his seat.

"What was that? Where the hell are we?"

"A long way from those fighters." He pointed at the moon. "Swing around to the far side."

"What did you just do?"

"We jumped like they did."

"But how?"

"I'll explain later. Right now, we need a better ship. This thing's an antique"

Morpho appeared from behind a panel and swung onto Geddy's shoulder. Verveik regarded him curiously. "Who have we here?"

"This is Morpho. He's a Sagacean, one of the good guys like Eli. His body's a synthetic they developed as a weapon."

Verveik frowned. "Hmm. Funny, we've never run across anything like that." Morpho gave Verveik a salute, earning him a bemused grin. "Thanks for the dust-off back there, Morpho." He raised his eyes back to Geddy. "So, all this business with the Zelnads and the Sagaceans ... That's really true?"

"I wouldn't lie to you."

"So, right now, there's an ancient alien listening to our conversation."

"Two, technically." Geddy reached over and patted Morph.

"And what do they have to say about all this?"

"That the only way to beat the Nads is to rebuild the Alliance."

Verveik rolled his eyes. "Then I seriously question their intelligence."

"When they tell me this is the only way, I believe them." Geddy asserted.

He was a military man. A master negotiator. A no-nonsense, let's-get-it-done leader. Geddy's tale of alien spores as old as time, and the rift between them, was hard for even the most whimsical person to wrap their head around. He needed a different tack.

The old man's eyes fixed on a point in space only he could see. "Okay, Starheart. Let's say the Alliance is magically reborn. What then?"

"We gather evidence against the Nads. Make sure everyone knows what they're up to. When the Coalition falls apart, we pick up the pieces and stop them. Together."

"Do you have any idea how long it would take to build a multi-world army from scratch?" He scoffed and shook his head. "You're probably one of those Ring War buffs who knows every ship and every battle, aren't you?"

"My old man was. I was more fascinated by ... well ... you."

Verveik cocked his head and looked at Geddy over the tops of his eyes. "You can't be serious."

"Every story my dad told me about the War, everything I read ... it all came back to Supreme Commander Verveik. Your battle tactics. And your strength! My god, I still watch the footage of you snapping that rifle in half."

During a speech to the Alliance high council at the height of the War, a Screvari assassin ran onstage, firing a pulse rifle at him from point-blank range. Verveik bolted *toward* the guy and ripped the weapon from his hands, then socked him so hard, he flew offstage. He was so fired up, and so sick of war at that point, he broke the rifle over his knee and threw the pieces at the dazed assassin, then continued his speech. To this day, it was the most baller thing he'd ever seen someone do.

Not many kids his age knew or cared who Verveik was. But for whatever reason, young Eddie Kepler latched onto his legend and never let go. It couldn't have all been bullshit. His hero had to be in there somewhere.

"If all you know is the schoolbook version, then you know nothing. History is unreasonably kind to wartime leaders."

— *You have his ear now. Speak from your heart.*

"Commander, this ... this is for all the marbles. For all we know, our galaxy is the last one standing. Every invention. Every picnic. Every family tree might just disappear like on all those other worlds. You can't be willing to sit by and watch that happen."

"Why not?"

His throat tightened. "Because it would mean I didn't believe in the right hero."

Verveik guffawed. "I'm no hero. I'm a coward who left others to clean up his mess."

Geddy leaned back. "You mean Kigantu."

Verveik jerked his head to him, surprised, then gave a knowing look. "Tretiak told you."

"You lived in the south desert for *sixty-six years?* How is that even possible?"

The big commander gave a weary sigh. "A prison of my own design."

A flash of inspiration hit Geddy. "Like Melpf Lowderthistle."

"Who?"

Geddy excitedly related the story of Parmhar's fable about rumination. Verveik didn't exactly have a healthy connection to the past, either.

"As Jeledine likes to say, the only days that still matter are today and tomorrow."

His lips pursed and his head worked slowly up and down. "Wise words. Did you really read some old Ornean book?"

Geddy's cheeks flushed. "No. But when this is all over, you, me, and a buddy of mine are gonna get drunk and read it together."

"Something to look forward to." The big man allowed the tiniest of smiles.

CHAPTER FORTY-TWO

MY LOVE FOR YOU IS LIKE A TRUCK

THE MOMENT the Berzerker cleared the moon's turbulent atmosphere, Verveik tapped something on the jump device, and the scene before them changed again. What had just been open space was now an impossibly vast expanse of ionizing radiation that appeared as a purple cloud.

Geddy stared at it in disbelief. "Is this the Karrea Ion Cloud?"

Verveik's entire manner had changed. He was less guarded now, seemingly confident in their safety now that they were in the Berzerker. He leaned way back in his chair and put his feet up on the console, tapping his bratwurst-sized fingers together as the ship entered the dangerous formation.

Like Verdithea, it made comms and scans impossible. Most ships avoided it, but if you needed to disappear for a while and knew the way out, it was just the ticket.

"You still don't understand, do you?"

"Guess I'm a little slow on the uptake," Geddy replied.

Verveik narrowed his eyes and held out his empty palms.

"We jumped. Just like the Zelnads do."

"Yeah, but *how?*"

Verveik sighed and looked sideways at Geddy as he folded his arms. "Boy, you really are slow."

The flurry of emotions the past couple hours had clouded Geddy's mind, but as soon as Verveik said the words, the memory snapped back like new underwear. It was what Zirhof theorized and the quantum cubes had proven — the story of how humans came to the galaxy was a lie. A Project Rearview scientist named Dr. Birgit Nilsson was, in fact, host to a Sagacean just like Geddy, only she was much smarter. Together, they built an entirely novel technology that cross the infinite void in the blink of an eye.

"Rearview," Geddy muttered. "This is the tech that brought humans to the galaxy."

Verveik leaned toward him, his expression grave. "Geddy, what I'm about to tell you may change everything. For better or worse, I can't be sure."

— That doesn't sound ominous.

— *Are you sure about this?*

— I'd say we're all in at this point.

"Zereth-Tinn said the same thing back on Xellara. Next thing I know, I've got skysnakes and Darkstars flying up my ass and my crew is missing."

"I assume you are aware of Dr. Nilsson?"

"The JPL scientist we think invented the jump tech."

Verveik nodded. "One way or another, it wound up on board, and at some point, a whole fleet of transports found itself in a galaxy they couldn't have known existed. Next thing you know, we have humans."

He held up a cautioning finger. "But Dr. Nilsson faced a

difficult choice. One option was to share her tech with the world. Usher in a new age of interstellar travel and go down in history as its inventor. Or, she could use it to make humans the dominant new kids on the block. She chose option three."

"Which was?"

"Hide it in the remotest part of Earth 2 where no one would find it."

The rest of the story was already filling in. "The Ice Castles."

Verveik gave a slow nod. "Fast-forward a few centuries. A young, adventurous major and his wife take a romantic journey north."

"My parents ..." Geddy's heartbeat echoed in his ears. This is what Tretiak had talked about.

Verveik continued. "We don't know how they found the device, but they did. And, dutifully, they brought it to your father's commanding officer."

"Colonel Pritchard." Geddy's head was spinning.

"Somehow, he knew it was there, which could only mean he knew what it was. About a year after your parents disappeared, he did, too."

Geddy clenched his jaw and fought the tears building in his eyes. "You think he ...?"

Verveik's eyes drifted to the floor. "We can't know for sure. But it wasn't long before Zelnads were everywhere and nowhere, buying up all the tukrium in the galaxy."

"They got the jump tech from us."

Geddy was gutted. All this was connected to him somehow. The Zelnads' long campaign against civilization had been going on for thousands of years, but thanks to Dr. Nilsson, it had accelerated.

"How the hell do you know all this?"

"We've pieced it together over many years. You and your quantum cubes filled in the blanks and showed us how to build this device."

"Okay, but how do you have it?"

"You brought it to me."

Geddy was so certain the case was just for the Scimitar that he hadn't so much as lifted the foam out of it. There was plenty of room for a small device underneath. Apparently, Zirhof had done a bit more than just find what he needed on the cubes, and Tretiak had one last item for him to deliver.

"So ... what are we doing here?"

He gave Geddy a knowing grin. "I told you there were other ships."

Verveik tapped something on the screen and sat back to watch Geddy. Outside, in the roiling, electric purple vastness of the storm, the running lights of nearby fighters popped to life, the likes of which Geddy had never seen. Adjacent ships lit up as well, blooming across his field of vision until a vast matrix glittered in the void like a mirror ball.

There were fighters and interceptors, light transports and heavy escorts, battleships and freighters and forward recon ships. More Berzerkers than he could count. Thousands of them, spanking new and bearing the Alliance logo.

Until that moment, Geddy had never cried and gotten hard at the same time.

"Dude ..." Geddy laughed like a child on Christmas morning. "Are you kidding me right now?"

"You're looking at the never-deployed Alliance First Fleet. Two more were planned. The Alliance folded before these ships could be commissioned."

They didn't know how big the Zelnad fleet was, but these were top-shelf ships armed to the gills. It didn't mean they'd stand much of a chance against the Zelnad technology, but it was a helluva lot better than what Geddy expected.

Which was the point, of course. The Alliance was down but not out, and Verveik wanted him to know it. If he couldn't inspire Geddy, what about the men, women, or hermaphroditic alien pilots he'd have to recruit?

"Who's gonna fly them?"

Verveik's expression darkened. "Whoever we can find. But those are worries for another day. Our priority now is retrofitting every ship with this jump tech so we stand half a chance. That'll take an army in itself."

The initial thrill of seeing a brand-new Alliance fleet was tempered by the size of the task ahead and the urgency it demanded. They had ships, but nothing else. Just a leader and a vague idea what the enemy was planning.

"Does this mean you're back in the fight?"

Verveik gave a rueful shake of his giant head. "I never stopped fighting, just forgot what I was fighting for. You reminded me."

Geddy's face felt hot, and he pulled at his loose-fitting collar. Again, the tears threatened, but he stood his ground. He couldn't lose it. Not in front of this man.

"You're my fucking hero," he blurted.

"No, Geddy." Verveik's face was as stony as a statue of mighty Zeus, but his tone was almost fatherly. "At this moment, you're mine."

Building tears blurred his vision. "Um, what?"

"I heard what you did over Gundrun. Pushing that satellite out by hand? That took some rocks. I mean, it was foolish and ultimately pointless, but brave."

His mouth hung open. "How ...?"

"I'm not quite as tuned out as Tretiak thinks. There are still people I can trust."

Of course, he still had people out there. Powerful people who weren't just rich. They'd need a lot of them.

Emotion overtook him, and he threw his arms around Verveik, sobbing uncontrollably. It was like hugging a granite statue. Tretiak, his parents, humans, even Verveik — he'd been wrong about almost all of it. He'd never stopped fighting either, but in that moment, he finally understood that his worst enemy was the man in the mirror. Eli tried to tell him in the Morpho-bubble over Kigantu, but the meaning of the parable about a man forever at war with himself only half landed. Now, thanks to Doc and Verveik, he knew exactly what it meant.

Verveik indulged Geddy for a minute then patted him on the back. "Okay. Pull yourself together, man."

Geddy sat back, noting the foamy schlogg of snot that now decorated Verveik's doublet. "Sorry," he sniffed, clumsily wiping it off. "I don't suppose you have a tissue?"

Verveik shook his head. "Right now, I have work to do, and you have a crew to find."

He took a deep breath and wiped his face, embarrassed to have literally cried on the Commander's shoulder, but he felt much lighter.

— *You needed that.*

"Right," Geddy said. "Guess I'd better get back before someone misses me."

This time, Geddy paid close attention to the jump.

Verveik even did a countdown before engaging. Despite that, the scene before his eyes of an untouched Alliance fleet was instantly replaced by the strange, stormy moon whence they'd come like a cut in a film.

Verveik dove through the thin upper atmosphere and spiraled his way back down toward the landing pad as it rose out of the dusty earth.

"How does one start rebuilding the Alliance, exactly?" Geddy asked.

Verveik cocked an eyebrow. "One ally at a time."

"I guess that makes sense."

Even on full manual, the big ship was perfectly compliant in the big Gundrun's hands. It settled onto the platform like a butterfly.

"I never knew you did much flying."

"My first post was the Air Guard. And I've played Ponley Point about a million times."

Geddy sucked in a sharp breath. "*You play Ponley Point?* I won at the Point about a month ago! Like, the real one."

"See? My hero," Verveik declared with a smirk.

He shut the Berzerker down and the platform lowered once again. As it did, he cleared his throat and started pointing to areas of the cabin.

"Okay, kid, listen ... This thing was designed to be flown by just about anyone. As soon you take off, just activate the New Pilot Wizard and it'll walk you through everything. Controls are controls, and the menu system is pretty intuitive. As far as her handling goes–"

"Wait," Geddy interrupted, shaking his head. "Why are you telling me all this?"

"Because I'm taking your Kailorian antique and you're

taking this," he said obviously. "Anyway, she's well-balanced in atmosphere, but it shifts quite a bit as you fire, so be ready for kickback. The AI's named Seth, but that's the default. You can change it to anything you want."

Geddy wanted to jump for joy, but two things stopped him. One, it didn't feel right taking a badass gunship from Verveik, and two, the *Dom* was the *Dom*. Yeah, it was eighty-plus years old, and he didn't know what all the buttons did, but she handled like a dream and had sentimental value now. It was bad enough not knowing where the *Fiz* was, but swapping out the *Dom* in order to look for it felt like cheating.

"What's unclear about this?" Verveik asked. "You need to go hunting, I need to stay under the radar."

"But–"

"We're trading ships, Captain. That's an order."

Geddy sat up straight, a strange sense of duty flooded his body. "Order?"

"You want me to lead, then you'd better learn to follow."

The thought that Verveik might be joking only lived for a moment. The look on his face slayed it.

"Yes ... sir?" he mumbled.

He cupped his hand behind his ear. "Did you say something? I'm very old."

"Yes, sir!"

Geddy felt the surge of purpose, and it felt good.

— What the hell is happening right now?

— *You've been swept up in a fire you lit.*

— It's the good kind of fire, right?

— *The best kind.*

Verveik smirked and patted Geddy's face. "Congratulations, Captain Starheart. Welcome to the Alliance."

CHAPTER FORTY-THREE

WHAT'S THIS BUTTON DO?

GEDDY SCOFFED at the New Pilot Wizard, but it turned out to be the most intuitive, idiot-proof system he'd ever seen for spinning up a pilot on a new platform. It projected a hologram on top of your actual body, taking you step by step through the activation of various functions, the list of which only became more impressive as Geddy learned his way around the ship.

Seth, the default AI profile, got the boot first thing. Cherie with a British accent was a little more Geddy's style.

The state of the art had moved well forward since this ship was made, but not where it counted. Apart from handling beautifully in atmosphere, it was half again as fast as the *Dom*, had better scopes, and showed superior attention to detail throughout. It might have been built long ago, but it felt like piloting the future.

The Alliance's military intervention in the Ring War had wound up defining it, but this ship was the product of rich collaborations between worlds. The kind that might yet happen again.

Even Morpho was impressed. After crawling through every nook and cranny, he reported that everything was pristine and working perfectly.

Geddy then checked the ship's transponder for a name, but of course, it had never been activated. Verveik wouldn't have wanted anyone to run across it on a scan and know what it was. The only ship Geddy ever got to name was the *Penetrator*. What would he call this one? Berzerker was cool, but it was just the model.

Without a crew, though, he was just a pilot and the Berzerker was just a ship. That needed fixing.

He'd sent Jel half a dozen hails across the band of thieves but hadn't heard back, which worried him. What if she didn't jump away like he said?

Whatever snatched Oz off the ground in heavy atmosphere was new to him. It had to be the Zelnads. But if that was true, what were the Darkstars doing there?

And then there was the *Fiz* and the rest of his crew. If Denk felt the ship was in jeopardy, its only real defense was to jump away. That's probably what happened, but where? Why hadn't they established an emergency rendezvous point in case things went south? So dumb.

The ship's bright, beautiful display pulsed to indicate his hail was being returned. And because he'd actually paid attention during the New Pilot Wizard, he proudly pushed the correct button.

Jel's face faded up, flat and expressionless. Relief flooded his body.

"Jel! Thank the stars!"

"Where the hell did you go? You vanished and left me to the fighters *I* warned you about."

"You jumped away, right?"

"I'm here aren't I?"

"Boy, I don't know what we would've done if you hadn't shown up when you did," Geddy said.

"Who's 'we?'"

He'd almost forgotten she had no idea what they were doing on Verdithea or who they were trying to find.

"You wouldn't believe me if I told you."

"Try me."

"Not here. Let's meet. Where are you?"

Jel chewed on her lower lip a moment, studying him. He didn't blink. Finally, she rubbed her face in her hands, heaved a sigh, and keyed in her coordinates. She was in orbit over Doxx-Mora, half a parsec away.

Ordinarily, it would be tricky to find a vector for a destination that far away, especially somewhere so hemmed in as a planet with eighteen moons. But thanks to this new jump tech, he didn't have to worry about that.

"Okay. I'll be right there."

Her face wrinkled in confusion. "Right here? I can't just wait for you to find a vector, Ged. I've got work lined up."

"Just trust me, okay. Two shakes."

The tablet did its thing and verified the jump was safe, which it was only able to do because they were in charted space.

EXECUTE POINT TO POINT? flashed on the screen.

Even though he'd done it with Verveik — twice — he still found it hard to trust. He inhaled and pushed the button.

CHAPTER FORTY-FOUR

ALLIANCES

For a few amusing seconds, Jel didn't even look up. She had her head in her hands and was staring down at the console running her fingers through her long, white hair. Not until Hughey Twoey, her shape-shifting robot, reached up and tapped her elbow did she lift her eyes.

She jumped back in her seat, her mouth agape as their eyes met.

"'Sup, girl?"

Jel gave her head a slow shake. "How ...? What ...?"

"Me first. How'd you find us?"

"A job on Myadan went south, so I decided to come surprise you guys on Xellara. I was waiting for clearance to land when I saw your transponder headed toward the wormhole. I was about to hail you when I saw those ships follow you in. I had a bad feeling, so I followed you."

"Do you know where the *Fiz* went? Or Oz?"

"I never saw the *Fiz*. Why? What happened to Oz?"

"You're sure you only saw four ships?"

"Yeah. But you jumped here. Like, *right here*. Whose ship is that? And where's the fargate? How could you know you wouldn't ..."

"Let's dock. I'll explain everything."

She rolled her eyes. "Oldest pick-up line in the galaxy."

He checked the scopes. At least for now, they were alone. No ships besides those coming and going from Doxx-Mora, which was still quite a ways off.

"This time, it's not a corny line."

She sighed. "Okay, but only because it's you."

Jel activated her docking sequence, and the *Bogart's* microthrusters] maneuvered it into position. Her airlock was aft and his was on the port side, so when the docking was completed, they wound up at a right angle. He unconsciously smoothed his hair before opening the door between the rear two seats and waited for her to come through. Morph followed him inside along the ceiling and dropped onto his shoulder.

A minute later, the airlock hatch opened and Jel crawled inside with Hughey in tow. They embraced warmly, and he relaxed further.

"I'm glad you're okay." She gave a long sigh. "Hey, Morph."

Morpho saluted as Geddy released her and thumbed over his shoulder. "You, ah, want the dime tour?"

She looked at him sideways, then gave an exasperated shrug. "Of course."

He showed her the small but well-appointed galley and pulled them both cups of eighty-year-old coffee from the multi-bev unit. There was a food recombinator, too, which he was unreasonably excited about. After eating a metric ton of nutrimush, even the thought of making new food from digested food sounded fantastic.

She took a cautious sip and flared her eyebrows. "That's actually ... good."

Like the galley, the crew berths were compact but thoughtful, with roomy bunks that allowed for total privacy but still had access to all the ship's systems. In an emergency, each bunk doubled as an escape pod or safe room not unlike what Morpho had built into the *Fiz*.

They entered the cabin, and he walked her through a smattering of the ship's long list of features and armaments.

"Tell me what happened to Oz."

"Some kind of beam snatched her into the clouds like a dog hitting the end of its leash."

She frowned. "A tractor beam?"

"Yeah, but powerful enough to work in atmosphere. Ever hear of anything like that?"

Jel's eyes darted back and forth, searching her memory, but there wasn't an immediate hit. "I dunno. Maybe. But what are you doing with this sweet-ass ship? Most importantly, how the hell did you just ... appear?"

"Remember when I told you we were going to rebuild the Alliance and you laughed?"

"Yeah ..."

"You're standing in a gently used Alliance ship. One of a thousand, in fact."

She was about to call bullshit again on him, but apparently the look on his face overcame her doubt. "You're serious." He nodded. "How do you know all this? And what the hell were you doing on *Verdithea*?"

"Two questions, one answer. Otaro Verveik."

He caught her up on the Committee, Verveik, Verdithea, and magical jump tech and how it came about. The fact that the presumed leader of the Zelnads, Colonel Pritchard, likely took out his own parents to keep it secret was the icing on top of his rage.

Her eyebrows arched sympathetically. "Jeez, Ged, I had no idea. You never talked about this stuff."

"I know. But this isn't about them, or us, or even Verveik. This is about stopping the Nads and exposing their whole plan. This ends here, in this galaxy, now."

"What are you supposed to do while Verveik puts the band back together?"

There was only one next step.

"First, we find Oz and the *Fizmo*. After that ... we'll figure it out."

"We?" she said, her eyebrow cocked.

"You and I make a pretty good team. Hughey and Morph, too." The two synthetics were nowhere to be seen. "The point is, I need you. *We* need you."

" ... and at long last come the magic words."

"Verveik said we can't rebuild the Alliance without allies. Whaddya say?"

She jutted her chin at her modified racing ship. "What about the *Bogart*?"

"I'm sure you know someone who could look after her for a while."

"What's it pay?"

"Nothing."

"Benefits?"

"Room, board, and witty repartee."

"Any opportunities for advancement?"

"Please, Jel."

Her pursed lips swished back and forth. "Please? Boy, you are really pulling out all the stops." She sighed. "Okay, fine. I'll help you. But I have terms."

Geddy made a beckoning motion with his hand and crossed his arms, happy to indulge her. "Lemme have it."

"You're not my captain, I'm not your crew. We are two in a box, and we don't do shit unless we agree on it."

"Just to be clear, you mean 'do shit' figuratively, right?"

"We only sleep in shifts, which means we're never in quarters at the same time, for reasons I hope are obvious."

"Let's put a pin in that one for now."

"And I get to fly fifty percent of the time."

"Not a chance."

She gave a sly grin and shrugged. "Can't blame a girl for trying. But there is one more, Ged, and it's a big one."

"Okay."

"We always tell each other the truth."

He pretended to hem and haw over this, but in fact, he had the same expectation of her. "Now that I can handle."

She stuck out her hand, and the deal was made.

"So, what's this fancy-ass ship called anyway?"

"The model is a Berzerker. She's never had a name."

"Any contenders?"

He hadn't given it much thought, but only one name would do. His other, long-dead hero. The stories of Verveik came from his dad, but his mom had another favorite.

"I was thinking *Armstrong*."

— *An excellent choice.*

She tilted her head, considering this a moment. "*Armstrong*. What is that?"

He grinned. "A character from an old parable."

"I like it." Jel clapped her hands. "So where are we off to first?"

"After we drop off the *Bogart*, we figure out who took Oz and where. Then we track down the *Fiz*."

"Sounds like a plan." Over her shoulder, she hollered, "Hughey, whatever you and Morph are doing, finish up. Momma's gotta help save the universe."

She left the cabin and headed for the airlock to find her synthetic companion Hughey already waiting by the threshold. Morpho reappeared from somewhere behind him and, again, settled onto Geddy's shoulder. He was getting used to the weight of him there.

"Meet you at the spaceport." Jel squeezed through the narrow opening between their ships. "We'll drop off my ship, maybe grab a few drinks before hitting the road."

"The ideal start to any perilous journey."

After she crawled through, he closed the hatch behind her and waited for hers to turn green. The ship gave a shudder as she undocked, and he meandered back out into the cabin in time to see her race off toward the surface.

"Well, Eli, looks like we're finally in the Zelnad-stopping business."

— Yes, Geddy. I am glad.

Without asking, Morpho snaked a tendril into his ear. It didn't hurt, but it always felt weird. This was his life now.

— I agree. This is an excellent arrangement.

"Do I even want to know what you and Hughey were getting up to?"

— **Hughey is powered by an AI. All it wants to talk about is math.**

— *Math is sexy.*

If it were possible for Eli and Morpho to talk amongst themselves without him having to lose sleep or hearing every word, Geddy would have done it in a heartbeat. But Sagaceans were not telepathic and needed matter and energy to communicate. The ideal medium for that was, unfortunately, the addled wad of meat and water he called his brain.

"I never thought I'd be a medium," Geddy said.

— **More like solid large, maybe even x-large.**

"Cute. Don't change the subject."

— *Yes, Morpho. Do not change the subject. We were talking about you and Hughey.*

— **We may have transferred a … small amount of energy.**

"And?"

— **And … it was not unpleasant.**

Normally, Geddy would switch to full manual and take her down the old-fashioned way, but there would be plenty of time to do that. He set a course for the Doxx-Mora spaceport, engaged the autopilot, and put up his feet.

"So, just out of curiosity, who was giving this 'energy' and who was, you know, receiving?"

THE END

THANK you for reading *Ship Show*. Geddy and the crew will return in early summer 2022.

In the meantime, head over to reassembly.cpjames.com and nab a complimentary copy of *Geddy's Gambit*, a prequel novella from Geddy's henchman days.

Please, please give Ship Show a rating on Amazon, if not a short written review, but only if you liked it. If you didn't, please email me at cp@cpjames.com and tell me why or I'll just keep writing books you hate.

The Cytocorp Saga: A Dystopian Adventure

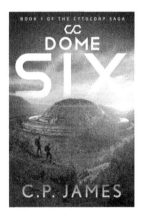

The discovery of a strange signal makes a young technician and his uncle question all they know about their utopian refuge. Now, they must solve the biggest mystery of all: Is there life beyond Dome Six?

Dome Six: Book 1 of the Cytocorp Saga is a high-concept,

engrossing dystopian adventure with influences from *The Island* to *Logan's Run* and *1984*. Grab your copy today and begin *The Cytocorp Saga*.

Available now at Amazon

ALSO BY C.P. JAMES

Printed in Great Britain
by Amazon